The wind had become a full-blown gale, howling like a cemetery banshee

Ryan paused, blinking the ocean spray out of his eye, and stared upward. He could see only a few feet ahead, but he made out the sharp edge of concrete only a half-dozen rungs above his head.

Drained by the struggle of leading the others into unknowable blackness, Ryan finally heaved himself over the rim and collapsed on hands and knees onto smooth stone. Krysty joined him a moment later, her breath surging harshly.

"I've done easier things, lover," she panted. "Hope the others can make it."

"Only one way. Can't go down," he replied, feeling the strength already seeping back into his body.

Ryan moved to explore the rear of the platform and found a small iron door covered with lichen. He pushed, and the door swung easily open. His eye winced at the brightness of light, startling after the long blackness.

But he could see enough to make out a slackly grinning mouth and shadowed eyes . . . and the twin barrels of a sawed-off shotgun.

Also available in the Deathlands saga:

JAMES AXLER

DEATH LANDS

Dectra Chain

A GOLD EAGLE BOOK

London · Toronto · New York · Sydney

First published in Great Britain 1989
by Gold Eagle, Eton House, 18–24 Paradise Road,
Richmond, Surrey TW9 1SR

© Worldwide Library 1988

Australian copyright 1988
Philippine copyright 1988
This edition 1989

ISBN 0 373 62507 3

25/8911

Made and printed in Great Britain

"Elegantiae arbiter," said Tacitus of Petronius. It could apply equally well to Feroze Mohammed. This book is for him, with my thanks for his ceaseless help, advice and encouragement.

They that go down to the sea in ships and occupy their business in great waters; These men see the works of the Lord and his wonders in the deep.

—*The Book of Common Prayer*, Psalm 107

Chapter One

RYAN CAWDOR OPENED HIS EYE, then closed it again, feeling the certainty that to try to move would make him throw up. He took several rapid, shallow breaths, fighting the nausea, swallowing hard. Sweat beaded his forehead, and his stomach was cramping. A mat-trans jump through one of the gateways always resulted in unconsciousness and a gut-churning sickness as every molecule was sucked into infinity and then reassembled in another gateway.

Ryan had never made an attempt to understand the technology of the hidden mat-trans chambers. Indeed, virtually all knowledge of anything technical or scientific had vanished on that January morning when the world disappeared under a nuclear haze, about a hundred years ago.

He could hear someone moaning and retching on the far side of the hexagonal room, which was protected with thick walls of colored, armored glass. Ryan still didn't feel confident enough to risk opening his eye again. All but one of the six people with him had made several jumps before and they knew what to expect.

But for one it was the first time.

Man Whose Eyes See More had been until very recently the wise man, or shaman, to a subtribe of the Mescalero Apaches, who lived among the jagged red canyons of the land that had once been called New Mexico. He'd never been more than fifty miles from his birthplace in Drowned Squaw Canyon, but now he didn't know where he was. All he knew was that his head was spinning, as though Ysun, giver of all life, had scooped out the pink-gray mush that filled his skull and taken it into its mouth only to spit it out again.

His mirrored sunglasses had fallen from his face, and he fumbled for them, not wanting to risk opening his eyes in case he saw... What? Nothing? Death? An endless darkness beyond all time? The shaman didn't know.

Very, very cautiously, he eased open his dark brown eyes.

"Nothing," he said to himself, conscious of how harsh and dry his voice sounded, as though it hadn't been used for several days. "Nothing has happened here at all."

They were exactly where they'd been when Ryan Cawdor, known to the Indian's people as One Eye Chills, had closed the ponderous door. His new companions sat or lay just where they'd been before the swooping raven of blackness had come and plucked away his mind for a while.

The metal disks in the floor and the ceiling were no longer glowing, and the tendrils of pale mist had long evaporated. The shaman recalled a distant humming that had seemed to come simultaneously from inside and outside the chamber and had hurt the head.

He sighed, swallowing to clear the pressure on his ears. Then he noticed that something *was* different. Even though the six-sided room looked precisely the same, the walls had changed color. When they'd entered the gateway in New Mexico, the glass walls had been a rich golden hue. Now they were a deep turquoise, tinted like old Navaho jewelry.

"All right?" someone asked from his left. Man Whose Eyes See More nodded, regretting the sharp movement and the pain it caused him.

"I am not yet dead," he said carefully.

"Good."

The Apache knew that the speaker, John Barrymore Dix, was a man of very few words, never using two when one would be enough. Short and wiry, J.B. was the Armorer of the traveling group of friends that the shaman had joined. His sallow face rarely showed any emotion unless he was talking about blasters—about weapons of any sort. His blue eyes would glitter behind his wire-rimmed spectacles, and he would push back the brim of the battered fedora he habitually wore. He could tell you all there was to know about rifles, carbines, automatics, revolvers and muskets.

Next to J.B., whom the Indians had christened Weapons Strike Fear, was the slumped and unconscious figure of a boy. Eyes of Wolf had been his name, but the Mescalero knew his proper name was Jak Lauren. He was only three inches over five feet in height, nearly two feet below Man Whose Eyes See More's towering seven feet, and weighed in at 105 pounds.

The boy's eyes were ruby red, and his hair was as pure white as the snow that dappled the high peaks of the distant Sierras. In his lap, Jak was clenching a massive .357 Magnum with a six-inch barrel. He was a brilliant hand-to-hand fighter who the Indian knew had killed an amazing number of men.

He also knew that Jak Lauren was just fourteen years old.

Feeling a little better, the shaman stretched out his long legs, bare feet scraping on the floor of the chamber. He was wearing his favorite pair of pants—seersucker, with one leg missing. His brocade vest had a cherry-red kerchief dangling from it, and he sported a silver stickpin in a scarlet cravat, its claw setting empty of a stone. The shaman's own decorated .50-caliber Sharps buffalo rifle lay at his side.

Next around the chamber, lying together, both showing the first signs of recovery, were the two women in the group. Man Whose Eyes See More came from a warrior society where women came third- or fourth-best—if they came anywhere at all.

One of the women moaned, clenching her fingers. Her name was Krysty Wroth, called Fire Hair Woman by the Mescalero. Man Whose Eyes See More was a priest of the Apache, with a mutie power of seeing a little into the future, of sensing things that others couldn't see. He knew that this woman with the bizarre, fiery crimson hair also had something of that doomie power.

She was tall, close to six feet, and was dressed in khaki coveralls. Her feet, pointed toward the shaman, were shod in dark blue leather cowboy boots that had chiseled heels and were ornamented with silver spread-wing falcons. The sharp toes were also silver. Her pistol was plated and polished—a Heckler & Koch P7A-13 9 mm blaster that fired thirteen rounds. And the Apache had firsthand knowledge that the girl knew how to use her gun.

He was a little scared of Krysty Wroth.

As he looked at her she blinked, opening the startling green eyes, managing a smile.

"Hey," she said quietly. "Enjoy your first jump with us?"

"No," he replied honestly.

"Mebbe you should have stayed where you were, shaman," she whispered.

Jak sat up, coughing, a thin string of bile dribbling from his slack lips, and dripping onto the front of his canvas camouflage jacket.

"Bastard jump makes feel ill every time," he said, shaking his head, the long white hair floating around his narrow skull like winter smoke.

The other girl also sat up, burying her face in her hands. She was one of the most beautiful women the Apache had ever seen. Indeed, on the strength of that she had been gifted by the Apache with the name of Keeps Night Warm. Her Anglo name was Lori Quint, and she was in her sixteenth year of life. She was even taller than Krysty Wroth, topping the six-foot mark by close to an inch. Lori was a startling blonde with blue eyes.

"I want to feel best, but I always feel badder than best," she said, smoothing her dark navy cotton skirt over her long thighs. As she shifted her position the shaman heard the silvery tinkling of the tiny spurs on her crimson high-heeled boots.

"How you feeling?" came a voice from the shaman's right. It was the leader of the small group, Ryan Cawdor. He was an imposing sight, built like the killing machine that he was. The man stretched two inches above six feet, weighing just on two hundred pounds. His right eye was a deathly, melt-ice blue, the left hidden beneath a patch of black leather. A savage scar furrowed his face from his right eye to the corner of his mouth. Both injuries, the Indian knew, were the result of a deadly fight between Ryan and an older brother.

"My head is still in space," replied Man Whose Eyes See More. "I will be pleased when it catches up with the other parts of me."

"Doc's still out cold," Krysty put in. "He takes it harder than the rest of us."

Doc Tanner was the last member of the group, someone whom the shaman found disturbing. Normally his seeing power enabled him to weigh up strangers, but not the gray-haired, skinny old man in the green-mottled frock coat and cracked knee boots. When Man Whose Eyes See More talked with Doc, he had the feeling that he was seeing a misty, unreal person. He had refused to allow Doc to carry an Indian name, and the old man hadn't seemed unduly surprised. From hints dropped by the others, the shaman suspected that Doc Tanner had come, somehow, from another time.

And, of course, the Apache was right.

Dr. Theophilus Algernon Tanner had been born in South Strafford, Vermont, on the fourteenth day of February in the year of our Lord 1868. Married, the father of two young children, a leading scientist of his time, Doc had been "trawled" forward to the year 1998. He was the first and, as far as he knew, the only successful subject of a time-travel experiment, which was a part of the infamous Cerberus Project.

Because he had caused the twentieth-century scientists such trouble, they used him once more as the unwilling subject for an experiment. This time they sent him forward to the bleak scenario of Deathlands, nearly a hundred years in the future. By a fluke of good or bad luck Doc was chron-jumped only a couple of weeks before the fire and light that swept so much of the United States clean of life and living. He had been rescued by Ryan Cawdor from the ville of Mocsin, up in the Darks, saved from Baron Jordan Teague and his supremely evil sec boss, Cort Strasser.

In recent bloody fighting, with Ryan and his companions siding with Man Whose Eyes See More and the Mescalero against killers in cavalry uniforms, the wheel had come full circle. The gang of butchers had been led by Cort Strasser.

Gradually all seven within the glass-walled chamber managed to struggle to their feet. Doc was the last to come around, helped up by Lori on one side and young Jak on the other. He was coughing and gasping, doubled over.

"By the three Kennedys! I fear that I am too far gone in years to relish this mat-trans jumping. The blackness grows ever deeper, and my heart sinks when I think of all the jumps to come."

"Mebbe there won't be any more jumps, Doc," Ryan suggested, running a finger around the collar of his long, fur-trimmed coat.

"Sure," Krysty added. "And this might be the very place in all the Deathlands where we can find what we're looking for, a place, mebbe, with a future."

"Maybe pigs fly, was what Father said." Jak grinned.

"How d'you feel, Man Whose Eyes See More?" J.B. asked, automatically checking the action on his mini-Uzi, cocking the Steyr AUG handblaster that he wore in a holster on his hip.

The shaman noticed that each member of the group was taking out their armory of weapons, doing so with a casual, professional ease that told much of how they had all survived so long.

The albino boy hefted his cannon, which looked too big for him to even hold. Lori, on the other hand, was reloading a delicate little Walther PPK .22 with polished pearl handles.

Ryan favored a SIG-Sauer P-226 9 mm pistol with a built-in baffle silencer that fired fifteen rounds.

Slung across his shoulders was a gun like nothing Man Whose Eyes See More had ever seen before. It was a pale gray rectangular automatic rifle. Jak had told him that it was a Heckler & Koch G-12.

Doc was the only one of the group who carried a gun that most of the Apaches would have recognized. It was a monstrously heavy and outdated blaster, called a Le Mat, a conventional revolver that fired nine rounds of .36 ammo. But there was also a second barrel that could be used to fire a single round of .63-caliber scattergun ball, like a sawed-off shotgun. Doc told the shaman that the gun was "just about as old as me, son. About as old as me."

Man Whose Eyes See More realized that he had allowed his thoughts to drift as he stared around at the weaponry of his six new friends.

"Sorry, J.B., what did you ask me? My mind was elsewhere."

The Armorer adjusted his fedora. "Asked how you were feeling, Man Whose Eyes See More."

Ryan stepped toward the door to the mat-trans chamber, then paused. "Man Whose Eyes See More?"

"Yes, Ryan?"

"Your name."

"It is the one given me because I have the power that—"

"I know, I know. Just that it's too long to say. If we're in a firefight, and I want you to cover me, by the time I shout your name, I'm likely dead meat."

"I don't—"

"We've all got short names. Ryan, Jak, J.B., Doc, Lori, Krysty and...Man Whose Eyes See More. We can't call you 'Man'...it'd be confusing."

"Don't have other name?" Jak asked, rubbing his finger across the side of his nose.

"No," the tall Indian replied.

"Must be a name you'd like to be called," Krysty suggested. "Some special reason for a name. Know what I mean?"

"I know what you... There is a name, but you would think me foolish." He shuffled his bare feet on the cool metal disks, looking down in embarrassment.

Ryan laughed. "You want to ride with us, brother, then you learn not to feel bad about anything. Tell us. If we laugh, then we laugh. That's all."

"It won't signify," Doc said kindly, baring his excellent front teeth in a rather frightening smile.

"Well... We had an antique ceedee player in the rancheria. I don't know where it came from but it was old, years before my time. And there was music. One that was my favorite."

"Go on," Lori prompted. "We gotten lotsa ceedees in our redoubt. Keeper's favorite was Barry someone. I doesn't remember. I liked Scum Legion and old Brucey. What did you like?"

"They were very old, I think. Brothers. I played their disk over and over until I knew all their songs. Such harmonies that even White Painted Woman could not imagine."

Doc pointed a gnarled finger at the Apache. "I know them. Two brothers from Kentucky. Can't rightly recall . . ."

"The Everly Brothers," the shaman said, with an almost reverential awe.

"You want to be called 'Everly,' do you?" Ryan asked. "That's almost as long as your real name."

"No. I have always loved their given first names. They were called Don and Phil. But it runs together as one name. Donfil. Like that. If you don't think it's too foolish then . . ."

"Fine with me," Ryan said, looking around at the other six. "No objections, I guess?"

Jak walked over to the Indian and reached up to shake his hand. "Welcome to Deathlands Six, Donfil More."

Krysty laughed. "Course. He has to have a second name. Man Whose Eyes See More. More. Donfil More."

So it was.

RYAN SOMETIMES WONDERED how many gateways were scattered throughout what remained of the old United States of America. He knew from his travels with the Trader that some regions were gone forever, mainly along the earthquake-flawed West Coast, with the whole of Baja California sliding into the lapping Pacific. Over the years their explorations had revealed many of the redoubts, some of which held the secret chambers locked within them. But without the uniquely specialized knowledge of Doc Tanner, their mysteries would never have been solved.

Even now, to use them for making a journey along the invisible waves of the mat-trans chain was to risk life. Even Doc didn't know the codes that were needed to control destinations. All that could be done was to enter the chamber and trigger the mechanism by closing the door.

A number of the gateways had to have been totally destroyed or vandalized over the past century, and Ryan's first fears had been that the group might materialize in the suffocating center of some fallen mountain, or a mile beneath the unforgiving sea. Now he had come to hope that the devices somehow resisted sending a person to any gateway that wasn't still functioning adequately.

But that didn't mean it was possible to escape from the redoubt that contained the gateway, nor even to use the gateway to escape again.

And when the gateway door was opened, no one had any idea of what dangers or horrors might be waiting on the other side.

Ryan set his finger on the curved trigger of the G-12 and reached for the handle of the chamber door. "Ready? Then let's go."

Chapter Two

THE LIGHT that had filtered through the turquoise walls had been dimmed, like a far-off lamp glimpsed underwater. As soon as the door began to ease silently open, the light flooded in, dazzlingly bright.

"Fireblast!" Ryan cursed, shading his eye. "There's some special kind of power source working here, Doc, giving out this much energy."

Like the others, Doc had at first also turned his head away, then squinted through watering eyes into the room beyond the gateway chamber. "Upon my soul, friends! The power of many a candle here. I have not seen... nor can I imagine why. Unless this gateway had some special function."

"Like what?" Krysty asked.

"I fear that I can't even make what one might call an educated guess, my dear Miss Wroth. There were some special sections that I could not, on a need-to-know basis, involve myself with."

"But you were on Cerberus, Doc?" J.B. queried.

"Indeed. But you must recall the concept of the Russian doll, my dear fellow. There is a huge doll, and when you open it there is a large doll within, and when you open that one, there is a medium-size doll within, and when you open that one there is a smaller doll within and—"

"We get the picture, Doc," Ryan said, fearing that the old man's mind was going to slide off into one of its lateral spirals that brought him perilously close to madness.

"Yeah, we see," the Armorer added. "Russian dolls. What's that got to do with Project Cerberus?"

"What's what got to do with what?" Doc asked, his forehead furrowed with confusion.

"You said about special gateways not being part of Project Cerberus," Ryan explained, barely managing to keep his patience.

"Correct," Doc beamed. "Give that customer a large coconut. Cerberus was the doll within Over-project Whisper. In its own turn, Overproject Whisper was concealed from the eyes of the public and the media beneath the accommodating skirts of our country's Totality Concept. You understand?"

"Yeah. Double-clear, Doc. Some things you knew, and some you didn't."

Ryan turned and pushed the door open farther, his eye becoming accustomed to the brightness. Every single mat-trans chamber he'd seen had been part of an identical setup, though the shrouding redoubts were all different in design.

There was the small anteroom opening off the glass-paneled chamber, which measured about five long paces by three and contained an empty table against one wall.

Beyond that Ryan knew there would be a main control area, all whirling comp-wheels, disks, dials and flickering lights.

"Look." Lori pointed. "What's it saying, Doc? Can't read loopy words."

"Called graffiti, it was. Some poor devil scrawled this generations back, my dear, lovely child. It says 'I don't have a drinking problem, except when I can't get a drink.' It's a joke."

Nobody laughed.

The words had been scrawled on the pale cream wall just at the side of a row of bare shelves. It was the only decoration in the room.

"Ready, Ryan?" J.B. asked, the mini-Uzi braced against his hip.

"Go."

It was just as Ryan expected, but the room was much bigger and brighter than any of the others they'd come across. The chamber measured a good hundred paces long by forty wide.

"By the three Kennedys!" Doc exclaimed, pointing at one side of the doorway they'd all just stepped through.

There was a *second* gateway chamber.

The usual message had been printed above it in stark black lettering on a white ground: Entry Absolutely Forbidden to All but B19 Cleared Personnel. Mat-Trans.

"Not quite the same, Ryan," Krysty said. "The gateway we came from says B12. That one says B19. What's the difference, Doc? Any idea?"

"Nineteen's a much higher classification. Nabobs from the Pentagon personnel privy to Whisper would have been 19s. I wasn't ever leaked that high. Couldn't be trusted."

"So, what is it?" Lori asked.

"Something new that they were working on?" J.B. suggested.

Doc shook his head. "I confess myself utterly bewildered by this. I never heard of any such development in any redoubt. Ryan, my dear friend, have you ever heard of anything like this?"

"I never even heard of one gateway, Doc, never mind two."

"One way find out," Jak said softly.

The anteroom connecting the control chamber to the actual gateway was larger than usual. Unlike any others they'd seen, it was split in two, with a separate section to the left that contained a number of benches with hooks above for clothes, as well as dark green sec-plas lockers with slatted doors.

Jak led the way, his blaster gleaming brightly in the harsh, metallic glare of the lights. J.B. came second, followed by Doc and Lori. Donfil More padded along on his bare feet, eyes darting from side to side. Krysty and Ryan brought up the rear. All of them had their guns up and ready.

The girl hesitated, catching Ryan by the sleeve. "Hold it, lover," she said, with a quiet intensity in her voice.

"What?"

"Hold up," she called, halting the others.

Ryan knew from his months with Krysty that her mutie powers came and went, sometimes strong and sometimes weak. From the look on her face, he knew that this feeling was a strong one.

"Yeah?"

"Someone's been here. Recent. So recent I can almost taste their sweat."

"I feel the scent of men," the stooping Indian announced. "Close and yet far away. Cold deserts away from here."

Ryan didn't have any mutie extra sense, but he had all the instincts of a hunting killer wolf. As he stood in the doorway, he knew that Krysty and Donfil were both right. The faint prickling at his nape told him the same damned story. The redoubt wasn't empty.

"Shall check lockers?" Jak asked, almost dancing on the balls of his feet with the sudden tension.

"Later, mebbe," Ryan replied. "Doc, you seen anything like this?"

"Indeed, I have not. All gateway complexes were built, as far as I know, to an identical pattern. Every one."

"Check the mat-trans chamber itself?" J.B. suggested.

Ryan nodded.

Just to the right of the doorway there was another scrawled piece of graffiti, in what looked like the same hand.

"The large print giveth and the small print taketh away," it read. Beneath it, in a different hand, someone had neatly added "Tom Waits said that."

Ryan wondered who Tom Waits had been, guessing it was probably the name of one of the men who'd been working in the redoubt when infinity had beckoned.

The shaman paused and turned around, mirrored glasses reflecting the doorway and the main control behind them. He looked at Ryan.

"You think of infinity, my brother." It was a statement, not a question. "Do you know what infinity truly is?"

Ryan nodded. "I read it once, years back, when I was a kid, 'bout the age of Jak here. I read that to understand infinity you have to imagine that the whole damned planet is a sphere of polished vanadium steel. Once every thousand years a butterfly comes by and brushes the metal ball with its wing. *Very* gently. Imagine Earth wearing away, and you get a kind of glimpse of infinity."

"That's fucking loveliest!" Lori exclaimed, shaking her long blond hair in wonderment. "Fucking loveliest, Ryan."

"Watch the bad-mouthing language, my sweet little enchantress," Doc warned.

"Sorry." She grinned. "Mebbe you'll spank my buns for it tonight, huh?"

"Yeah, you do that, Doc," Jak cackled, hopping around from foot to foot like a snow-headed dervish.

"Button your lip, young fellow," Doc demanded, blushing deep crimson. "Can't we get on with going into the hornswoggled boondocked gateway?"

Jak couldn't stop giggling, leaning helplessly against one of the lockers, so Ryan pushed to the front and stood in front of the control panel. "Three-five-two to open it, Doc?"

"Who knows, Ryan? Since it has a higher security coding, I doubt very much if it will be the same numerical cipher."

Ryan reached out with the end of the barrel of the G-12 caseless and the door swung open. The silver glass walls of the gateway were shimmering, showing that it was actually in use!

Chapter Three

"FIREBLAST!"

"Gaia!"

"Dark night!"

"By Ysun!"

"Doc! What's...?"

"Damn, oh damn!"

"By the three Kennedys!"

It was one of the biggest shocks Ryan and his friends had ever encountered. Bigger than the mutie alligator or the stoning or the Russians in the snows.

Ryan felt for a heart-stopping moment like a fond father who'd gone up to his child's bedroom to reassure the frightened toddler that there *really* wasn't a bogeyman in the closet. He'd opened the door with a broad smile and seen...seen a squatting, dribbling creature, all raw head and bloody bones, reaching for him with soft fingers that ended in ravening points of ragged horn.

The armored glass walls were almost opaque, but the glowing disks in floor and ceiling flared through, and frail tendrils of white mist crept out beneath the door. There wasn't the least moment of doubt that someone, or something, was using the gateway for a jump.

"Coming or going?" Ryan asked J.B.

"Can't tell. Can't see inside. Can you tell, Doc? Doc, come on!"

The old man was standing like one stricken, hand pressed to his chest, all the color drained from his lined cheeks.

"Leave him," Ryan snapped. "Everyone out. Find cover in the main control room. Move it!"

Lori dragged Doc out on stumbling feet, through the side room, pulling him into hiding behind one of the banks of comp-disks. Jak was kneeling next to them, his pistol as steady as death in both hands. Krysty and Ryan went the other way, finding space where they could take cover and watch the main gateway chamber at the same time. J.B. and Donfil darted around the corner to wait in the other gateway, the Armorer's Steyr blaster poised like a cobra waiting to strike. The Apache held his clumsy great Sharps rifle braced against his hip.

Even at that moment of heightened tension, it crossed Ryan's mind that the tall shaman needed a decent handblaster.

"See anything?" Jak hissed. "Can't hear nothing."

Ryan held his breath and cautiously edged his good eye around the corner of a control console, peering across into the mat-trans chamber. He blinked and then checked again what he saw.

"Light's fading," he called. "Don't move yet, but it looks like whoever's going and not coming."

He counted a hundred slow, measured beats of his heart, carefully checking again, easing around the edge of the cover, not taking a chance.

One of his first memories of joining War Wag One and the Trader was a firefight against some hillies up in the Zarks, most of them armed with two-hundred-year-old muskets. The man at his side had stuck his head up a touch careless, and Ryan would never forget the warm, sticky splash of brains and clotted blood that had darted into his face as the back of the man's skull exploded.

"What's it look like, lover?" Krysty whispered at his elbow.

"Light's most gone."

"Could still be coming," J.B. called. "We get well blacked out of it when we jump. Could be they're in there."

It was a good point. Ryan kept them for another fifteen minutes, watching the clicking digits of his wrist chron. "Man hurries when he doesn't have to gets himself an early chilling and gives the buzzards a free lunch," Trader used to say.

"Come on. Cover us," Ryan said, beckoning to Krysty and J.B. to follow him.

The glass walls were blank, with an impenetrable silvery sheen. Ryan put out a hand and touched one with the tips of his fingers.

"Still warm."

When they'd been making a jump he hadn't noticed any change in the temperature, but the feeling of having your brains curdled meant you weren't too aware of what was going down around you.

"Shall I open the door?" J.B. asked.

Ryan licked his dry lips. "Guess so. Slow and easy."

"Sure."

The mat-trans chamber was completely empty, not a speck of dust or a bead of moisture. No hint that it had just been used. Ryan called for the others to join them. "Watch you don't touch anything," he warned. "This might operate differently than the other gateways."

Doc paused to study the control panel near the entrance door, shaking his head. "I swear that I have never seen aught like this. Quite different from anything I worked on with Cerberus. It has most definitely been used for transmitting someone to somewhere. But the good Lord alone might know who and where."

"No point in hanging around here," Krysty said. "Nothing to see. Best we move out. Get us some food, if there is any. Break out for the day."

"Or night?" Lori asked quietly.

ANOTHER OF THE TRADER'S RULES had been that you only split your forces when there was no help for it. "Half your men and you got half your power," he would sometimes say.

Though Krysty, Doc, Lori and Jak were all for proceeding into the rest of the redoubt, Ryan insisted they first spend a little time in checking out the lockers that lined the second anteroom.

Most of them were empty. One had a porno pic of a slant-eyed girl with enormous breasts, touching herself with her left hand while the right held the engorged cock of a massive pit bull terrier. The laser-holo caught Jak's attention for several seconds.

"Never seen nothing like it," he said, turning away reluctantly.

At the bottom of one of the narrow cupboards J.B. found a spent cartridge case. "Forty-four," he said, dropping it with a metallic thunk.

The most amazing discovery was in the second last locker in the row. The lock had jammed, and Ryan had to pry it open.

"Well, look at this," he breathed.

The locker contained a black zippered bag, which looked like it contained some kind of bulky uniform. Ryan left that until last. On the top shelf was a pair of worn combat boots with steel tips to heels and toes. Tucked in behind them was an Eickhorn combat knife with a seven-inch blade, rusted and frail from being kept there for so long. A rubbed leather strap held a holstered pistol, a customized Smith & Wesson Distinguished Combat .357 Magnum.

"Model 686," the armorer commented, hefting the gun, testing the action. He thumbed back on the hammer and eased it down, checking to see if the revolver carried a full load. "Not bad. Not bad at all. Soft on the trigger. Bit of wear around the cylinder. Got a ball catch added in the crane. Mat fiber-blast finish. Nice blaster. Got the Wichita rib sight added for accuracy. Standard six-inch barrel, six rounds. Stocked up with Silvalube bullets.''

It was rare that the slightly built man ever spoke more than two consecutive sentences, other than when you got him talking about blasters. Or weapons of any kind.

Ryan took it from him. ''Donfil could do with a handblaster, J.B. How'd this be for him?''

''Plenty of gun. Extra sight's a big bonus. Looks like a box of hollow-nose on that shelf up there. Yeah. What d'you think?''

The skeletal Apache stooped and took the blaster from Ryan's fingers, feeling the balance, extending his arm and squinting along the barrel. He finally nodded and tucked the gun into his belt.

''What's this, Ryan?'' Jak asked, pulling out a cotton vest that nearly fell apart in his hands. There was writing across the front in faded red lettering. Life Sucks and Then You're Chilled.

Jak crumpled the garment and threw it into the locker.

A denim jacket carried the multiheaded dog that was the symbol of Project Cerberus. Ryan checked through the pockets in case there was anything that might cast some light on the mysterious gateway but found only a torn candy bar wrapper, a handful of loose change and a sliver of card that had once held a condom.

He reached out and zipped open the plastic bag, the whisper of sound seeming almost deafening in the stillness of the chamber. All of them jumped as something shapeless and gleaming came toppling out, arms and legs flailing toward them.

"Nearly fucking chilled it." Jak grinned down at the empty, hooded garment that sprawled at their feet.

"Looks like a diving suit," Krysty said. "Had a pic of one in an old book back in Harmony. Book 'bout a subsea boat from real old times."

"Doubtlessly Jules?" Doc suggested.

"No," she replied. "No jewels, no gold, no treasure at all."

"Let it pass," the old man said.

Ryan stooped and picked up the suit, seeing that it was covered in all sorts of numbered and lettered patches, pockets and straps. The material shimmered in his hands and was surprisingly light. There was some sort of screw connection around the neck where it looked as though a helmet had once been fixed, confirming Krysty's guess that the garment had been used for diving. But there was something about it....

"I don't think..." he began, but Doc interrupted him, snatching at the suit and peering at it shortsightedly.

"No!" the old man yelled, voice cracking in his excitement. "No, it's not a diving suit! Course it's not."

"Then what is it?" Lori asked.

Ryan knew the answer a jagged shard of iced time before Doc spoke.

"It's what we used to call a space suit," Doc told them.

The idea that this particular gateway could be used as a portal for travel off the planet into the silent deeps of space didn't, somehow, surprise Ryan Cawdor. He'd read in old books about the way the United States, as it had been called before the name of Deathlands overlaid it, had been dabbling in the exploration of space from the 1950s or so. And in the ten years before nuke-cull, they'd been pouring more and more trillions of dollars into setting up circling stations that would eventually become self-supporting. Just how far some of those plans had gone was unknown. Guesses replaced facts as government censorship bit heavily into the freedom of the media in the nineties.

Now here was clear, undeniable evidence that this secondary gateway had been used as a link, not only with other gateways across the land, but also outward.

Everyone wanted to talk about it, but Ryan stopped the excited chatter. "Come on, friends! Nothing more here to see." He took the space suit and threw it back into the locker. "Let's go find us some food and somewhere to rest up after that jump."

"But, my dear Ryan, do you not realize what this discovery means?"

"Sure, Doc. Means someone, apart from us seven, knows how to use a Gateway. Mebbe they know better than us how they work. But we just missed 'em by the width of a knife blade. They've gone—" he waved an arm in the vague direction of the brightly lit ceiling "—somewhere out there. We keep moving long enough and far enough, we'll likely come across 'em one day.''

DONFIL SLUNG his Sharps .50 across his shoulders by its braided strap, gripping his new Smith & Wesson blaster in his long fingers. Ryan shook his head as he glanced at the immensely tall Apache, thinking what a raggle-taggle band they were.

"Smell like swamps," Jak said, pausing suddenly, sniffing at the cool, recirculated air like a pointing hound.

Ryan also took in several deep breaths through his nose, as did the others.

Only Krysty noticed anything. "Sort of rotting plants and salty and... Can't place the smell, but Jak's right. There's something around."

The door out of the main control section of the redoubt opened on a simple manual switch. In the corridor beyond, Ryan immediately noticed that there were prepared firing points for defense, with side walls cutting out at angles to give cover to riflemen. That was something new as well, strengthening the feeling that this place was, somehow, real special.

"Smell's stronger," Ryan said. "I can taste it now."

The passageway forked after a hundred paces. To the right was a flight of stairs going upward, with a door at its top. To the left was a massively solid pair of titanium-steel doors, surrounded by thick black rubber sealing strips.

"Stop a battalion of war wags, doors like that," J.B. said.

Lori shivered and Doc hastily put his arm around her shoulder. "Feel colder and wet." She screwed up her face to show her discomfort.

"Yes. There's the sensation of a long-closed tomb down here, Ryan," Doc commented. "Best we try to go upward, I think."

Ryan shook his head. "Those look like outer doors to the redoubt. Best thing is to find out what kind of place we've landed up in. J.B. can use his sextant, and we'll have some idea, mebbe, of what to expect. There's the main control lock to the right of the entrance."

It was a chromed steel wheel, which was obviously linked to some system of gears that would swing open the huge doors. At a nod from Ryan, the Armorer went to lay a hand on the wheel. "Real cold," he said.

"Everyone back and ready for trouble," Ryan warned. "Could be . . . Just take real good care."

They all heard the faint hiss of hydraulics engaging—the whirring of long-static motors grumbling into reluctant life. Above the sounds Ryan detected the noise of cogs not quite meshing, metal grinding ominously.

"Not good, J.B.!" he called.

But the face beneath the shadowing fedora hat didn't turn toward him, and he realized that the Armorer wasn't able to hear him.

The polished wheel started to revolve slowly, J.B.'s knuckles white with the effort of moving it around.

"It's real hard and . . . No, it's going now. Yeah, there she . . ."

The words were drowned out by the great green-white gusher of water that jetted between the opening doors, bursting among the group with the power of a fire hose and knocking them off their feet.

Ryan opened his mouth to yell for them to make for the stairs, but he was nearly choked by the rush of freezing salt water that filled his throat.

He rolled over and over, fighting to get to his feet, clawing his way up the wall until he could find his balance. The wave was already three feet deep, swirling around the tops of his thighs. He'd automatically hung on to his weapons as the sea tumbled him down. To his enormous relief, Ryan saw that the inrush had hit him harder than the rest, since he'd been standing near the center of the passageway.

Doc had Lori by the arm and was already leading her up the stairs toward the high set of doors. The girl was barely able to walk, her long blond hair hanging limply across her shoulders.

Jak was on the second step, scarcely knee-deep, brushing back his mane of snow-white hair, peering down for the others. J.B. was clinging to the chrome wheel, braced against the wall, hat tugged immovably down over his forehead. He shook his head as he turned to face Ryan. Above the thunder of the deepening water, Ryan couldn't hear him, but the shape of his mouth and the movement of the head made it clear that the control was jammed. Nothing could stop the sea from continuing to pour into the redoubt.

Krysty came bursting up from underwater, hair like a spurt of fire around her face. She managed to stand alongside her man, putting her lips close to his ears to shout "You all right, lover? Make for the stairs? Only way."

"Yeah!" he bellowed, wondering how deep below the sea the doors of the redoubt lay, and if the other exit from the corridor, some thirty feet above them, would be open.

Out of the corner of his eye he spotted Donfil, brandishing his new blaster, the incoming waves hardly reaching to his knees as he picked his way toward the staircase with the ungainly delicacy of a feeding stork.

Ryan clutched Krysty by the hand and they battled together across the corridor, joined by J.B. just before they reached the line of steps. The sea had already reached their waists.

"Jammed solid!" J.B. yelled. "Couldn't shift it an inch."

"Best hope we can open those doors at the top. Or we're in the deepest shit."

"Unless the waters stop rising."

The doors proved immovably locked. As the seven huddled wetly together on the narrow landing, all they could do was watch the dull gray waters rise inexorably higher toward them.

Higher and higher.

Chapter Four

DESPITE THEIR IMMEDIATE DANGER, Ryan kept trying to remember whether he'd closed the doors that led through to the main gateway control room. If he hadn't, then there wasn't a scintilla of doubt that the whole place was now at least ten feet underwater, for the corridor had been fairly level. All the electrical equipment would be fused into a barren silence, and they would have no hope of ever using the mat-trans again.

But as the sea kept insistently and steadily rising, he became more occupied with the threat of the dreadful death that confronted them.

The gap in the doors didn't just allow a ceaseless torrent to flood into the passage—it also allowed life to come in from the deep waters beyond the buried entrance.

Jak had been sitting on one of the steps near the top with his booted feet dabbling in the bubbling water when something like a snake, whip-thin, darted from the darkness and attached itself to his arm. It wound itself around, tiny head with needled teeth striking blindly toward the boy's face. Before anyone else could make a move, the teenager drew one of his con-

cealed throwing knives, slashing with the honed edge,
and cut the creature's head from its flailing body. Its
grip weakened immediately, and it fell back into the
seething torrent. Its light green corpse sank slowly
until it vanished into the murk.

"Best keep clear," Ryan advised.

"Long as we can," Donfil replied, standing on the
top step, looking doubtfully down as the water lapped
at his bare feet. His head was bowed to avoid touching the oppressive metal ceiling with its fan of strip
lights.

"How long?" Jak asked J.B., who'd been obviously taking a count of the speed of the rising waters with his chron.

"One step in thirty-eight seconds. Step, near as I can
figure it, is 7½ inches. That's one inch every 5.06 re-
curring seconds."

"How many inches to gone before we get sinked?"
Lori asked, still clutching Doc around his waist.

"I vanish at around another seventy inches. You
make it another four inches. Means you get nearly a
half minute over me. Donfil, there, could last clear
until the water reaches the ceiling."

"Bastard way t'go," Jak said. "Like rat in trap."

Ryan leaned against the unbudgeable doors, feeling the seawater rising over his ankles. The kid was
right about that. If he could have picked the manner
of his passing, then Ryan would have gone down in a
firefight, taking as many to hell with him. Not like
this.

Doc cleared his throat. The landing was relatively quiet, the noise of the rushing water drowned by its own depth. The surface rose calmly and inexorably toward them. "A man could choose a good deal worse company in which to greet his Maker," he said.

"If only I'd kept some ex-plas. A high-ex gren. Least we could have had an ace on the line. This way, we got nothing."

The water was above Ryan's knees.

He was conscious of the increased air pressure, squeezing at his ears, as the space became ever more constricted.

"Wouldn't mind it if you gave me a last kiss, lover," Krysty said quietly. "Sorry we gotta end like this."

"Me too." He hugged her tightly.

The water was touching his belt. One hand around the girl, he automatically held his G-12 above the sea with his other hand.

"Ears hurt," Lori moaned.

"Of course!" Doc shouted, his voice sounding peculiarly dead and flat in the waterbound space.

"What?" Ryan asked, hoping there weren't any more of the venomous sea snakes seething around his submerged groin.

"Her ears hurt because of the air pressure. We've got a chance, friends. Chance of time, at least. Unless we're way, way deep, hundreds of feet, this air'll save us. These doors here are sealed tighter than a nun's... Pardon me. But the air can't get out. So it holds the water off. Hurts our ears. Keep swallowing hard, chickadee. But the water'll soon stop rising here."

"Better be quick," Jak panted, nearly six inches shorter than even J.B.

"You can ride my shoulders, Eyes of Wolf," the shaman offered.

"Shouldn't be necessary," the old man said, clapping his gnarled hands together.

"But it won't get us out, Doc," Ryan said, suddenly aware that the rise of the sea had definitely slowed.

"It'll give us time to think of a way."

The water stopped rising just above Ryan's waist. As an experiment he dipped his head below the surface, straining his hearing to try to catch the sound of the sea gushing through the gap, twenty feet or so below them. But there was silence, which was broken only by the surging noise of his own blood pumping through his head.

Doc kept mumbling to himself, trying to work out some hideously complex sum in his head, linking the pressure of the air around them with how deep the sea might be outside.

"Hundred and forty-six miles," he concluded. "Damnation and perdition! That can't be right. No. Can't be too much deeper outside than in. If this is high tide, then we do have some small hope of escape when it falls again. Particularly if we are anywhere near the northeast coast. The tides there are exceedingly large. The Bay of Fundy...born on Monday, christened on Tuesday and...What was I saying?"

The old man's voice faded away.

The coldness was chilling, cutting through to the bone. Ryan made everyone keep moving, stamping their feet and slapping hands, fighting off the insidious enemy.

Once he felt something move close by his legs, swirling past him, grazing his pants. Something that felt a whole lot too large for his peace of mind. At his warning, everyone who carried a knife drew it, and they moved even closer together on the cramped, narrow landing. It was a sign that the doors of the redoubt must have opened wider than he'd thought.

The creature didn't come back.

"IT'S GOING DOWN," Donfil said.

Ryan hadn't noticed any sign of the water level dropping, but he didn't propose to argue with the seven-foot-tall Apache.

"Yes," Krysty agreed after a couple of minutes. "He's right."

Three hours passed before the water dropped enough for them to be able to see the gap in the jammed doors. From above, it looked to be about fifteen inches wide—just enough for them all to be able to squeeze through. But they still had no idea what was on the other side. The sea was out there; that was all they knew.

The redoubt could be on some uninhabited island, miles from land. The doors might open at the foot of unscalable cliffs. Ryan knew that their chances of getting out of this mess alive weren't much better than even.

"Light's fading out there," Jak Lauren observed some time later, his red eyes being more sensitive than anyone else's to such changes. "Must be night starting."

The water at the foot of the stairs was barely a foot deep. Ryan was conscious of the risk that they might miss the turning of the tide and leave it too late to make their move. But he still hesitated at leading his six companions out into the unknown and threatening darkness.

"Gaia!" Krysty shivered. "My bones are turning into pack ice, lover. Doc and Lori won't make it through another tide. Maybe I won't. We'll die if we stay here."

He nodded, feeling the stiffness and deadly numbness sapping his energy. "Sure. Let's move out."

Ryan led the way, wading to the doors. The gap was festooned with long tendrils of leprous-pale weed, and he was aware of sand beneath the soles of his combat boots. It was impossible, with the dazzling lights of the redoubt at his shoulder, to see anything at all outside, beyond the gleam of water on rock a couple of paces beyond the entrance.

J.B. went to the control wheel and threw his weight against it. He shook his head grimly. "Locked for ever an' a day."

"I'll go first," Jak said. "Follow tight."

The young albino had excellent night vision, and Ryan was happy for him to take the lead, moving easily between the rubber-sealed doors. J.B. went second, with the rest of the group close behind. Ryan brought up the rear, glancing back down the bright corridor, wondering whether they might have done better by going back and trying the gateway. But the water seemed to be rising once more, and if they got trapped again, the cold and wet would surely take its toll among them.

"Nobody ever gets anywhere going backward," he said quietly to himself. He pushed past the fronds of seaweed and walked out into the cool night breeze.

They stood on the crumbling remnants of an old jetty, with huge, rusting iron mooring rings set in the weathered concrete. The turning tide was already a foot or more over the surface, and Ryan guessed that the vicious nuking of the last of wars must have caused a local earth shift. When it was first built, the quay would have been a good many feet proud of the high-tide level.

The night was piercingly black, with only scudding white clouds staining the oppressive darkness of the sky. Ryan found it difficult to see through the blown spume off the ocean, but he had the impression of a vast distance out beyond the edge of the jetty, and of monstrously high cliffs scraping upward behind them.

"Stairs. Iron. Up there." Jak pointed up by the side of the pair of doors. "Not safe. All rotted down."

"Just what I needed," Ryan said, baring his teeth in a mirthless grin. "Always loved climbing up a crumbling ladder in pitch-dark over rocks and sea. Nothing fucking nicer in the world."

THE RUNGS AND side supports of the ladder had been worn down until many of them were thinner than a child's finger. Despite the bitter chill and the rising wind, Ryan found himself sodden with sweat, which was running down the small of his back and was making his hands even more slippery.

He lost track of how long and how high they'd been climbing. For the first few minutes he'd been able to peer down between his boots and see white water breaking over the quay's rough edges. The next time he looked down, all that had vanished. There was nothing to be seen above him and nothing below.

Every now and again Ryan felt Krysty, climbing second, touch his foot, but for most of the spidering ascent he felt utterly alone, suspended in the yawning chasm between Earth and Heaven. Once a rung broke under his foot, and he swung for a heart-stopping second by his hands, conscious only of the frailty of the metal and the appalling distance he would fall.

The wind was rising, tugging at his clothes, trying to jerk the G-12 off his shoulders. His hair blew about his face.

A large gull burst shrieking from a cleft in the rock, nearly dislodging his grip and sending him spinning into the void. But he held on and kept climbing remorselessly upward.

The ladder could only possibly have been built there for emergency purposes. There was no human way of making the climb, except in the direst of needs.

The wind had become almost a full-blown gale, howling like a cemetery banshee, deafening him to every other sound. It blanked out all of his senses except the ones that gripped the rusting iron and hauled him painfully upward, a trembling step at a time.

Ryan paused and blinked the spray from his eye, staring up. He was able to see only a few feet, but seeing...thinking he was seeing...the sharp edge of concrete only a half dozen rungs above his head. It had to be the top of the climb.

The sides of the ladder rose up and over in a semi-circle of freezing, pitted metal. Ryan, drained by the struggle of leading the others into unknown blackness, clambered clumsily over the rim and collapsed on hands and knees on smoother stone. Krysty joined him a moment later, her breathing surging harshly.

"I've done easier things, lover," she panted. "Hope the others can make it."

"Only one way. Can't go down," he said, feeling strength already seeping back into his body.

It seemed an eternity before the next head loomed into sight, mirrored glasses making it appear like a bizarrely mutated stick insect.

"Doc's...close behind. Near falling. Lori tied herself to him with belt. Told him if he let go he'd...take her with...with him. Been pulling from above. I would not do that again for immortal life."

With a great effort the three of them managed to heave the old man and the girl over the brink onto the flat platform. Doc collapsed, totally exhausted, and Lori fell behind him, retching on hands and knees, threads of vomit dangling from her sagging mouth.

"Five up and two to go," Ryan said.

Jak was next, hair plastered to his angular skull like a snow-plas mask. He was sobbing for breath, and he joined Lori, doubled up.

Last was J.B., his trusty fedora jammed down the front of his jacket. His glasses were totally misted with sea spray, but he climbed the last few steps as sprightly as if he'd been out for an afternoon scramble with a pair of maiden aunts.

Ryan had found a small iron door, covered in lichen, at the rear of the platform, and he left the others and pushed at it, finding that it swung open easily. His eye winced at the brightness of light inside, startling after the long blackness.

But he could see enough to make out a slackly grinning mouth and shadowed eyes that seemed to mutter brain death. And below that the twin barrels of a sawed-off shotgun.

Chapter Five

"HI. WHOOOOO YOU?"

The fluting, owllike voice was like that of a young child. But the face above the scattergun was at least sixty years old, lined and furrowed, with a pale, unhealthy sheen to it, overlaid with a gray patina of dust and grease. The crazed eyes stared at Ryan out of pits of scoured bone, deadly flat and so dark a brown that they blurred into black. There were no teeth in the yellowed gums that leered at Ryan Cawdor. His hair was the color of rotting corn, pasted thinly over the crumpled scalp. Both ears pointed backward instead of forward. The man wore a shapeless suit of crudely woven wool, dyed a sickly green-yellow. Ryan wrinkled his nose at the foul smell of damp and decay that billowed around him.

"Whooooo you?" the voice repeated.

"Name's Ryan Cawdor. What do they call you?"

"Don't knooooow. Nooooo name for meeee. How you come?"

"Up the ladder. Had a boat wrecked below on the rocks. Climbed up. Long way, ain't it?"

The head nodded, but the gun never shifted. The stranger's finger never moved off the twin triggers of the battered Remington.

"Long waaaaay. Sure is. Upanupanup."

The man was a perfect target for anyone behind Ryan, with that bright light haloing him, and he wouldn't be able to see any of the others in the blackness outside. However, any of the other six would also be able to see the shotgun pointing just below Ryan's breastbone. It was way better than evens that a bullet through the toothless mouth could also mean a hole in Ryan's guts.

"Why the gun?" Ryan asked, taking care not to let his own fingers stray toward the blaster in his belt.

"Why not? There's a riddle, innit? Riddlemereeeeee. You come the ladder?"

"Yeah."

"Up it?"

"Sure."

"Now you gooooo down it."

"How's that?" The muzzle jabbing toward Ryan made it clear what the mutie meant.

"Down, down." The movement stopped. "You got any Cokes?"

"Drinks, you mean?"

The face split wider in a smile of delight. "You know it."

In a few of the redoubts that Ryan Cawdor had helped to uncover, there'd been rooms full of supplies. The familiar red-and-white cans were sometimes there, still good and drinkable after all the long years.

"Could have," Ryan said cautiously, hedging his bets for the crazie.

"Where?"

"In the boat. Out there." He pointed behind him, where he could sense the others waiting, tensely, for a chance to chill the stranger.

"I been here lotsa days. Found a room with cansa Coke innit. Had—" a look of concentrated effort crossed the man's face "—had meeee same cans as fingers every day. More lotsa times. All days been here all life been here."

Ryan's mind boggled. If this gibbering dotard had really been in this redoubt all his life and had been drinking ten cans of soft drink every day, he must have finished off...hundreds of thousands of them. Somewhere there must be a graveyard of tins bigger than a dozen war wags.

"Not had any for days now. Lotsa days. How many you got?"

"Lots." Ryan held up both hands to show ten fingers, clenching and opening them, drawing the sunken, mad little eyes.

The barrels of the scattergun wavered for a moment, which was all that Ryan needed.

He slashed down with his left hand, parrying the blaster away, simultaneously diving low and to his left, inside the doorway.

"Chill him!" he yelled.

The blast of gunfire filled his ears, and he was conscious of the all too familiar warm rain of blood and bone splinters cascading over him. The mutie didn't even have time for a proper scream as he saw his own passing—a muffled cry and then the clatter of the Remington hitting the floor, followed by the loose flailing as he went down after the blaster. One of his feet kicked Ryan in the ribs before he could roll away.

"You can get up, Ryan," J.B. said. "He's going nowhere."

He stood up, dusting himself off, seeing that J.B., Jak and Krysty were all holding smoking blasters. The dead mutie lay in a jumbled heap of torn flesh, dark blood puddled all around him.

Jak picked up the fallen shotgun, flicking it open. "Empty," he said laconically. "Not fired for fifty years by dirt."

"Is that a mistake?" Donfil asked, stooping to get through the doorway, out of the screeching wind and spray.

"No," Ryan answered. "Mistake would have been if it had been me down and done for. No. No mistake at all, friend."

DOC WAS IN A PARLOUS STATE. The shock of the climb—after the immersion in freezing seawater—had carried him beyond the level of exhaustion. And, as is often the case, the mind had gone along with his body.

Lori and Ryan carried him in, while Krysty finally closed the door on the bitter storm that raged outside in the night. The old man was talking incessantly, in a ragged monotone, half inaudible, the rest complete nonsense.

"Cape Cod, summer of '95. Bitter chill it was. The crabs for all their feathers were... Emily, belly swollen like a milkmaid, smiling in the sun. Rachel tarryhooting around like a heathen savage. We went so gentle into the far-off beating of a slackskin drum." The eyes snapped open and stared with a fiery intelligence into Ryan's good eye. "You lied who told me time would ease my pain. I miss them in the turning of the tides. I miss them in the weeping of the rain. There's a wind on the heath, Brother Ryan. Life is very sweet. Who would wish to die?"

His eyes closed and he fell deeply asleep, even as they carried him into the depths of the isolated redoubt.

For reasons that nobody would ever know, it seemed that the nameless mutie had been living alone in that section of the complex for most of his life. There were rooms filled with empty and rotten self-heats and ring-pulls. It had been the storage section, and there were still enough racks of food and drink to keep a small army supplied for months.

There was also a whole wing of the redoubt equipped as dormitories, with partitions dividing off small rooms, each with half a dozen metal-frame bunk beds.

They laid Doc on one of them, and Lori crashed out on the bed beside. J.B. and Jak joined the shaman in a room just along the passage.

"We need a guard, Ryan?" the Armorer asked.

"Doesn't seem to be any sign that the crazie had any company here. After the past few hours, I figure we all need some sleep real bad. Let's take a chance. The doors are bolted at both ends of this dormitory. We got our blasters at our sides."

J.B. nodded his agreement. "Fine. I feel kinda tired."

Ryan grinned at his old friend. "That's a first. I swear I can't recall ever hearing you say before in all the years... You *must* be tired."

Krysty called to him. "Couple of beds here pushed together, lover. Not used, neither. Double spread of blankets."

Ryan closed the flimsy hardboard door and switched off the light. There was still plenty of glow from the main overhead lamps that were never switched off in any redoubt.

He felt bone weary. "You getting undressed?" Krysty asked from where she lay sprawled on the bed. Her sentient hair framed her pale cheeks limply, setting off the startling green of her eyes.

Ryan shook his head. "Nope. I'll peel off what's wet and... Guess that's everything. Fireblast! Yeah, why not?"

She didn't move, watching him as he unlaced the combat boots, cursing the seawater that had tightened the knots. He peeled the socks off his pale, puckered feet, carefully unburdening himself of his armory of weapons: rifle, pistol and panga, the hidden slim-bladed flensing knife. He unwound the white silk scarf with the strangler's weights at both ends, then removed the heavy coat with the white fur collar and the rest of his clothes, until he stood, swaying with tiredness, magnificently naked in front of her.

"Very good, lover," she said softly, clapping her hands gently together. "Now you lie down here and watch me."

"Krysty," he warned her, "I'm not going to be up to this tonight. Leave it lay until the dawning. I can't do a thing until I've slept."

"We'll see." She licked her lips very slowly, and despite his protestations, Ryan felt a tremor stirring at his groin.

He moved past her and lay on the bed, not bothering to pull up the blankets. As in most redoubts, the automatic temperature control kept conditions comfortable.

Krysty glanced across at him, admiring the planes of muscle across his lean torso, noticing, as she always did on the rare occasions she saw him nude, the seamed scars and weals of old wounds that mapped his body from temple to heel.

The woman pulled off her dark blue leather boots, throwing them down by the bed, the silver points on the toes gleaming softly. The khaki coveralls peeled away from her and fell about her bare feet, leaving only the sheen of her bikini pants, strung across her hips.

"Want me to keep these on?" she asked, hooking her thumbs in the elastic and posing like a border gaudy house whore for him, her breasts like fire-tipped cones of firm flesh.

"Told you. I'm too damned tired," he insisted.

She grinned impishly, pointing at the part of his body that was insistently giving the lie to his words.

"That's not tired, lover." Krysty grinned.

"Let's just sleep now. Make love tomorrow, when we wake up."

Farther along they both heard Doc cry out, an anguished yelp of terror and despair, torn from his sleeping mind.

"Poor old bastard," Ryan said. "Hope he feels more himself tomorrow."

"Lori'll help him do that."

"Yeah."

Krysty walked to the bed and folded herself onto it, leaning against Ryan's raised knees. She ran her hand gently up his leg, stroking the inside of his thighs.

Higher.

"What d'you say, lover?" she whispered.

"I say that I can't. Not tonight. I'm sorry, love, but I can't."

Higher, her strong fingers proving him more of a liar.

"I can't, Krysty."

But he could.

Chapter Six

THE BATTERING ON THE DOOR of their dormitory sent Ryan's hand scrabbling for the butt of the SIG-Sauer blaster, feeling the chill of the metal against the warmth of his palm.

But the voice outside was Doc's and he relaxed again, Krysty cuddling up against him under the blankets.

"For gentlemen in England now a'bed will think themselves accursed they were not here and hold their manhood cheap... Upon my soul, friend Cawdor, friend Glamis, are you in there with yon wanton maiden, holding your manhood?"

"If Doc knew I *was* holding it, he'd go fire-red with embarrassment," Krysty whispered.

"He sounds in good voice." He called out to the old man. "You got first food cooked and waiting for us, Doc?"

"Of course. Eggs fresher than tomorrow's sunrise done just the way you like 'em. Fluffy and full of get-up-and-go goodness. Rashers of orange-cured ham so thick you need a forklift to get them to your mouth. Honey-roasted chicken pieces and crisp link patties. Peaches and melons that fell off the trees five minutes ago. Coffee strong enough and black enough to float a six-shooter. Bread that hasn't even finished being baked yet awhile. And butter that was in the cow less than a half hour since."

"Doc," Ryan said, swinging his long legs out of the bed and starting to pull on his pants, "you got yourself a couple of hungry customers. It really is good as you say?"

"Sure! Come and get it! Come and get it!"

A few minutes later Ryan cautiously lifted the brittle off-white plastic spoon to his lips, grimacing at the familiar gray texture and stodgy consistency of the dull mess resting like a sullen reproach in the middle of the plate.

"You lying old bastard!" he shouted. "It's just fucking self-heat, like it always is."

Doc cackled with merriment, eyes glinting at the success of his small joke. "Yes, dear Ryan, yes. But you had a good couple of minutes there anticipating it, didn't you?"

A decent, uninterrupted night's sleep was such a rarity in the Deathlands that all seven of them were in high spirits as they ate their breakfast, with the possible exception of Donfil More, who was tenderly rubbing the lower part of his back, complaining that the bed was a foot too short for him.

"Every bed too short f'you," Jak sniggered.

APART FROM DONFIL'S Smith & Wesson, there didn't seem to be any worthwhile armament sections in the vast, rambling redoubt. Even the first superficial survey of the morning made it clear that the land, wherever they were, had definitely been subject to a major shift and drop. Whole sections of the complex had totally disappeared, corridors ending in blank walls of smeared earth, as though a gigantic knife had hacked through them.

Some of the redoubts that had been totally abandoned at the time of the long winters had been scoured clear with fine combs; every single artifact, notice, instruction or plan had been removed. But that wasn't the case here, as they found when they finished their dreary breakfast and set out to explore.

Every main passage and junction area had its own 3-D holo map of the entire redoubt that showed where they were at any given moment, as well as tappable info about how to move around both inside and outside.

Since there was no sign of any danger, Ryan agreed that they should split up. Doc and Lori were accompanied by Jak, and J.B. went on a recce with the Mescalero shaman. Ryan went with Krysty.

After studying one of the plans, Ryan realized that the gateway section could be totally cut off from the rest of the redoubt, only accessible now down the tottering ladder at the lowest turning of the tide. Once again there came the nagging doubt that he'd closed the outer sealing doors to the mat-trans section.

The map also showed, at the highest floor level near something marked as Main Entrance, a rectangular building called Visitor Center and Initial Indoctrination Module.

"Sounds worth a look, lover?" Krysty suggested.

"Yeah. Doesn't sound like there's all that much around this place worth a look. It's kind of funny in a way."

"What is?"

"We've seen redoubts cleared right out, and yet you still can find something mebbe useful around the place. You know?"

"Yeah."

"This looks like it was in use right up till the nukes started falling...."

Krysty shook her head. "More than that, lover. We already saw that there's somebody around somewhere who's *still* using the redoubt—least the gateways—to jump."

"I know. But apart from the big landslide, this place is filled with food and everything. We could live here the rest of our lives and never need to go outside again."

"Call that living?"

"No. Call it existing. Once saw some old vid, back around bloody Kansas, with some friends who got holed up in a kind of ville. Muties all around them trying to get in. They sort of existed."

"What happened to them?"

Ryan shook his head. "No idea. Vid player broke before we got to the end of the story. I guess they all died."

Krysty reached in her pocket and drew out the small, gleaming black Apache tear, the smooth stone she'd brought with her from the wilderness of the

Southwest. She threw it up in the air and caught it, bringing it to her lips for a gentle kiss. "How 'bout we all go up and get us some fresh air. What do you say to that?"

"Yeah," Ryan said with a noticeable lack of enthusiasm. "Why not?"

None of the others had found anything of great interest in the parts of the redoubt they'd been exploring. Donfil had been fascinated by a room packed from floor-to-ceiling with boxes of tablets.

"They were called... What was their name, again, J.B.?"

"Tranks and sleepers," the Armorer replied.

"Yes." The shaman nodded. "Pills to make you sleep and pills to stop you worrying. It is not the way of my people to take such things. There is wrong in the balance if such 'pills' are needed."

Doc laughed, still sounding a little weak after his ordeal of the previous day. "One pill to make you larger and one to make you small," he chanted. "Go ask Alice, but I think she doesn't live hereabouts anymore."

Ryan didn't take much notice, figuring the old man's skull was still a couple of rounds short of a full mag.

THE DEAD MUTIE had obviously been an old loner, a packie, hanging around the corpses of old buildings for what he could suck out of the ruins. By far the greater threat to their safety was the mysterious, unseen stranger who'd been able to manipulate the controls of the gateway with such apparent ease. He *could* be dangerous.

So Ryan led them along in full firefight order, blasters at the ready, fingers on triggers, nerves drawn as tight as bowstrings. J.B. brought up the rear of their patrol, with the rest of them strung out between.

The journey up toward the surface was trouble-free and uneventful, and they followed the explicit maps at every turn and junction. The walls were gently curved, with the overbright lighting fading to normal as they climbed into the highest levels. It crossed Ryan's mind that it was odd the redoubt contained no corpses. Where were all the dead? The atomic generators had been built and programmed to provide air, heat and light for a thousand years. But they weren't programmed to shift what must have been several hundred iced bodies.

"This is it." Ryan held up his clenched fist in the signal for them to stop and beckoned them all forward into the large open space. Oil stains marked the concrete floor.

"Usual control," Jak commented, pointing to the green lever.

Unusually it was pointing in the up position, meaning that the main outer doors had been opened from the inside, which was probably the handiwork of the deceased mutie.

"Ready to go out, friends?" Ryan asked, glancing around.

"Let's do it," Krysty said.

The door swung open with a greased silence, letting in a wave of cool, fresh air, which was such a contrast to the dull recirculated air of the redoubt that it tasted like a heady, sparkling wine.

"My word," Doc breathed, stepping through the entrance. "That is just so beautiful it makes you..." He shook his head in mute wonderment at the scene.

They stood near the crest of the hill, a rounded slope that was at the center of a small island. The sea was spread around it in a dark gray expanse, touched with dappled weals of bright silver. It looked as if the island was about four miles across and barely two miles wide, the flanks of the hill speckled with stands of larch, pine and fir.

Down to the left they could see the flash of a waterfall, among an expanse of aspen, maple and live oaks. Ryan had never seen anything quite so brilliant as the magnificent show of color from the trees. Every imaginable shade from dark green, through dull brown, to fiery reds and startling orange. It was almost as if the mountain was ablaze from sea's edge to the beginnings of bare, gray rock.

"New England fall," Doc told them.

"It's beautiful," Lori said, kneeling down on a bank of soft, cropped turf.

"Road there." Jak pointed to where the blacktop, partly overgrown, wound across the flank of the hill toward the shattered remains of a stone harbor.

"Never saw anything so bright and strong as those trees," J.B. said quietly, taking off his glasses and polishing them on his sleeve.

"What makes them that color, Doc?" Ryan asked.

"The bright reds and golds? I recall reading in some...some time back. The soil and the season brings it on. All that brave array of brilliant hues and tints is simply the last scene of death. The leaves die back for the winter, and before they die they display all their rich panoply. That is what we see here, my friends. The brightness of death."

There was an infinite calm about the morning. Away to the north they could make out either the mainland or more islands. Around the granite headland below them they could see great circling clouds of cormorants, rising like smoke from the sea. Farther out, Ryan thought for a moment that he spotted some vast creature moving through the sullen waves, broaching for a moment, then disappearing. But he couldn't be certain, and it didn't reappear.

Donfil joined Lori, sitting cross-legged and gazing around him, eyes hidden by the mirrored sunglasses. He looked like some skeletal hunting bird, waiting patiently for its prey by a quiet forest pool.

"This is the first place I have seen in many, many moons," he said. "There is a word in the tongue of the lost Navaho people. They speak of *hozro* in their language."

"What's it mean? *Hozro?*" Krysty asked the shaman.

He paused as he considered the question. "*Hozro* is to be as one with your world. With your...what is the Anglo word?"

"Environment?" Doc offered. "Big buzzword way back when."

"Environment. Good word, Dr. Tanner. Yes, it is to be free from all worry and anger. To relish the day and all in it for what it is. If it is a day of rain, then *hozro* means to enjoy the day for its rain and not moan about the wet."

"Sounds good to me," Ryan said. "Lotta times I could've done with some *hozro* myself."

"You must seek it within yourself, Ryan Cawdor," the Apache said solemnly. "Seek within and you shall find it."

THEY COULD SEE from immense fault lines in the granite slopes of the mountain that concealed the redoubt where major earth slippage had occurred during the nukings of the war. No more buildings were visible.

From high above Ryan thought he could detect the remains of a long causeway stretching out toward the distant land, but some earth shift seemed to have dropped it below sea level. For the first time it came to him that they might have serious problems in trying to get off the island.

Halfway down the rippled roadway they found a stone shelter, roofless, at an overlook.

Acadia National Park. Scenic View, said a wooden notice, deeply carved, set into the landmark wall.

"You might be interested, Jak," Doc said. "The Acadians, or Arcadians, were what became the Cajuns from down around your part."

The boy nodded, the light breeze tugging at the white froth of hair that tumbled over his narrow shoulders.

"Look at burn bits." Lori pointed at the sill of the great open window. The wood was charred and scorched, rotting where a hundred years of rain had penetrated it.

"Must have been some heavy hot spots around here," J.B. said.

"One of the bad parts, if we're truly in New England, here," Krysty replied. "Uncle Tyas McCann was real wise. Said the west and southerly-west got burned badly by the missiles. But the long winter came hardest up this way."

"Let's settle it." The Armorer reached into one of his capacious pockets and pulled out the tiny, folding sextant. He took a sight at the sun and then busied himself with his creased maps and calculations. "Yeah," he said finally. "Nearest big ville I can work is Boston."

"Acadia was up in Maine," Doc said. "As near as I can recall."

"Look." Krysty pointed to the back of the rough shelter. There was a silvery metal plaque, around five feet long and eighteen inches deep. It had an etched map of the coastline across from the harbor, with names on it, and a few lines of text.

"It's called Ile au Haut," Ryan told them. "This island we're on."

Ryan scanned the lines of text about the national park. "Says here that there's a mountain over there on

the big island. Cadillac Mountain. The first rays of
sunlight to touch the old United States used to brush
the top of it. Talks about all the hiking trails there are
around this island.''

"Looks like someone tried to chisel this last bit
away,'' Krysty commented, stooping to peer at it.
"You can still read it, though.''

"Where?'' Doc asked.

"There.'' She indicated the last section of the in-
cised text.

"Ah, yes.''

All of them could read it, though Lori and Jak had
problems with some of the longer words on the in-
scription.

Ile au Haut was once part of Acadia National
Park. Founded in 1919, it was the first such park
in the east and remained the only one in all of
New England. For nearly eighty years the forty
thousand acres of Acadia provided a haven for all
lovers of nature. In 1996 the government—in its
wisdom—pushed through the bill that took Ile au
Haut away from the national park system and
handed it to the military for the building of a
massive, secret establishment.

"They mean the redoubt,'' Lori said.
"Yes,'' Doc sighed. "Right, child. They surely do.''

There was nationwide outrage at this decision and
protests by environmental groups from all over

the world. An attempt by Greenpeace to thwart the plans ended in tragedy and the deaths of dozens of protestors. This taking of Acadia was followed in the next months by the government's assuming control, through the Pentagon, of all national parks. Be warned all who come after.... This is only the beginning.

Doc Tanner rubbed absently at the scratched metal. "The times were changing, friends," he said quietly. "Wasn't any use to block up the hall. The wheel was in spin."

"No success like failure, Doc," Krysty said. "And failure's no damned success at all."

Doc nodded. "He had it right, ma'am, and no mistake. And here's all that's left. Nature coming back and covering it all up."

"Surprised the military left this here," Ryan said, pointing at the plaque.

The old man sniffed despondently. "They'd got what they wanted here. Why bother anymore?"

J.B. moved outside the ruined shelter, peering down towards the water. "If we're getting off this island today, we'd best start."

Ryan joined him. "Looks like it might not be that easy."

Chapter Seven

THE QUAKES THAT HAD SHIFTED the coast of Maine a hundred years ago had destroyed the lower part of the military blacktop, reducing it to a corrugated ribbon of weed-scattered rubble. The seven friends picked their way carefully over it, nearing the rolling breakers of the sea. The closer they got to the high-tide level, the more the mist-shrouded coast of the mainland seemed to recede from them. Ryan's first guess had been a couple of miles of open water. Now it looked like five. Maybe more.

"Don't want get caught night," Jak said, glancing up at the sky.

The bright sunlight had gone, vanishing behind a purplish haze of thin chem clouds. Even as they all looked up, a piece of age-old nuke debris came searing back into Earth's atmosphere, burning up in a dazzling golden crackle of light. Simultaneously there came a long, bone-quivering rumble of thunder, bouncing off the rocky slope behind them. Without the sun, the fall colors of the trees were oddly muted and dull.

"Be dark in about three hours," J.B. informed them, checking his wrist chron. Like the others, he'd

altered it as soon as they hit the outdoors, making sure
everyone had the right time. The only guide was the
sun. If they ever hit any sort of civilization they could
alter the chrons to fit in with what they called time
there.

"Be pushed to find some way of getting across there
in that time." Ryan nibbled at a piece of rough skin on
his thumb. "Wouldn't want to be stuck halfway
across. Can't tell what kind of currents there are between the island and the land there."

"Try and build boat and then sail at first dawning," Donfil suggested.

Ryan glanced up and down the boulder-strewn
beach. "Like I said. Talk's cheap. Action comes a lot
more expensive. Don't see much to build a boat from
along here."

They agreed that they'd split up. Ryan would go
west with Krysty and Donfil, the other four would try
east, scavenging along the desolate shoreline for anything they might be able to use.

"Meet back here in an hour and a half," Ryan said,
watching the cormorants circling and dipping a quarter mile out.

THE APACHE KEPT breaking away from them to explore the wealth of rock pools that fringed the long
beach. "Man would not starve here," he said. "All
kinds food. Shellfish and weed."

"Better than self-heats?" Krysty asked.

"Anything's better than self-heats." Ryan grinned. "We can go back up the road to the redoubt for the night. Mebbe cook up some sort of stew?"

"Easy," Donfil agreed.

But the first priority was to find something that would float. Anything.

Doc had once, months back, been talking to Ryan about a vacation he'd enjoyed at the seaside with his wife, before the first trawling. Ryan recalled the old man mentioning the interest in what he'd called "beachcombing," scavenging the shore for anything the storms might have washed up from its copious bounty.

Now, a century after Armageddon, there were few men left to sail the oceans. And little for the hungry waters to feed on and cast up on the land.

The first stretch of exposed beach had nothing larger than a man's hand; only a few splintered pieces of wood. A long way up among the rocks they saw the trunk of an immense pine, its end feathered and worn by the sea. But it was at least a hundred feet long, just as useless as the scattered twigs.

"Around the headland," Krysty called, raising her voice over the ceaseless rumbling of the waves on the shingle.

"Could be," Ryan replied, knowing that the currents would often swirl about such places. If they were to find anything that might help them off the island, then it could be around the narrow spit of protruding land.

"It is a good day, my brothers," Donfil yelled.

"Looks good," Ryan agreed, jogging after the barefooted Indian, picking his way between the smaller boulders.

The movement of the sea had funnelled all sorts of rubbish and driftwood into the narrow bay, piling it around the rocks. There was also a number of dark blue plastic drums that looked as if they might once have held some kind of chemicals.

A tangle of cords and ropes was wound all about the detritus, holding it together. Ryan stooped and tugged at it, testing it for strength, finding it gave a little but wouldn't break.

"Could make a good raft out of all this, lover," the girl said, folding her long red hair back out of her eyes.

Now that he was close up, Ryan could see lettering on the drums, white, stenciled, faded away over the decades until it was almost illegible. He traced them with his finger. Acetylcholine . . . ammonium carbaryl ester. Then came a string of letters and numbers and the name of a town—East Rutherford, NJ. That was all. Each of the drums looked as if it had once held about twenty-five gallons of liquid. Ryan rapped one with his knuckle, hearing it sound flat and hollow, like a shovel of earth on a coffin lid.

"Empty. We can use some of that wood and lash it all together with a coupla dozen of these. Find us some paddles or use blankets for a sail. One way or the other, we can do it."

He kicked again at the drums, jumping back as he disturbed a large crab, three feet across its gray-green shell, eyes on waving stalks. Its pincers looked as though they could easily have sliced through a horse's leg.

"By Ysun!" the Apache yelped, hopping sideways with remarkable speed and dexterity. His shades nearly fell off as he dodged the skittering monster, vaulting over a jagged hunk of granite.

"This some Indian way of hunting supper?" Ryan laughed, watching as the shaman put as much distance between himself and the mutie crab as he could. Despite his amusement, Ryan took the precaution of drawing his blaster. Just in case.

But the crustacean made its shuffling, lateral way down into the edge of the surf, its eyes the last part to disappear.

Ryan wondered what other mutated creatures the Lantic might be hiding out yonder.

By the time all seven had got together again and started work on their raft, darkness was creeping across the sea toward them like an assassin's velvet cloak.

Jak showed great skill in cutting away the net of plastic ropes and dragging clear the drums and the lengths of timber. He darted around as their clumsy craft began to take shape, lashing the empty drums together, rejecting any that were damaged or leaked.

"Tide'll turn soon," J.B. said, checking the waterline.

"Best make sure this is well moored and anchored down. Or we'll come here at first light and find she's long gone," Ryan said.

It was more than half-done, a ramshackle creation that rested heavy on one side. But it looked as though it would float and carry all seven of them across the miles of darkening water toward the mainland.

"The tide's rising fast," Doc warned. "I fear it will be on us in a scant hour."

They all redoubled their efforts.

"Enough!" Ryan finally shouted. "Got her tied to those big rocks, Jak?"

"Sure. Take hurricane to shift it."

"Then let's go back up to the redoubt. Get some self-heats and some sleep. Doc, you lead us on."

"A loaf of bread, a jug of wine and the redoubt will be heaven enough. Not that ring-pulls and self-heats quite qualify as the food of the gods, do they, Ryan?"

"Just get moving." He glanced at their raft, shaking his head at the thought that they were considering using it to cross the menacing stretch of sea.

In less than twelve hours' time.

RYAN SLEPT BADLY. It was always a gamble with self-heats. When you remembered that they'd been around for all those years, it was something of a miracle that more didn't die of food poisoning after eating them.

But his stomach was disturbed, and he had to go to the small, shadowless cubicles at the end of the dormitory. He could feel sweat rolling down his back, and he was gripped with savage pains that clawed at his guts. Krysty slept through it all.

When he eventually slithered into sleep, it was to find nightmares waiting for him. He was clambering over rocks near pounding waves. The spray lay slick and salty over the gray stones, making them treacherous to the touch. Tiny worms writhed everywhere, miniature jaws lined with needle teeth, snapping at his feet as he crushed them with every clumsy, staggering step. Ryan knew that if he fell they would immediately overwhelm him and fill his eyes, nose and throat.

Overlying the noise of the roaring surf was a sinister clicking, like giant claws snapping together.

It drew closer as he ran and slithered, on the sharp edge of losing his balance, arms flailing, feet slipping. There was a bright, serene moon floating low over the sea, highlighting the veil of blown spume, silver-white across the tops of the long, rolling waves.

Ryan didn't dare to look back over his shoulder, knowing that to do so would be to fall, knowing the frightful creature was scuttling behind him. The moon threw its shadow ahead of him, with the jointed, angular legs.

And the incessant clicking of the claws.

He woke curled into the fetal position, back wet with perspiration, hair matted to his head. With an effort he managed to slow his breathing, trying to relax. Eventually he succeeded in falling into a deeper and more restful sleep.

Morning came all too soon.

THERE WAS A FINE MIST on the sea's face, and a ceaseless drizzle sweeping in from the east carried the taste of salt. Visibility was less than a half mile, and the sun seemed reluctant to put in any kind of appearance.

The tide was still high and the seven were able to haul their raft in, using one of the lengths of plastic cord that tied it to the rocks above the high-water mark.

Lori shivered. "Cold, Doc."

He shuddered with her, hunching his shrunken shoulders against the damp. "Phew! Someone's walking over my grave," he muttered crossly. "Not the jolliest of boating weather, is it?"

Ryan squinted across the sound toward where he remembered the land lay. "Figure we can hold a true course on that?" he asked J.B.

"Doubtful. Can't judge currents, directions, wind, tide. None of that. Could get swept out into the Lantic and not know it."

It was true. While they'd been building the raft on the previous afternoon, Ryan had been watching the water, noticing a vicious rip current just about where the ebb tide turned, a mile or so across, with a swirling undertow and ominous areas of flat, oily sea. If they ran into it, then their makeshift raft could break up like a paper boat.

"Best wait," Krysty advised. "Drizzle could stop in a while and then the mist'll burn off."

"Getting soaked to skin here," Jak complained, squatting in the glistening shingle, rain trickling through his snowy hair and turning it the sodden gold of a polar bear's pelt.

"No point going all the way up the blacktop to the redoubt. We'll wait."

Ryan was the leader, so they waited.

Krysty's feelings about the weather turned out to be right. Around seven the rain drifted away across the gray sea, and the mist began to clear from the east.

"I can see the mainland," Krysty said, shading her eyes.

"Long as the fog stays away we should make it. Everyone got their paddles?" Ryan held his own rough-hewn oar.

The raft bobbed at their feet, and he looked at it dubiously.

Krysty read his mind. "This or nothing, lover."

Ryan found that the idea of nothing seemed almost attractive at the moment.

"All aboard that's coming aboard!" Doc yelled in a bluff, mock-nautical bellow, stepping on the nearest of the chemical drums, which rolled under his feet like the release of a logjam, nearly throwing him clear over the other side.

"Have some careful, Doc!" Lori shrieked, hurling herself on the raft and grabbing at the old man's waving ankles, pulling him back to a perch of precarious safety near the center of the craft.

The rest of them slowly climbed aboard, Jak remaining on the beach to untie the final tethering rope from the cold rocks. He ran down and hopped on with a nimble ease that made Doc spit into the sea in disgust.

The ebbing tide carried them quickly away from the shore of the island and into the open sea.

Chapter Eight

To RYAN'S RELIEF there didn't seem to be any current in the sound that they couldn't handle. Though the raft of plastic drums was clumsy and difficult to steer, their combined efforts with their paddles kept it going in roughly the right direction, toward the misty shore of what had once been known as the state of Maine.

"Sea's damned cold," Doc complained as their craft butted into a long, gray roller, sending up a shower of bitter salt spray.

Slowly Ile au Haut began to fall away behind them. Ryan took a moment to see that a lot of the top of the mountain had gone, leaving an awkward, crooked shape that concealed the main entrance to the redoubt. He guessed that this had been a result—direct or indirect—of the nuking and probably accounted for the fact that they'd never been able to find the Visitor Center and Initial Indoctrination Module. The earthslide had whisked it into a smear of stone.

"Stop lazing, lover," Krysty panted. "Many a mile to go before we sleep."

"How far d'you figure we've gone?" he asked J.B.

"Not far enough, Ryan."

"Halfway?" Jak gasped. It wasn't entirely clear whether it was a question or a statement.

"More than half," Donfil replied, still digging in his clumsy paddle with a rhythmic, almost mechanical drive, the water swirling in tiny circles about the tip of his blade.

"Yeah. Half is done. Two halfs done, way I feel now." Lori pushed her blond hair out of her eyes and continued paddling.

Doc was resting, chest heaving. "I was never much of an oarsman in my university days, I fear."

"More of cocksman, Doc?" Jak grinned. But the old man was so tired from his labors that the crude joke didn't even prompt a blush.

"Just shut up and keep rowing," Ryan ordered. They were about two-thirds of the way across, and it was now possible to make out the trees above the shoreline. But the tide was turning, and their progress seemed to be slowing.

"GONNA MAKE IT," Ryan gasped, lips peeled back off his strong white teeth in a feral grin.

The raft was bobbing along steadily, now only a quarter mile or so off the beach ahead of them. Every yard of progress was harder than the one before as the swirling tide worked against their efforts. Some of the ropes were becoming loose, the drums rattling and banging against one another. Also, Ryan noticed that they were slowly settling deeper in the water, indicating that some of the chemical containers had tiny leaks.

Lori and Doc had both given up, tired out from paddling. Krysty, Jak and Donfil were all laboring, breath rasping, sweat-soaked. Only J.B. and Ryan kept up a steady stroke, plowing their way remorselessly north.

Away to their left and a little beyond them, Ryan had noticed some kind of disturbance of the sea. But the rise and fall of the long Atlantic rollers made it hard to see what was happening. There was some spray and tossing white water, and a horde of screaming black-capped gulls.

But the muscle-tearing effort of fighting against the pitching of the raft distracted him from trying to investigate the incident any further.

Two narrow promontories of jumbled granite boulders stuck out into the sea for a couple of hundred yards, sheltering the beach from the wind, giving an area of calmer water. Once they were within the horns Ryan relaxed a little, knowing they could almost glide in from there. The others also felt it, smiling at one another. Donfil spread himself across the cans, allowing his long arms to dangle into the sea, peering down.

"Very clear, the water," he said, voice lifted above the lapping of the waves on the nearby beach. "Must be thirty feet deep, but you can see nearly all the way to the bottom."

"Any buried treasure?" Doc asked, lifting himself on one elbow.

The Apache shook his head, his jet-black, shoulder-length hair trailing into the water. "No. Lot of sand and some rocks."

Doc was chirpier now that they were so close to safety. "I dabbled somewhat in ichthyology in my youth."

"You what?"

"Ichthyology."

"What's that, Doc?" Krysty asked.

He dabbed spray off his face. "It is, my dearest flame-headed lady, the study of big fishes that have little fishes to bite them. And little fishes, smaller fishes and so on, ad infinitum." He cackled with laughter at a joke that nobody understood.

"You read all 'bout fishes?" Jak asked. "How they kill?"

"Yes. I recall that these chilly waters off the northeastern states were particularly fruitful for the larger fish and mammals of the oceans."

"Sharks and whales? We had them not far from my ville when I was a boy," Ryan said. "Some big bastards, so the fishermen said. I never saw none of them that big."

"I never saw *any*," Krysty corrected.

"You haven't done that in an age," he complained, keeping the rough paddle dipping and pulling.

"Haven't needed to, lover." She smiled.

"This used to be a big center for the Yankee whaling industry when I was a shaver," Doc reminisced. "New England's bravest. Battling monster whales from cockleshell dories. All done now. They got hunted near to destruction. Right whales, blues, sperm whales. Lots of species, I'm ashamed to say. Man's inhumanity to his fellow creatures that— What was that?"

The raft tipped suddenly, sending solid water across its rough deck of bound timbers. As quickly as it had rocked, it became still again.

"See anything, Donfil?" Ryan asked, half standing, holding his hewn branch like a harpoon, hefted against any threat.

The shaman rolled over, water dripping in slow beads from his hair. Behind the glasses his eyes were invisible, but his voice was slow, and oddly, artificially calm.

"You asked if I saw anything, Ryan Cawdor?"

"Yeah. What . . . ?"

"I saw grinning death, my brother. *That* is what I saw."

Krysty had one hand just on the edge of the raft, barely touching the surface of the icy waters. But she gave a sharp cry of shock as she felt something brush against her.

"What?" Ryan said.

"Gaia! Something very big, lover. Skin rough as sandpaper. But . . . Oh, so big."

"Fish," the Indian managed to say. "Bigger than any fish I ever heard of. Bigger than me. Bigger than this raft. Maybe bigger than the island. Moved slow on us, and I saw its eye look up and eat into my soul. Coldest deadest thing I ever saw."

"Where is it?"

Lori was standing, pointing ahead of them, where the calm water lapped toward the shelving beach, now mocking them from a hundred yards away.

"Saw the water move like folding in on itself," she said quietly.

"Big whales and sharks can be curious," Doc offered. "It's possible he's just nosing around us. Nothing better to do."

"Turning," Jak said, pistol drawn, the long barrel of his satin-finish .357 glittering in the cold sunlight as he pointed to their right.

"Get ready," Ryan warned.

"Holy..." Doc began, but the word was choked back in his throat.

It was another feigned attack, the creature swimming ponderously under the raft, its back scraping on the bottom of the chemical drums, making the whole thing rock from side to side. Ryan peered down at it, holding the G-12 ready in his hands, the control set on full-automatic. It wasn't an occasion to mess around with single shots.

"Maybe it'll fuck off," Lori said hopefully, voice an octave higher than usual with the tension.

"Maybe," Ryan agreed. "You're the damned expert, Doc. What d'you say?"

"I say it's some sort of mutie crossbreed monster, half *Orcinus orca*."

"What?"

"Killer whale. The black coloring and head shape show that."

"What's the other half?" J.B. asked, mini-Uzi in his right hand, eyes scanning the placid waters of the bay.

Doc cleared his throat nervously. "From the look of the rest of it and the way it rolled as it made its pass at us, I fear that it might be *Carcharodon carcharias*."

"What the hell is that?" Ryan asked. "Sounds like something you'd pick up in a frontier gaudy house, doesn't it?"

There was no answering smile. "That would be a blessing compared to this, Mr. Cawdor. *Carcharodon carcharias* is the proper name of the great white shark."

"A PAINTED SHIP UPON...upon...I forget what." Doc glanced at the still water.

Ryan had ordered them to stop paddling, guessing that the splashing might be attracting the beast. The raft was wallowing lower in the sea, the small waves kissing its sides, occasionally lapping clear over its top. The tide seemed to be turning, holding them in place. Not easing them in toward the shore. Not sucking them back toward the open Lantic Ocean.

More than ten minutes had trickled by, without any further sign of the monster whale-shark. All of them were trying to watch for it, but a light wind had sprung up, sending ruffling cat's-paws across the surface of the water, making it impossible to see below.

Ryan's finger was still tight on the trigger of the automatic caseless rifle. He was about to tell the other six to begin paddling again.

The creature came up almost directly beneath them, like a nuke exploding from its silo. The only hint of warning was the circling, wailing gulls.

Ryan's razor-honed reflexes saved him from being thrown off the raft. He and J.B. were the only two able to cling on; the other five were hurled into the frothing water.

Ryan glimpsed the little doll eye that stared blankly at him from inches away. There was an exhalation of stinking air and the gleam of row upon row of serrated teeth. The raft was pitched over, heeling vertically, then pulled back to the level by the weight of water in the leaking drums.

A flash of polished black skin, dappled with white, and then the monster was gone again, sliding with an awesome, effortless power beneath the turbulent waves.

A head count showed four swimming. Five, as Doc popped up like a cork from a bottle, gray hair lank around his face, arms flailing, legs kicking desperately.

"Back on the raft!" Ryan yelled. "Quick. 'Fore it comes back."

"Can't see the bastard!" J.B. shouted, head turning from side to side, the muzzle of the Uzi tasting the damp air like the tongue of a snake.

Jak was nearest and hauled himself aboard, shaking his hair like a terrier. He gave a hand to Donfil. The shaman balanced on the timbers like a waterlogged stick insect, his glasses hung over one ear, fumbling for his new Smith & Wesson.

Krysty reached the raft, looking over her shoulder, green eyes wide in terror of the creature lurking invisibly below and behind her.

Lori was helping Doc, but neither of them was making much progress. The old man seemed to be trying to persuade the girl to abandon him and save herself. She was ignoring him.

"There!" Jak screamed, his voice loud enough to shatter crystal, cracked with horror.

Ryan saw it.

A huge dorsal fin, rolling lazily out of the sea, was fully fifteen feet long, which meant the predator had to be unthinkably large. Sixty or seventy feet was the hurried guess. The sunlight shone on the skin, showing the tiny shellfish dotted over it.

"Wait as long as you can!" he yelled to the others. There was no way of knowing what effect their bullets would have on such a beast.

Krysty was aboard, hands shaking with shock. Lori and Doc were still a dozen yards away, laboring toward the raft.

"It'll roll on its back before it finally strikes!" Doc shouted, straining to keep his face clear of the water.

"Let it have it when it rolls!" Ryan bellowed, trying to steady himself against the raft's uneven movement.

The whale-shark was closing in, and Lori and Doc weren't going to make safety.

"Now!" Jak cried as the black body turned, revealing the white throat and belly, and the massive gaping jaws that snapped open in a cavernous grin.

It was no time for subtlety. Ryan squeezed the trigger, feeling the G-12 buck against his hip, blowing the entire magazine in a couple of seconds. He tried to keep the rifle trained on the same spot, below the tiny black eye, where he hoped there might be something vulnerable, like a spine.

J.B.'s mini-Uzi coughed out a full mag, and both Jak and Donfil fired their handblasters again and again, the heavy-caliber bullets ripping out chunks of bloodied flesh.

But the mutie was so enormous and its functional system so primitive that the rounds from the two Magnums did no more than mildly irritate it. The Uzi was a little more effective.

The Heckler & Koch G-12 destroyed it.

The self-lubricating, nylon-coated rounds were fired at nearly three times the normal velocity. Their lethal peculiarity was that the rounds themselves stopped quickly, but their kinetic energy carried on, sending deadly shock waves rippling through the body, pulping flesh and muscle into torn tatters.

Fifty bullets hit the vicious predator in an area little larger than a soup plate. At less than fifty-foot range their effect was extreme termination.

The creature immediately lurched away from the swimming couple, tail beating, lashing up a great wall of spray, behind which Lori and Doc totally disappeared. Blood jetted from the mutie monster's body, staining the gray waters red-pink.

"Got it," J.B. said laconically, throwing away his empty magazine, slotting in a fresh one from one of his many capacious pockets.

The water foamed and boiled as the huge creature continued to thrash around in blind circles, blood flooding from the great body, darkening the ocean.

"Totally," Ryan said. His own coat's pockets held spare caseless ammo for his G-12, enough for one full reload and a few left over. Once they were gone, he knew he'd have to dump the unusual blaster and pick up something more conventional.

Lori came aboard, clots of blood streaking her yellow hair, pulling Doc after her. The old man was grinning apishly and he blinked away the water, watching the death throes of the leviathan as it dived and broached, dived again.

"Wonderful specimen, my dear Ryan, quite wonderful. But such a shame you had to butcher it. Necessary, I suppose."

"Yeah, Doc. You fucking suppose right."

By the time they eventually grounded the raft on the beach of the mainland, the whale-shark lay still and dead in the bay, its carcass wallowing under the attention of thousands of seabirds.

Chapter Nine

THE PATH WAS STEEP and narrow. There were the remains of old steps, blocks of crudely carved stone set in the loose earth. But time and weather had eroded many of them, sending them sliding down the hill toward the beach.

With a great struggle Ryan and the others managed to haul their waterlogged raft high enough up the shore to keep it clear of the seaweed-strewn tidemark. The drums began to leak silvery drops onto the piled shingle, drying out.

"With luck it'll float again when we need it. Long enough to get us back to the Ile au Haut and the gateway," Krysty said.

Jak tethered it to some frost-riven granite slabs, holding it fast against their eventual return. "Now what?" he asked.

"Now we go inland a ways. Find us some food and some way of getting dry. Look around some. That's what we do next," Ryan replied.

"Must have been many small hamlets scattered about this part of New England, back before the darkening of the skies," Doc said, shivering in his soaking clothes. "Some of them were allegedly places of inbred oddities. I recall a writer called Hodgcraft, or some such...wrote of blasphemous entities and colors beyond space. Set many of them in this region. I strongly recommend that we be most careful."

"Know what steps take if see real horror, Doc?" Jak asked, grinning impishly.

"No, young fellow. What steps should I take?"

"Long ones." The boy laughed.

The cliffs had fallen in sometime in the past hundred years. The final ninety feet of the path had vanished in a blur of tumbled pines and furrowed mud slides.

When they finally reached the top, Ryan paused and looked backward, across the stretch of ocean to the lopsided island. He saw that the other predators had scented the death of the mighty whale-shark. They were almost hidden by kicking spray, but he could make out the indistinct shapes of other sea creatures, tearing at the streaming corpse. The agitation had driven the gulls from the feast, leaving them to circle, screaming impotently, in a whirling cloud of hunger.

"Which way?" Donfil asked, peering around at the shrubs and stunted trees that angled toward the land, away from the sea's gales. "Looks something like a road over there."

They all followed the direction of the pointing finger. Among the scrub and trees, visible as it coiled over a low hill, there did indeed seem to be the dark ribbon of a highway.

DESPITE THE COOLNESS, their clothes were drying on them as they walked. If it had been nearer winter with the prospect of a hard frost, Ryan would have made sure they lit a fire immediately to dry out and warm up. Cold and wet were the two biggest killers in the Deathlands. Far bigger than stickies or crazies.

"There's some sort of direction post up ahead," Doc called. Now fully recovered from the ordeal, he was striding along with Lori on his arm, pointing out interesting features of the land to the girl.

The seven were strung out in a loose patrol formation, on what the Trader would have called a "condition green" assignment, where there were no signs of any threat or danger—which didn't mean that you ignored any possible threat. It meant you didn't bother with someone out at point or using flank scouts or a distanced rear guard.

The post had fallen over at an angle, propped against the tumbled end of a picket fence. To have lasted so long in such a harsh climate the wood must have been amazingly well seasoned and protected. Doc and Lori were there first, and the old man bent to read the names on the four pointing fingers.

"Dunwich one way. Miskatonic University next one around. Of course, we don't know which way the sign originally pointed so we aren't really any wiser. The third name is Castle Rock."

"Doc," Lori said, as though she were trying to point something out to him.

"Shh, my sweet youthful bird. The last name is Jerusalem's Lot."

Ryan was next up, bending over the broken signpost, peering at the moss-covered boards. He straightened and looked at Doc, who was sniggering like a schoolboy.

"There's nothing on any of them, Doc. All worn off and blank."

"Yes, Ryan. Just one of my little jokes. You know me."

"Sure, do, Doc. Don't suppose you could explain this particular joke? All the names that don't exist nowhere. I mean, anywhere." He glanced at Krysty.

"No, Ryan. I don't believe I can. Perhaps the truth might be found in a certain arcane volume, bound in human skin, written by the mad Arab, Alhazred." He smiled gently. "Then again, Ryan, my very dear friend, perhaps it might not."

"So, which way?" J.B. asked. "Could do with shelter with the night closing in."

"Where there is a sign, then once there has been a road," Donfil said. "Where there is a road, then there are life and people. Even if much has gone, we shall find something." He stooped and picked his way around for a few paces. "Here. The road ran that way. Blacktop. Other was only dirt." He pointed farther along the green path. "Another sign."

This one hadn't faded to illegibility: Consequence, Maine. Population 843.

"Hope there aren't any of those inbred oddities you talked about, Doc," Krysty muttered.

"OLD HOT SPOT," J.B. commented, checking the small rad counter on his lapel. "Only just touches orange. This gotta be the edge of one of the original craters. Don't see that many you can tell so easy. Like a damned big dish carved out of the stone."

It looked as if it had been a stray, medium-sized Russian missile. Maybe an AS.B.18, launched form one of the old Oscar-class submarines lurking off the Atlantic seaboard.

The saucer-shaped hole was a little more than six hundred yards across, dipping around fifty feet deep. A pond of stagnant water had collected at its bottom, reflecting the orange glow of the setting sun. Unusually, there was little vegetation sprouting from the shattered stone.

"That can't have done much for the population of 843 in the ville of Consequence," Ryan observed.

It looked as though Consequence, Maine hadn't ever amounted to much. One road ran in and the same road ran out again. The derelict ruins of a light engineering factory were set back to the left, and a smaller workshop specializing in brake linings for tractors was opposite.

The Peter Pan Adult Motel—quadruple X-rated movies and one water bed—had its flat roof folded in like a concertina. Its neighbor was the Church of the Last Coming, linked with the Fellowship of the Blessed Saint Bubo of Ishmaelia. That roof was utterly gone, all four walls tipped in on one another, rotting from the bottom up. What looked to have been a general store was flattened completely.

The seven began to wander cautiously through the ruins, and Ryan looked down through the dusty glass of an unbroken window. There was a hand-lettered notice.

Waltzes and shuffles. Down-home music for friends and neighbors. Milt Tyson and His Cowboy Quartet. Pies and punch. For Claggartville General's Scan Fund. Tickets—five dollars. Doors open at Church Hall at seven o'clock. Last day of January 2001. Be there or...

The corner of the poster was missing.

"Be there or be dead," Ryan finished. "World died a week before they had their dance."

He turned and gazed up what must have been the main street of Consequence. There was hardly a house left standing, time and weather continuing what the missile had started.

"Getting cool," Krysty observed, threading her arm through his.

"Road goes up, then down. Any blast might've been deflected by that. Best chance of shelter's over the ridge."

"Found old wag!" Jak called.

Ryan was sometimes surprised at how few vehicles survived from before the long winter. There must have been tens of millions of wags around, but all anyone ever saw were rusted wrecks. Only the wealthiest barons with access to a gas supply could now afford to drive for pleasure.

This vehicle was like the others. It looked as though a garage had once sheltered the pickup truck, but that had gone and the winters had stripped off the layers of paint. Tires had rotted; the gas tank had been hacked open; the glass shattered; seats removed. What remained was only the shell of a Chevy K2200.

The others gathered around the wag in silence. Somewhere out in the woods they all heard the mournful cry of some hunting animal. The reminder that night was near prompted Ryan into action.

"No time to hang around here," he said. "Best keep together now and get shelter."

The temperature was dropping fast. Once the sun had gone there was the first frosting of ice lipping the puddles. Breath streamed out like wood smoke, hanging in the still air. The sky was fading to a velvety purple-black.

Ryan's guess was right. Once they were over the hill, several of the houses looked better preserved. The street eventually petered out in a dead end, the overgrown remnants of a dirt road winding up into the forest to their left.

"One of these?" Lori asked, shoulders huddled against the cold.

"Yeah."

"I dream of stumbling over some old, long-lost ville," J.B. said, "and finding in a sealed garage a mint, fresh, oiled and gassed-up Jeep. Figure I never will, but it's nice to think on."

Ryan looked at his old comrade, jaw dropping. It was so unusual to hear the Armorer talk about anything other than weapons or food that he didn't know what to say.

CONSEQUENCE DIDN'T LOOK as if there'd been an awful lot of money working there. Apart from a couple of old frame houses, which had suffered particularly badly from the weather, most of the dwellings were single-story shacks or cabins. The one exception stood foursquare at the end of the road, as though daring it to go any farther.

It was based on granite, gray and strong, wood-framed, with screened windows and pointed turrets to the four corner bedrooms on the third floor. The porch was pillared and ran the whole length of the front of the building. From the scraps of paint that cowered in sheltered crevices, it seemed that the house had been dark brown and cream. The gravel path was bordered with shrubs, rampant, and on either side of the wrought-iron gate were rusting columns of metal, each carrying an iron ball the size of a man's head.

"Looks like the Baron Big of Consequence must have lived there," Ryan said. "Good enough for him, good enough for us."

All the windows on the top floor had been broken, but most of those lower down were intact, which must have been a result of the blast pattern of the missile that had left the crater down the way.

"How come it's not been ripped apart?" Donfil asked. "Place like this must have had its share of freak survivors. Why didn't they hole up in this house? Built like a fort."

"Could be that this is one of the regions that lost all the population. The way it looks from outside, the house might be empty," Ryan suggested.

It was.

The main lock on the front door had been kicked in, but the interior was completely stripped—not a stick of furniture on any of the floors. Ryan assumed that anyone coming in after the nuking wouldn't even have bothered to vandalize the house.

"There's some junk mail here," Doc said, pointing to a corner of the entrance hall behind the door. "All dated December and January. Just before they...you know. The owners must have moved out and maybe put the place on the market. Never found a buyer."

"You mean letters from that long ago?" Krysty exclaimed. "I've never..."

The old man stooped with a sigh, picking up the dry, dusty, scattered envelopes. "Junk, my dear. All junk." He ripped them open and threw the contents to the cracked parquet. "*Reader's Digest*, Time-Life Books, magazines and ceedees. A restaurant opening in Claggartville. The town's only about ten miles off from this sketch map, unless it was nuked to ashes."

Ryan took some of the envelopes from Doc's hands, looking at them himself, intrigued by this odd little peephole into the long-dead past.

There were invitations to buy this and that—ceramic statues of shepherdesses; facsimile clocks from Europe; devices to make your rooms dryer or less dry; books that would make you richer, happier, sleep better, make love with endless energy, read faster; flesh-colored Christs that were luminous when you turned out the lights; blasters of all sizes and shapes and prices. "Protect your home and the ones you love. A dead intruder won't be back."

"Is this the kind of stuff the mailman used to bring, Doc?" he asked.

"Guarantees . . . fire-damaged stock . . . Shown half actual size . . . No deposit required . . . Ask our area manager to call . . . Complete satisfaction . . ." Doc snorted and crumpled the brittle paper in his hands. "Satisfaction! By the three Kennedys but this makes me want to vomit, my friends. This was the peak of thousands of years of civilization! A free condom with every meal at this eatery! Offer conditional on being alive after world madness! Oh, these were such times, my brothers!"

The old man threw the paper to the floor, where Jak started to pick it up. "Good for starting fire, this. Break off some that stuff side stairs. Plenty good dry wood. Yeah, Ryan?"

"Yeah, Jak."

All of them were used to sleeping on bare earth, so the lack of beds didn't bother anyone. After some discussion, Ryan and J.B. agreed that there didn't seem to be any feeling of danger. But they'd set single guards.

Two hours each, just in case.

Like Trader said—nobody ever got dead from being careful.

Chapter Ten

THE SMOKE DREW THEM to the big, empty house at the end of the street.

It snaked through the frosty New England night, weaving out of the remnants of the township of Consequence, in among the silent sentinels of oak, pine and maple. To the hillside where they lived.

Where they'd always lived.

Where they had their twining caves of earth and stone, where they all existed together. Sometimes one would kill another. They were hunters. Stealthy, cunning in the arts of stalking and trapping.

They never came close to the tumbled buildings of Consequence, where their forefathers and mothers had lived an eternity ago. The buildings were linked with death in their memories, those who had any memories for anything but dung and death.

They coupled with any other of them who happened to be there. Many of them bore babies that never drew a breath.

But some of them lived.

Strangers never went to that area. Claggartville folk knew of the dark region and avoided it as though the plague dwelled there.

But now there were outlanders come to Consequence.

And they were in the big house.

It was the flavor of the smoke that brought them there.

RYAN CAWDOR WAS ON GUARD. He'd picked the duty from two till four in the morning, the time of the soul's dark night, when sleep is deepest, when sickly babies lose their frail hold on life and when the breathing of the elderly becomes slower and falters and fails.

When a sentry is at his most careless and nocturnal attacks can be most successful.

Ryan had the G-12 slung across his shoulders, the white silk scarf tucked down into the fur collar of his long coat, a barrier against the cold that filtered all through the old house. Only in what had once been the music room, where a merry fire blazed, was the chill held at bay. On the upper floors, with broken glass crunching under the soles of his combat boots, Ryan whistled beneath his teeth at the bitterness of the night.

The SIG-Sauer P-226 pistol was on his right hip, balanced by the weight of the panga with its eighteen-inch blade on the other hip. The salt on his skin had made the thong of the eye patch chafe his temple, and he eased a finger beneath it.

A pallid moon rode low on the horizon, smudged behind galloping banks of dark clouds. Once there was a fluttering of hail against the wooden walls of the house, but it passed quickly off toward the south. All around the mansion were only darkness and the still night.

Ryan picked his way among the sleeping figures, his shadow dancing madly off the farthest wall, between the curtainless windows. Lori was cradled, inevitably, in Doc's arms. Jak was curled up like a young puppy, his damp jacket still steaming slightly from the heat of the fire. The wood in the empty house was so old and dry under its layers of varnish that it burned quickly with a ferocious heat. Donfil was stretched out straight near the bolted door, arms by his sides, mirrored glasses reflecting the yellow flames. Krysty was asleep near the wall, where Ryan had been lying. As he stooped to look at her, her long sentient hair curled protectively about her calm face.

Though Ryan moved like a ghost, he woke J.B. The fedora hat was pushed back off the sallow forehead and his eyes glittered like specks of onyx.

"Anything moving?" he whispered.

Ryan shook his head. "Just me," he replied, pitching his voice low.

"My turn?"

Ryan turned the left cuff of the coat to check his chron. "Nope. I'll wake you in another fifteen minutes."

The Armorer slipped easily back into sleep.

Ryan decided on one last slow turn around the creaking floors and stairs of the old house. There was the big main staircase, and the narrow back flights, which brought him through what must have been the kitchens to the unlocked door to the music room.

The cramped top floor with its attics for servants seemed even colder. He checked one of the turret rooms again.

And felt something burst toward his face, slashing and tearing, hot blood on his cheek, near his ear.

"Fireblast!" he cried, staggering back and nearly falling, his right hand punching up at his assailant, feeling the satisfying jar of an impact with flesh. There was a muffled squawk of pain, then the flutterings of great wings.

He watched as the huge owl panicked its way through the empty frame of the window, flying off into the safety of the night.

"Bitching gaudy-whore bastard," he muttered, dabbing at his cut face with the back of his hand, feeling that the cut wasn't much more than a surface scratch.

But the shock had been real enough.

Ryan walked to the casement and leaned on the frame, sucking in the cold air, steadying his breathing and his nerves. He stared down into what had once been the back garden of the house, past some over-grown apple trees and currant bushes.

He saw movement, a flicker among the deep pools of shadow that surrounded the mansion.

After the false alarm of the owl, Ryan wasn't about to open fire and find he'd smeared a rabbit all over the ground.

As light as a big cat, Ryan picked his way down the main stairs, arriving in the entrance hall on the first floor. The door had an old stained-glass pattern to it, acanthus leaves, twined with some unidentifiable purple flowers. The moonlight came and went as the wind drove clouds across it, and the colors flowed and merged on the dusty floor. The only sound was the bright crackling of the dry wood in the hearth, beyond the locked door to Ryan's left.

His pistol was in his hand, a round ready under the hammer.

There were heavy iron bolts at top and bottom and a rusting sec chain near the broken mortise. Ryan opened the top bolt first, wincing at the thin screech of corroded metal. He stooped to release the lower bolt, checking that the chain was still in place, hooked over the hasp.

He waited a moment for the return of moonlight. When it came he turned the ornate brass handle and put his good eye to the gap, squinting out into the garden.

But his view was blocked.

The cold moon was to his right, free from clouds, making the porch almost as bright as day.

They were out there, ringing the front of the house, standing quite still, like a scattering of obscenely grotesque statues, born from the crazed imagination of some long-dead, demented gardener.

The nearest of them was actually on the porch, less than a yard away from the front door.

It wasn't possible to tell either the age or the sex of the mutie, who stood several shambling inches taller than seven feet, with shoulders broader than an M-16 rifle. Its hair straggled down either side of its face, lank and matted with glittering streaks of orange clay. One lidless eye, weeping a colorless liquid, was roughly in the middle of its left cheek. There was no nose, just a semicircular hole above the chin, fringed with tendrils of pale skin that trembled in time with the thing's breathing. Ryan saw that it didn't actually have a proper chin. The lower jaw was missing, and a row of jagged stumps protruded from the set-back upper jaw.

It wore a long, shapeless sack of filthy material that reached clear to the planks of the wooden porch. Where it had moved up from the garden, Ryan could make out a trail of thick, jellylike slime, like that left behind by a gigantic snail.

The mutie had two seemingly ordinary arms that ended in crooked fingers. The right hand gripped a gnarled club of wood, with several pieces of iron hammered into it. Beneath the normal arms Ryan saw that the mutie had several sets of paddlelike, residual arms, becoming progressively smaller.

During his travels in the Deathlands, Ryan had seen some appalling cases of genetic mutation, resulting initially from the nuking of 2001. But never anything quite as gross as this.

For several moments of stopped time, Ryan and the mutie looked at each other. In those steady, beating seconds, Ryan looked past it, running his eye over the remainder of the group, which numbered about twenty. The moon flickered and died, but Ryan had seen enough to know that whatever stood on the porch was a prince among its peers. Some of the others were unbelievably monstrous in their mutations. And all carried some sort of rudimentary weapon.

"Goodbye," Ryan said, slamming the door, immediately yelling out a warning to the others. "Muties! Up and at 'em! There's muties!"

The colored glass in the top half of the door imploded, splinters of crimson, deep blue, yellow and sea-green scattering over the hall floor. The tip of the great club appeared in the hole for a moment, disappeared, then came crashing down a second time, knocking the door clear off its frail old hinges. The mutie stood there, stooping to enter the house. Its face was in deep shadow.

The door to the music room swung open and Ryan saw J.B.'s face in the gap, peering out behind the stubby barrel of his mini-Uzi.

"Dark night!" he exclaimed, not really sounding that surprised.

"Let's get the fuck out of here," Ryan called, spinning around and putting a triple burst through the middle of where he assumed the mutie's heart might be. The giant staggered back onto the porch, giving a roar of pain and rage, tearing away half the frame of the door as it went. But it didn't fall.

A second burst from the G-12 put it down, the club dropping with a crash. Ryan could hear a dreadful sound from outside, a confused, wordless shriek that mixed anger and hatred.

"Through here and out the back door," the Armorer said.

Ryan glanced over his shoulder, but none of the muties had yet appeared. He darted into the music room, seeing that the fire had sunk low. The others were up and ready, blasters in hands.

"Bad?" Krysty asked.

He shook his head as Jak and Donfil bolted the heavy door behind him. "Muties like you've never seen," he panted. "Real... But I figure they don't have the brains of a self-heat can between them. Mebbe best we outrun them. No point wasting good lead."

Lori appeared from the far door, at the bottom of the rear stairs. "They're out there, through the old kitchens. Five or six. No blasters. Axes and some getting knifes."

"Knives," Doc corrected automatically.

"More than that out front. Jak, pile all the wood we've got on the fire and set the floor burning. Place'll go like a torched gas wag. Give the muties something to think about."

While the boy scampered to carry out the orders, Ryan cautiously led the other five into the rear hall. They could hear a rhythmic drumming and pounding on the music room door, as the muties closed in on their prey.

A face appeared from the blackness, pressed against the glass of a small window opening off the kitchen area. It took a second to see that the skull was totally bald, covered with what looked like small pinkish-white worms or maggots.

Krysty snapped off a shot from her Heckler & Koch silvered P7A-13. The 9 mm round smashed the glass, sending the mutie out of sight in a spray of blood that was almost black in the moonlight as it splattered over the white walls.

"Two down," Krysty said, calmly.

Jak joined them, silhouetted in the doorway against the dazzling light. "Fire burn all. Floor and walls all burn. House gone real soon, I guess."

"You got much ammo, Ryan?" J.B. asked, checking his own pockets.

"Not that much. Forty-four in the G-12 and a few singles."

"I got more. Best I go first and clear the path. You figure these sons of bitches are slow on their feet?"

"From what I've seen, yeah, they are. Hey, that fire's going to catch us if we don't make a move now."

There was a gust of raw heat that scorched at the seven companions, huddled at the foot of the dark, spiraling staircase. For a moment Ryan considered trying to lure the muties into what would be an inferno in a handful of minutes, but the rule was always to get out when you could.

He motioned for the Armorer to go first. "I'll come last. Anyone falls, we stand and fight for time to get them up and away. Head out as far as you can. I'll hold off any pursuit. Right? Then let's do it, friends!"

The next sixty seconds were a blur of violence, noise and death.

There were seven of the creatures. One was probably female, as it was naked to the waist and had a cluster of dangling breasts across its chest. Another had arms so long that they scraped on the frost-rimed grass. A raking burst from the Uzi sent half of them spinning away in a tangle of normal and residual limbs. There was a harsh crying, choked with blood, as J.B. let loose at them, firing from the hip. The others were close behind him, picking their targets. But it was damnably difficult to shoot on the run, and only one more of the inbred monsters was hit.

Ryan hesitated a second, looking back into the burning room. Tongues of flame leaped eagerly at the old floorboards, climbing the paneled walls. Already a chunk of the ceiling was blazing. Through the other door Ryan glimpsed something, very low, near the floor, something pale and sluglike that moved on its belly in rippling movements. He aimed the G-12, then changed his mind, powering after the others into the cold night air.

The garden was filled with chaos. He hurdled a corpse and dodged a hissing blow from an enormous, scythelike blade. Another of the muties, who was gut shot, reached out and tried to grab Ryan as he darted by, but the man was too quick, dodging sideways and making for a break in the bushes where the others waited for him.

"We could chill them all," J.B. said, pointing to the rear of the house. It looked like most of the muties were there, watching them, fifty paces away, ignoring their own dead and wounded.

Even while the two sides stared at one another there was a great whooshing sound and a bursting sphere of flames shot out through the side of the mansion.

It wreathed around the heads of the muties, sending them into a gurgling, screeching, huddled group, several of them actually falling to the dirt.

"Time to move," Ryan said. "I don't figure we'll have any more trouble from them."

Nothing followed them as they circled back around the blazing house. Flames soared a hundred feet in the air, sending a fountain of golden sparks ten times as high. By the time they reached the blacktop that would take them away from Consequence, there was already the first gleaming of the false dawn showing low in the eastern sky.

JUST AS THE SMOKE had drawn them from their burrows among the trees, so the ferocity of the fire sent them crawling and stumbling back. Houses were bad. They should never have gone near them. That had been a bad thing to do.

At least some of them would have fresh meat for a few days.

The ashes of the old house smoldered quietly for three days and then died away. If anything ever walked there again, it walked alone.

Chapter Eleven

FORTUNATELY DOC TANNER'S sometimes muddled memory was functioning well. He could recall the details of the sketch map that he'd seen in the leaflet advertising a new restaurant opening, back in Consequence.

"Inland a half mile or so. Then you reach a road... Old County Turnpike, I think. Head west and loop back again toward the coast. It looked as though it were a more sizeable community, set in a valley. Harbor. Said something there about how Claggartville was one of the centers of the New England whaling industry. That would be around ... Goodness me! Around two hundred and fifty years ago. So many, many years, tears, fears and jeers, and tears and tears."

Lori stepped forward and put her arm around his shoulders, smiling up at him, lifting a finger and touching the old man on the lips, hushing the flow of words.

"I could use a shave," Ryan said, fingering the stubble that was beginning to thicken on his chin. J.B. never seemed to grow much of a beard on his pale skin. Jak sprouted an odd, long, embarrassing snowy hair from his chin. Ryan knew it was rare for an Indian to grow any sort of beard. Doc, on the other hand, was already showing the beginnings of a fine set of grizzled whiskers.

"I could use some food, lover," Krysty replied, "and my hair needs trimming."

The smile was a shared private joke. Because of the mutie genes that dwelt within Krysty Wroth, she possessed certain oddities. And the long mane of dazzling red hair, with a strange life of its own, was one of them. Cutting it at all was a difficult and often painful process for the girl. But she'd taught Ryan the best way of doing it, which involved her drinking plenty of alcohol or sniffing some lines of jolt. Anything to numb the sentience of her fiery locks.

"That'll have to wait. The haircutting, I mean. But my belly's been moaning since last night that it was feeling left out of things. Maybe there'll be something for us all in Claggartville. If we ever find it."

The rising sun didn't make their journey any easier. The road that Doc had seen on the old map didn't exist anymore. There'd been some kind of seismic shift, probably prompted by the deathly power of the hundreds of missiles that had ravaged the seaboard. But Doc was certain that Claggartville had been a ville on the coast, so they tried to turn their way southwest, back toward the taste of the ocean.

The woods grew thickly, making progress difficult. Just before noon, Krysty held up her hand.

"What is it, lover?" Ryan asked.

"Smoke. Wood fire. And meat cooking." She checked the direction of the light breeze. "Ahead a half mile or so."

"Spread out," Ryan called. "Forest like this we could walk right past a dozen ambushers. Around ten paces apart and keep your eyes open."

"And if we see your grandmother, lover, we'll make sure she knows how to suck eggs," Krysty teased.

"Venison," Donfil said quietly, when they'd gone a hundred paces or so. "If they don't take it off the fire real soon it'll be blacker than the heart of a pony soldier."

By now they could all catch the smell of meat roasting over a wood fire. Jak glimpsed smoke curling up among the trees, not far ahead of them.

And they could hear the noise of singing, sounding like two voices. One was thin and piping, the other an echoing bass.

"Can't make out the words," Ryan said. "Anyone else?"

None of them could pick out any recognizable words in the chanting.

From the location of the smoke, Ryan figured they were only fifty paces or so from the fire and the singers. He went straight ahead while J.B. looped left and Jak went right. The others stayed with Ryan.

The undergrowth was thick, but the soft earth and the compressed fallen leaves made for silent stalking. He dropped to a crouch when he spotted crackling flames, and two fur-clad figures squatting on the earth by the fire. Both of them had their backs turned to the approaching men and women.

Krysty tugged at Ryan's sleeve. When he turned to look at her she mimed notching an arrow and drawing a longbow, pointing ahead of them to the singing duo. Ryan couldn't see the weapons, but he trusted Krysty's keen sight.

Placing each foot cautiously in front of the other as if he were walking on eggshells, Ryan closed in, Heckler & Koch at the ready, eyes raking the surrounding woods for the possibility of a trap.

"Chill them," Lori whispered, her breath ruffling the short hairs inside Ryan's ears, making him start.

"Blood-drinker bitch," he whispered back.

"Safe," she retorted.

It was true. But that still wasn't quite enough of a reason to send a couple of strangers off to buy the farm. Not when they might be able to help out by telling where this elusive settlement of Claggartville could be found.

He moved to the edge of the clearing, waiting until he'd located Jak, almost invisible in his camouflage jacket, and J.B. Dix, both covering the singers. The smell of burning meat was much stronger. A light brown jug was being passed frequently between the two men. Ryan found himself beginning to salivate.

"Move and you're dead!"

The singing continued, both the huddled figures waving their short arms from side to side. Ryan couldn't believe that they hadn't heard him. But they both had dark fur caps on, with long flaps over their ears that tied under their chins, and they both looked and sounded drunker than skunks.

Shaking his head in disbelief, Ryan stepped out from cover and poked the barrel of the caseless rifle into the back of the nearer man, who leaped to his feet so fast that he nearly knocked Ryan over. He vaulted the fire, catching his foot on the spit that held the blackened haunch of venison, sending it spinning. He began to scream in the same puny little voice that Ryan had heard singing, moments earlier.

The other men also had lightning reactions, a knife springing from sheath to fist, cutting back so fast that he nearly slashed Ryan across the thigh.

"Hold it, you stupe!" Ryan bellowed as he took a couple of steps away, keeping both strangers covered. Jak and J.B. appeared like lethal phantoms from the other side of the clearing, the boy with his satin-finish cannon and the Armorer with his trusty Uzi.

"Stand still and keep your hands up. Drop that blade!"

Now that they turned to look at Ryan, he saw that both the men had rounded, brutish faces, with reddish eyes sunk in layers of weathered flesh. They had thin lips and short necks. Under their furs, both of them looked stocky and muscular. As far as he could see, neither was a mutie.

The one with the knife glanced sideways at his comrade, muttering something in his rumbling, deep voice. The other fluted something back and the knife thudded into the turf, a couple of inches from the toes of Ryan's boots.

"Don't push it, friend," he growled, lifting the muzzle of the G-12 toward the man's face.

"We don't want to hurt you," J.B. told them. "Just a little food and some directions. Give us that and you can go free."

There was no reaction from either man.

"They dumbies?" Jak asked.

"They were sanging," Lori observed.

"Perhaps they do not speak your tongue," Donfil suggested, staring intently at their two prisoners. "It is an arrogance to think every man you meet will speak your language. You understand me, One Eye Chills? Do you?"

Ryan nodded. "Sure, Man Whose Eyes See More. I know what you mean."

"Do you speak English?" Krysty asked, standing at Ryan's side.

The slitted eyes turned to her, but the faces showed no trace of emotion.

"Looks like they don't."

"Fireblast! If they can't help us, we'd better chill them. Safest."

Doc pushed past him. "Really, my dear Ryan, there are times that your chilling desire for chilling makes me concerned for your immortal soul. There are times that there could be alternative solutions to 'Chill him,' if you look for them."

"Such as?"

Doc stepped closer to the man who'd thrown the knife. As he did so the blank face lightened and he again mumbled something to his companion, who clearly nodded his agreement.

"Seems like they know you, Doc," J.B. said amusedly.

"Claggartville," the old man said very slowly and clearly. "Where is Claggartville?"

The one who had knocked over the venison opened his eyes a millimeter wider. Though his accent was barbaric, there was no doubt at all that he repeated the name. "Claggartville."

Doc shrugged his shoulders, miming someone who was lost, shading his eyes with his hand, looking around and saying the name of the ville in a puzzled tone of voice.

"Great performance, Doc," Ryan said.

"Claggartville," said the man with the high voice. He then tried a string of guttural words. Seeing that this failed, he relied then on pointing to the west, using his hand to indicate they should then curve toward the south.

"What we figured," Jak said dismissively.

"How about telling them we want to steal all their food and they can go," Ryan suggested.

"I'll give it a try. I was always rather a stunner when it came to playing charades at the Yuletide parties, back when I was . . . when the world was young," he finished, biting his lip. "I'll try, Ryan."

He stooped with cracking knee joints and picked a few pieces off the piece of meat, wiping his mouth in a vivid pantomime of appreciation. Then he took the two men, one by each arm, and led them to the edge of the clearing, to the east. He gently pushed them toward the forest.

Both stubbornly resisted his efforts to get them to leave the clearing. One pointed to his knife, the other to the pair of horn longbows that leaned against a tree.

Ryan shook his head angrily, gesturing at them with the rifle. "Tell them to get out of it, Doc."

"I don't speak their tongue. It sounds like some debased form of German or Polish. I don't know. They were probably a small community that was cut off by the bombing and kept elements of their mother tongue. Immigrants."

"Fuck off!" Jak shouted, cocking his Magnum and ramming the end of the barrel under the chin of the nearer man. The tip of the forward sight cut into the skin, leaving a tiny, perfect bead of bright crimson blood on the tanned skin.

The hand rose and brushed away the gaping muzzle of the massive handblaster, as if it were a mildly troublesome insect. J.B. laughed out loud. "Sure terrified him there, boy."

Lori took the next try, pulling the fur-covered men to the farther edge of the small clearing, coughing as she passed through the smoke of their cooking fire. She rubbed her stomach and mimed hunger, smiling at the venison, which was rapidly cooling on the grass. Then she pushed the men from her, with a wave and a sad smile.

One of them nodded, mouth breaking into a toothless grin, which made Ryan wonder in passing how he would have eaten the roasted meat. But the man was pointing again, this time to the earthenware crock of liquor.

"Yes?" Lori asked. Getting Ryan's smile of agreement, the tall blonde ran across, silver spurs tinkling, and picked up the jar, handing it to the primitive outlander.

He raised it to his lips and gave the teenage girl a deep bow. His companion also bowed low, offering a slightly cautious smile to the rest of the watching group.

Then the two turned and began to pick their way between the trees. Within a couple of minutes they'd totally vanished.

"Well done, my poppet." Doc grinned, hugging Lori and giving her a great smacking kiss on the lips.

"Yeah, Lori," Ryan agreed. "Jak, just keep a watch in case they decide to come back for their bows. Let's eat."

Apart from the outer skin of the deer, which had been roasted to charcoal, the meat was good, tender and succulent. They all sat cross-legged around the dying fire, chins slick with the juices of the animal.

Ryan sighed. "Food's good. If that map Doc saw is about right, we still got some miles to cover to try and find this ville down on the coast. Best be moving."

They left the bows where they'd found them, so that the two primitive hunters would be able to retrieve them after they'd gone.

The outskirts of Claggartville were reached just before sunset with no further trouble.

Chapter Twelve

A WHITE MIST CREPT off the Lantic Ocean, toward the shore. Already its first questing tendrils had reached a line of large boulders a hundred paces off the beach. The seven friends stood together on a low bluff surrounded by tall pine trees, looking down on Claggartville.

"Handsome little ville," J.B. observed.

Ryan nodded. "Looks clean." He counted the line of masts alongside the quay. "Eight sailers. Must be fishers and transports. They're burning coal in those houses. Must ship it in."

Claggartville looked as though it consisted of around seven to eight hundred houses, making it one of the largest villes that Ryan had ever encountered. Smoke poured from well over half of the chimneys, drifting their way.

The buildings were almost entirely white-framed, with red roofs. The streets looked narrow near the harbor, but wider farther up the hill. He could see the spires of two churches and a large windmill, its sails motionless in the calm of the evening.

"Several of the houses got a kind of platform on the top," Krysty said, using her amazing eyesight to scan the ville. "Rails around them, as well. Wonder what . . . ?"

"Widows' walks, my dear," Doc replied. "The women climbed up them to spy out across the sea for some sight of a returning sail. These whalers often were away for five years at a time. It was a bleak, harsh life."

"Any those ships whaling?" Jak asked.

"I fear that I can't tell, dear boy. The old peepers see less than once they did. Perhaps Krysty can . . . ?"

"What am I looking for, Doc?"

"Some evidence of small ovens on board where they would render the oil. Several long, narrow boats shipped aboard. Tough, seagoing vessels ready for any weather."

Krysty shook her head. "Can't see from up here, Doc. The fog's closing in on the ville. We should get down there if we want to find a bed and food."

"Best step easy. Those men with the venison might live here. Or it might be home to some relatives of the good folk of Consequence."

Ryan shook his head at the Indian's words. "Doubt that, Donfil. Hardly ever seen such a trim ville as this one. But it could be the sort of place with a heavy presence of sec men. Best we step slow and easy and avoid trouble."

"Put up blaster or I'll stick where sun never shines!"

"Cool it down, Jak," Ryan warned, fearing the confrontation was already fallen from their hands.

"You blaspheme, mutie outlander," the sec guard snarled.

"Don't know word, stinking bastard!" the boy replied, hand trembling over the holster that held his .357.

"Jak!" Ryan shouted. "Just button up the mouth and let me do the talking." He faced the angry sec man. "Boy's wild. Sorry for the way he speaks. He was orphaned when his family was taken by stickies. We rescued him."

It was a situation familiar to Ryan and to J.B. Throughout Deathlands there were all kinds of different communities. Large villes, ruled over by successful barons and an unknown number of smaller settlements, sometimes only a handful of scattered hovels. The difference between these and the villes was most often seen in their attitude to security and strangers.

The Trader and the war wags had frequently run foul of overofficious sec men, many of whom were swift and evil bastards, born and reared in an atmosphere of bullying and corruption.

But the trio of sec men on the main highway into Claggartville was a little different from the usual breed.

The mist had reached the houses along the quay, twisting and turning in the alleys and courts of the town. As they drew closer it had become obvious to the seven companions that Claggartville was one of the oldest villes they'd come across. Or it had been cleverly rebuilt to give the impression that it was extremely old. The houses had gables and small leaded windows, and the streets were narrow and cribbed.

"Sec patrol," Krysty had warned, seeing the three men standing by a kind of tollgate lowered across the road. All three wore black jackets and pants, with knee-length boots of black leather, and had trimmed mustaches and long side-whiskers that practically met under their chins. Two of three wore old-fashioned stovepipe hats like the one Doc had favored for so long.

That was the general impression. But from habit Ryan's eye went to the weapons the three men were carrying.

He blinked.

At his side J.B. whispered, "Can't be real, Ryan. They're remakes. Good ones. But they gotta be remakes."

The most modern was an 1848 Colt Dragoon .44-caliber revolver. That was carried by the tallest of the three sec men. He also had an 1819 Hall .54-caliber flintlock breechloader slung across his shoulders on a worn leather strap with a polished brass buckle.

One of the other men held a battered Kentucky flintlock musket in his hand, the stock resting on the ground. He also had a brace of smoothbore flintlock pistols at his belt, looking the same bore as the Hall musket.

The third man had a single pistol in his belt. It was the Harper's Ferry martial flintlock, the rare 1806 model, Ryan noticed, with the number 22 stamped on the barrel.

Apart from the Kentucky musket, all the guns looked in amazingly good condition. There were a few, a very few, original antique firearms in Deathlands. But these blasters were so good that they had to be, as J.B. had suggested, skillful remakes or rebuilds.

All three men looked to be in their mid to late thirties, and they were calm and self-possessed. Yet they showed none of the usual sec men's arrogance.

"The words of the young are as the falling of broken shards of pot," the leader of the patrol said to Ryan.

"And of less worth than the dry dirt that spills from the wheels of the dung cart," his colleague with the musket added.

"Yeah," Ryan said. "What can we do to help you folks?"

"Whither go ye and from whence? And what is your business here in Claggartville?"

The speech was old-fashioned and stiltedly formal, reminding Ryan of old books he'd read and old historical vids.

"We got us wrecked about ten miles back. Had a run-in with some muties near a ville called Consequence and—"

"Ye have been with the punished ones of Consequence and have come here?"

Ryan looked at the tallest of the trio. "Yeah. Had to chill us some and burn down a house. You know about them?"

"By the broaching of the flukes! They are sodden in evil and no man nor woman nor child goes there. It is forbidden. Ye have slain some of the blasphemous creatures, thou sayest?"

"Aye, that we did," Doc said, pushing to the front of their group. "The unbelievers perished at the hands of the righteous, for so it is truly writ, is it not?"

"Verily it is, brother." For the first time there was a visible relaxing of the tension. "Where were ye bound?"

"Out past Nantucket, but the wind rose and cast us upon the shore. We seek shelter and food from any person of charity."

"Charity, brother! Nay, thou seekest not charity here in Claggartville. But if thou and thy companions will work for thy keep?" His eyes roamed across them, settling on Jak. "Yon resembles the spawn of Satan. His hair and eyes . . ."

Ryan spoke, seeing that Doc was floundering. "Boy's fine, friend. Mother was scared by a blizzard when carrying him and the color white marks him. But he is honest and hardworking."

"I am," Jak agreed, lowering his eyes in what he hoped looked to be a suitably humble way.

"Have any of ye hunted the great fishes?" the third sec man asked.

Ryan glanced around. "We killed a mutie whale-shark only yesterday."

"Then you will find work in Claggartville. This place lives off the great fishes of the ocean for food, light and heat." The sec man's face assumed a pious expression. "Truly we are they who go down to the sea and occupy our business in great waters. We see the works of the Lord and all of his wonders in the deep."

"Amen to that," Doc said, attracting another approving glance from the tallest of the trio.

"All outlanders are allowed three days' free lodging and food, of the simplest. Then they must find work or they must leave the ville."

"Seems fair," Krysty said.

The oldest of the three stared at her. "A wanton woman is as a mighty splinter in the eye of an honest man," he intoned.

"Amen," Doc muttered, flinching at the venom in Krysty's glance.

The leader spoke again. "Ye must go to the place set aside for wayfarers. It is called the Rising Flukes Inn and is run by Jedediah Rodriguez. Follow this road until ye reach Welles Street. Down until ye see Try-pot Alley. The sign hangs where none but a blind man could miss it. Ye must sign the register there with your names and the day of your arrival. Sundown three days hence is your mark."

"Thank you kindly," Ryan said. "This is a most generous and welcoming ville."

The three road guards exchanged a knowing look with one another, but said nothing.

THE RISING FLUKES. The sign creaked as it swung to and fro in the dark, misty air. It depicted a delicate painting of a great gray whale, leaping into the sky in a shower of silver spray, dwarfing a tiny rowboat in the sea beneath it.

Owner Jedediah Hernando Rodriguez. Under License to Purvey Ales, Spirits and Tobacco under Claggartville Ordinances.

On the way down into the heart of the ville the seven friends had seen very few of the local people. Doors had slammed shut and shutters closed. Draperies had twitched, and they'd seen faces shadowed behind the small windows. Most of the homes showed the golden glow of oil lamps burning in their front rooms.

"What's smell?" Jak asked, wrinkling his nose. "Like lots dead fish."

Doc answered him. "This is a whaling town, lad. Seems likely that after the great bombing of the holocaust this is one of the places largely spared. It's in a deep hollow with hills all around it, only open toward the boundless ocean. No gas or electricity. No factories for work. So they turn to what they must have done here back in the mid-1800s—hunting the whale."

"You eat whales, Doc?" Lori asked.

"Me personally, or . . . Yes, you can. You boil them down for their oil. An awful lot of uses for the whale. In my time they were hunted damnably near to extinction. Only the wars saved them. Probably more out there now than ever before. And quite right, too."

The oak door of the inn had a top window made from the dark green bottoms of wine bottles. As soon as Ryan pushed the door open they all heard a great rush of talk and laughter. The smell of beer, cigars and sweat hung in the air, and for a moment they hesitated out in the darkness of Try-pot Alley.

"Wast thou born in a barn, stranger?" came a bellowing voice. "Come thou in or stay thou out and be damned to thee. But close the perditional door lest we all freeze to death."

Ryan led the way inside the saloon, peering through the fug of smoke that filled the place. He saw it had a low, beamed ceiling, stained and dirty. There was a bar at the far end, and a dozen or more tables scattered around the single room. In the farther corner, under a lattice window, was a jangling, out-of-tune piano, being hammered by a stout black man. A skinny woman in a head scarf was leaning on his shoulder, singing an old sea song.

"...of Liverpool that saddens me, it's my sweetheart that I must leave—" She broke off as she saw the seven strangers filing in. "Ware outlanders!" she yelled. "Jed! Outlanders for yer trade!"

The noise faded and every head turned their way. Ryan was conscious of dark sweaters and work pants; knee boots and beards; eyes turning toward them; stillness; pint mugs frozen, halfway to mouths; playing cards checked an inch from the scarred surface of the round tables.

"Hi. Told to ask for Jedediah Rodriguez. Sec men told us."

The sailor nearest hitched a thumb behind him, pointing to the bar. Ryan looked across the silent saloon.

"Rodriguez?"

"Me, outlanders. Come and sign the sweat-swilling register to keep them quaking sons of sec men happy. Don't rock the boat is my saying, friends. Come and have a drink on the Rising Flukes."

Jedediah Hernando Rodriguez leaned his hand on the top of the bar and grinned across at them, waving them over. The talk began to spring up again, in whispers, gradually swelling louder. The cards resumed and there was the chink of glasses on tables. The woman began singing, more quietly.

Ryan and the six companions lined up at the bar, the locals moving out of their way.

A large blue book had appeared, with a copper inkwell and a quill pen. "Jed Rodriguez welcomes you and asks you to name your poison. Put your monikers down here first."

"Monikers?" Donfil asked.

"Thy names, my tall Indian friend. It's a harpooneer thou art, or I miss my guess. Art thou kin to the Flathead tribes?"

"No. Mescalero Apache."

"And a tall one at that. They'll scarcely fit thee in a whaleboat, brother."

The innkeeper was a strange-looking man. His skin was sallow and unhealthy, stretched tight across the bones of his skull. Though he looked around thirty years of age, there was no trace of any beard on his chin. His eyes were dark brown, like limpid pools, under lashes as long as any gaudy whore's. His hair was cut neatly and curled, with some sort of scented grease on it. He was wearing a shirt of purple satin, open to the waist, showing a golden necklace and a medallion. His hands were long and slender, nearly every finger sporting a jeweled ring. Ryan noticed that he wore an ornate inlaid derringer in his belt and a long stiletto with a silver hilt.

The date on the register was the first day of October. The ink was still fresh, at the top of a clean page. Ryan was curious and turned to the previous page. It carried only one name and the ville of Portland. The date was April 17.

Rodriguez smirked. "We don't get many out-landers here, friend."

"But you have a triple patrol on the highway every day?"

"Sec men are for the risk of muties. Don't rock the boat is what I always say. Let's have your names and then I'll serve ye all a quart of the best ale and a pie of good whale meat and some taties to go with it."

They entered their names, Ryan taking the lead. In the column marked Ville, Ryan wrote Richmond, Virginia. The others followed, all giving the same ville's name. Rodriguez looked at their names curiously.

"What's your trade, friends? Women are cooks, I'll warrant. Cabin boy with red eyes, and the old'll be... Be what?"

"I'm a teacher, Mr. Rodriguez," Doc replied.

"Could find work here. But Mr. Dix and Mr. Cawdor. What might ye be? Mercies? Hired blasters? That's the cut of your jib as I spies it."

Ryan leaned across the bar and touched the man very gently on the cheek with the tip of his index finger. "What we do, *friend*, falls into the field of our business. Do you understand me? Good. Then serve us your food and beer, and show us where we're to sleep. That and no more."

The barkeep didn't speak for a moment. Then he brushed away Ryan's hand. "I've seen outlanders come to Claggartville, and I've seen them go. Go in many a different way, Mr. Cawdor. Keep thine own council, but step careful when thou goest from light into shadow. If thou takest my meaning. Now I'll fetch ye the food you're entitled to."

J.B. INHALED the cigar smoke, admiring the way the tip glowed brightly. "Been many a long day since I've enjoyed a smoke. The food was good and the beer better. We've been in many a worse place, Ryan, haven't we?"

"Yeah," Ryan said, stifling a belch. "Shouldn't have had a third helping of that pie. But I could manage another quart of beer. Anyone else?"

Everyone else had eaten and drunk enough. At Ryan's wave, the landlord bustled over to them, bringing another of the foaming mugs of the local brew. He placed it carefully in front of Ryan.

"Like to see your rooms now?" he asked.

"Sure."

"And on the morrow ye can set off to find yourself some work."

Ryan nodded. "See what's to do around the ville."

One of the men at a table near the window heard the conversation and called out something, but none of them could catch it.

"What was that?" Ryan asked.

Rodriguez smiled lopsidedly. "Japhet said Captain Quadde was seeking extra crew for the next whaling voyage. Replace those lost last time. Might be something there for you, Mr. Cawdor."

There was a burst of ribald laughter from all around the taproom of the Rising Flukes at his suggestion. Ryan wondered why, wondered who this Captain Quadde might be. But he dismissed the name from his mind, as he knew he was never likely to make the acquaintance of the gentleman. They wouldn't be in Claggartville long enough for that.

"And so to bed betimes," the landlord said.

Chapter Thirteen

THE ROOM WAS TUCKED under the eaves of the old
house, with angled beams and tiny dormer windows.
At its peak the ceiling sloped just high enough for both
Jak and J.B. to stand upright, but none of the others
could avoid bumping their heads. Donfil had to stoop
so low that his knuckles almost trailed on the wide
floorboards.

There were ten beds in the room. Single trundle
beds, narrow and hard. The room had the cold, damp
feel of not having been occupied for a long time.
Which, from the evidence of the register down in the
bar, it probably hadn't.

Ryan opened one of the windows, pushing hard, for
it was stiff, the hinges rusted. It finally squeaked back
and he was able to look out over Claggartville, toward the harbor a block or two away.

The fog had settled down over the lower streets,
courts and alleys, finding a level around the middle of
the second-floor windows. For Ryan, a whole floor
higher, it was an odd sight. The white mist writhing
and undulating below him, like a living blanket, with
the roofs of houses poking up like the prows of old,
wrecked vessels, their chimneys smoking. There were

lights to be seen, sometimes through the fog, like a host of drowned carriages. And voices, muffled, and the ringing of heels on cobblestones.

Just visible in the moonlight was the forest of masts, spars and delicate rigging of the ships moored alongside the quays.

"Anything to see, lover?" Krysty asked, leaning on his shoulder.

"Sailers. Always wondered what it must be like to go out in a small wooden water wag, right out of sight of land for days and weeks." He laughed. "Not that I ever want to find out."

Far below them they could still hear the noise of the inn—singing and an occasional bellow of merriment, the piano tinkling away and the constant buzz of talk.

"Another customer." Krysty pointed to the alley.

There was a black-cloaked figure, foreshortened by their viewpoint, stumping along toward the Rising Flukes, the metal ferrule of a cane ringing out on the damp stones. They could only see the man through a peekhole in the banks of fog, which swirled about the houses.

They heard the crack of the front door of the inn being thrown open and the sudden, instant, total silence that followed.

"Must be another outlander," Ryan guessed.

Through the open window they could hear a few barked, harsh words, the voice raised as though in a query. No audible reply came from any of the tavern's customers. The door banged shut, and they could hear the stumping of feet. But the mist had swept back, and the alley had vanished from their eyes.

THE NIGHT HAD PASSED peacefully. The companions dressed—although none of them had taken off all their clothes or weapons for the night—and made their way down into the main room of the tavern. It was a little after seven in the morning. The room had been swept and scrubbed, and the front door stood open to the bright morning sunlight. But the unpleasant odor of stale smoke and flat beer remained.

Jed Rodriguez was washing tankards behind the bar and looked up at the sound of their feet on the stairs.

"Good morrow, outlanders. Slept ye well?"

He didn't wait for the answer, pointing them to a table in a bay window, calling out back for one of the servant girls to come and bring them something to break their fasts.

"Going after work?" he asked.

Ryan replied for them all. "First we need to pick our way around the ville. Suss out the good from the bad."

"Nothing bad here in Claggartville, Mr. Cawdor! And thou might do well to remember that. Don't rock the boat is my motto, and it would be as well for thee to think on that."

Ryan noticed the unveiled threat. Or was it just a warning?

The food was plain but good.

While the girl laid out the wooden platters, the landlord explained the simple facts of their economy in the ville. The whale oil and meat were traded up and down the coast of New England for other items of food or drink.

"Don't grow much around here. Turnips and potatoes. Peas an' beans. Not much corn or crops like that. Few cows. Mutie chickens. And lots of fish. Here's your breakfast. Eat hearty."

The butter was heavily salted and the variety of smoked fishes oppressive so early in the morning. But the eggs, mostly double and triple yolked, were golden and good. There was also some fatback, which Ryan guessed was another of the commodities that Claggartville traded for their whaling produce.

The drink, in an orange enameled jug, was dark brown and scalding hot, and Krysty correctly identified it as acorn coffee.

Rodriguez came back as they were finishing off the meal. He beamed down at the empty plates. "Done good, outlanders. Eaten hearty. Give ye the appetite to go find some work."

"Who's Captain Quadde?" J.B. asked, wiping the remnants of egg from his platter with a hunk of bread.

The landlord of the tavern looked away, staring past them through the open door. "Looks like it'll be a goodish day. Fog's nigh lifted off the harbor already."

Ryan stood up slowly. "Man who rocks the boat ends up falling overboard, wouldn't you say, Jed? Eh?"

"Could be, Mr. Cawdor."

"Then I'd be obliged if you'd answer our question to you."

"Captain Quadde?"

"Yeah."

"Captain Quadde's one of the richest skippers ever sailed from Claggartville."

"And . . . ?" Ryan prompted, still facing the man.

"There's those as might say that to sail with Quadde is to buy thy pay with the skin off thy back and...maybe with thy mortal soul, as well. But I don't say that. I just say that it's best to keep well to windward of Captain Quadde. If thou catchest my drift on the matter?"

"Take your meaning, Jed. Thanks for it. We'll watch out for the captain."

DOC TANNER, with his sprouting side-whiskers and his old-fashioned manners, fitted seamlessly into the daily round of life in the town of Claggartville. Even his clothes, with the stained frock coat and the cracked knee boots, attracted no attention from any of the locals.

Ryan, with his eye patch and armory of weapons, was stared at from around corners and behind draperies. J.B. didn't catch much notice. Lori was openly ogled by the young men, as was Krysty. But the height and bearing of the women created its own immediate barrier. There was rather more awe than there was simple lust.

Most of the interest was reserved for Jak and Donfil.

The Apache was a full foot taller than anyone else in the ville, and his clothes made him stand out like a cockerel in a henhouse. As he stalked barefooted through the winding cobbled streets, reflecting glasses shielding his eyes, every head turned to follow him. Every jaw dropped and every conversation suddenly halted.

Then they noticed Jak, bouncing along behind the long-haired scarecrow. The young boy nodded and smiled to everyone they passed, quickly picking up the habit of bowing to all of the women and girls. There was a fresh breeze in off the Lantic, and it made his fine white hair dance and spin about his shoulders.

A pretty blind girl was playing a dulcimer on a balcony as they passed, and Jak called out a bright good-morning to her, making her blush and lay down her instrument, and run inside her house. Before they'd gone a dozen paces a man rushed from the white-painted building, face heavy with anger.

"Outlander dog!" he yelled. "Come thou here, thou mutie spawn!"

"Easy, Jak," Ryan warned, hand dropping, so casually, to the butt of the SIG-Sauer pistol.

"No problem," the teenager said, stopping and turning calmly to face the enraged man, who was several inches taller and a hundred pounds heavier than the albino.

"Thou hast given insult to my poor, afflicted child!" he screeched.

"Then sorry. Not deliberate," Jak apologized.

"Mutie demon! Thou shalt be beaten and driven from the ville for thy wickedness."

"Boy didn't mean anything by it, mister, and he's said he's sorry. Let it lay."

Ryan's attempt to pour oil upon the troubled waters was ignored. The man carried a stout cudgel, and he raised it above his head and aimed a blow at Jak's skull.

"Oh shit," Ryan sighed, hoping the white-haired youth wouldn't butcher the man in the street.

Jak dodged effortlessly, dipping under the crushing swing, one of his many hidden throwing knives appearing in his fingers like magic. He held the leaf-bladed weapon by its weighted hilt, point up, like all classic knife fighters. He waited in a half crouch, whispering to the man.

"Last warning, bastard. Said sorry, now get away. Cut you horrible. Peel face like skinning rat. Fuck off!"

The last was hissed with such fearsome malevolence that the angry father took three tumbling steps backward, tripping over his own feet and nearly falling. A muscle worked at the corner of his mouth, making his lips twitch and jerk. Ryan thought he looked like someone who'd been about to strangle a kitten and found he was holding a panther. From the way the man was standing, slightly bowlegged, he guessed that he must have lost control in his sudden terror and fouled his dark serge breeches.

"Best do like the boy says, mister," J.B. urged.

They left him there, still holding his cudgel, knuckles white, face drained of blood, and carried on with their walk around the streets of Claggartville in the brisk fall sunshine.

Twice they passed sec patrols. The first time they were stopped and questioned. With an infinite, oppressive politeness, the sec boss carefully wrote down their details in a small leather-bound notebook, using a stub of lead pencil—their names and when they entered the ville, that they'd registered at the Rising Flukes Inn, and that they knew the regulations about finding work within three days or they would have to leave.

"Tightest little ville in all Deathlands," Krysty said as they moved on.

They went past a shop selling fruit and vegetables, the contents spilling out on tables over the narrow sidewalk. The owner, a stout man with jolly red cheeks and eyes like small chips of Sierra melt ice, greeted them.

"Morning to ye, outlanders. A merry pippin to crunch? Punnet of blackberries? Lovely ripe pears from the Shens? What's your fancy, fine ladies and fine mariners? Come taste."

Lori reached for the golden pear that the shopkeeper held out temptingly toward her, but at the last moment he snatched it back.

"Why d'you did that?" she asked crossly.

"Show thy jack, lady. Handful of jack buys a handful of good victuals. No jack. No eat. Thy credit runs only with Master Jedediah Rodriguez and the Rising Flukes. And no place else."

"Then stuff it up your fat arsehole, you sad fat bastard," she said, knocking the false smile clean off the plump lips.

THE QUAYSIDE of Claggartville was bustling with action, men heaving casks and bales, pushing small carts with iron wheels over the clattering cobbles. Mongrels slunk around, snapping at one another, cowering from the blows and kicks aimed at them. As they moved through, Ryan and the others could catch the scent of tobacco and liquor.

"Git out th'way, outlanders," bellowed an enormous man in a stained white shirt, who carried a pile of baskets filled with fish on his head.

The ships loomed over it all, masts rocking in unison on the gently rolling waters of the harbor.

"She's a whaler," Doc said, pointing to one called *Rights of Man*. "There's the ovens on decks there."

"The one painted dark brown?" Donfil asked interestedly.

"Not paint. Blood," J.B. said.

The last ship along the line was another whaler, painted in somber black, with a narrow white stripe running all the way around her, just beneath the rails. False gun ports were etched in white along her sides, and a white flag hung limply from the masthead.

The men working on the dock seemed to be avoiding this ship. It was almost as though there were an invisible barrier erected on the quay. Nothing was being loaded or unloaded at that end of the harbor, and there was nobody to be seen on the deck of the dark vessel.

"Called the *Salvation*," Ryan said. "Fine name for a sailer."

The seven stood and watched the ship, admiring the elegant lines of her yards and the four slim twenty-eight-foot whaleboats that hung from the davits on either side.

"Everyone stopped," Jak whispered.

It was true.

Behind them, all along the dock, work had ceased as though a switch had been thrown. Every bearded face was turned toward them, staring in a fascinated stillness. The only sound was the sighing of the wind through the rigging and the scream of gulls, circling around a small shoal of herring a quarter mile out into the bay.

"Someone farted?" Jak asked, giggling nervously. "What d'they want?"

"Something about the ship?" Krysty suggested.

"She looks normal enough. Like the others. Sight cleaner than most."

"True, Ryan," Donfil agreed. "But there is something I like not about it."

Krysty nodded slowly. "Know what you mean. Feeling gets me across the back of my head and clear down my spine. Something about the *Salvation* just doesn't set right. Can't say what."

"Guess we can go," Ryan said. "Find out later. Mebbe."

As they neared the turning into Try-pot Alley they came across a ragged urchin bowling a metal hoop, striking sparks from the stones. Ryan reached out a hand and took the hoop from the boy.

"What art thou . . . ?" the guttersnipe began.

"One question. Who owns the *Salvation*?"

The boy spit against the wall. "Everyone knows that, 'cept outlanders. Captain Quadde, of course."

Ryan gave him back the hoop, and they continued on to the Rising Flukes.

Chapter Fourteen

"NO WORK?"

"No work."

"All day in Claggartville... seven healthy out-landers and no work?"

The incredulity of the landlord was going on and on, and Ryan Cawdor was already beginning to find it exceedingly tedious. Ever since they'd returned after exploring the ville he'd been on about work, counting off on his fingers the people that he knew personally who were almost begging in the streets and alleys to find men and women to fill vacancies for all manner of work.

"Rory Starbuck the chandler. Also runs the rope-making works. He could take on a couple of fresh hands with no trouble. The women would be welcome with their looks at Eleanor Goodman's gaudy..." He caught the eye of Doc Tanner and hastily changed his mind. "No, I didn't... There's many taverns'd take them as pot girls or cooks if they had the skill. The Indian could ship as harpooner on any vessel leaving harbor. There's jobs in some shops for... Oh, so many that it makes my head spin."

"Why don't you just spin off and bring us some food?" J.B. suggested, as calm as ever. As menacing as ever.

The supper was baked fish, what Rodriguez called "star-gazers' pie." It had a thick golden crust with the heads of a dozen mackerels protruding through the top, eyes open, staring ceilingward. With it came some fried greens and large potatoes roasted in their skins, with butter oozing over the platters.

They washed it down with bumpers of ale, perhaps the very same they'd seen being rolled in iron-hooped kegs along the quayside.

The piano was being played by a blind man whose forehead was furrowed by a huge scar. He picked at the keys with a soft touch, singing slow ballads of lost love and vanquished honor.

As Rodriguez came across at the end of the meal to oversee the removal of the greasy dishes and dirty glasses, Ryan caught him by the sleeve of his linen smock.

"What is it, Mr. Cawdor? The meal not to thy liking?"

"Tell us about Captain Quadde and the *Salvation*. What's so terrible?"

The innkeeper tried for a laugh that got lost somewhere between his throat and his mouth, coming out like a strangled yelp. "Terrible?" he squawked. "Why rock the boat asking that sort of question? Won't do thee good, outlander."

"Quadde and the *Salvation*," Ryan repeated, tightening his grip.

"Not good to blab 'bout it. Don't want to finish keelhauled or having my backbone laid bare by the cat. Let thee find someone else to tell thee about Quadde. Not me."

Ryan looked around the Rising Flukes, seeing that his conversation with Rodriguez had hushed every voice in the place. Every face was turned to him.

"Well!" he shouted. "Any of you chicken-shit bastards tell an outlander about the fireblasted mystery of the *Salvation* and her captain?"

Faces were averted, eyes downcast.

"Let it lie, mister," the landlord whispered. "There's a couple of men of her crew here."

Ryan stood up, feeling the familiar rise of anger, the crimson mist that flowed down over his brain when the rage took him. For most of his adult years he'd been able to control it. Most of the time. But now it was swelling again.

"Rodriguez says some of you are off the *Salvation*. So, what's so fucking frightening about her?"

"Outlander?"

"At last." Ryan turned to face the man who'd spoken. He was sitting in front of a half-finished plate of mutton stew at the long table nearest to the silent piano.

"I'm second mate on the *Salvation*. Been that for five years now."

He was a little taller than average height, with a smaller beard than was usual about the ville. Several scars lined his weather-beaten face, one of them pulling down the corner of his left eye. The middle finger was missing from his left hand. He wore the jumper and breeches that most of the sailors favored. There was a dirk in his belt with a hilt that looked as if it had been carved from a piece of bone or ivory.

"Then you can tell me why everyone shits themselves at the mention of your ship and your captain."

"Best keep thy prow out of waters that don't concern thee."

Ryan spit on the floor, shrugging off Krysty's warning hand, knowing with a surge of strange excitement that he wasn't going to be cautious. Not this time. This time he was going to see the quarrel through. Even if it meant pushing it all the way himself.

"You scared to tell?"

The man stood at that, pushing away the table, hands resting on his hips in a gesture that was provocative and also kept his right hand near the knife hilt.

"Scared, outlander? Jonas Clegg fears neither man nor beast. There isn't the man born of woman or the whale broaching from the deepest waters that scares Jonas Clegg."

"I say you're a liar. I say you're a liar, Clegg, and a white-gutted coward!"

The mate smiled at that, gesturing to the three men with him to step away. The rest of the customers of the Rising Flukes also got up from their tables, backing off to ring the walls. Rodriguez shrugged his shoulders and retreated behind the bar.

"Come on, lover," Krysty urged quietly.

Ryan glanced at her and she took a sudden, indrawn breath. She knew Ryan was a killer. That was his trade. But rarely had she seen his face glowing with the thrill of an imminent fight.

"Got to be, lover," he replied softly. "Had enough of this place. Polite on the surface and something stinking rotten underneath. Time to get that out here in the open."

"Careful, Ryan."

He kissed her lightly on the cheek. "Always am, lover."

"Finished saying thy goodbye to thy poxed whore, outlander?" Clegg sneered.

"Sure you don't want to run and get your poxy Captain Quadde and hide behind his skirts?"

"Hide behind...?" Clegg began, looking puzzled for a moment. "Then thou knowest not that much about the *Salvation*?"

"Get to the steel!" someone yelled, and the sailor grinned wolfishly.

"Aye, let us to the steel. Dost thou have a knife, outlander?"

Ryan drew the panga with its eighteen-inch cutting edge from its sheath, the sight of the weapon bringing a burst of whispering from around the taproom of the inn.

"Bring the blood-red roses to thy cheeks, Jonas," one of his shipmates cackled.

Clegg drew his own knife, showing it had a double-edged blade around eleven inches long. "My sticker'll draw the teeth of thy butchering cleaver, my chilled outlander," he called.

"Fuck the talk. Fight," Ryan gritted, his whole body twitching with the adrenaline rush. He was filled with the burning desire to annihilate the man in front of him. He didn't really know why, but that didn't matter much in the Deathlands, either. There was something inherently evil about the whaling ship *Salvation*, and he was about to remove a little of it from the earth.

The extra length and weight of his panga was outweighed by the difficulty of using it effectively against a lighter blade in the hands of a skilled man.

The sailor was a tough fighting man, veteran of dozens of tavern brawls and dockside melees. Over the years he'd killed at least a dozen men in eye-to-eye combat.

Ryan, approaching the near side of middle age, was a whetted, flawless chilling machine, with no idea of how many men and women he'd sent into the endless dark.

Sensing that the one-eyed outlander held himself like an experienced knife fighter, Clegg kept off, moving around in a slow shuffle, feet scraping on the worn boards. The point of his knife was up, threatening Ryan with a cut at groin or belly.

The panga wasn't ideal for this sort of cut-and-thrust, dancing standoff. It came into its own when tables were falling and chairs thrown and a dozen men tangled in a bloody shambles of hacking steel.

"Take 'im, Jonas!" a voice yelled from the blurred ring of faces around the room. Ryan's concentration was totally fixed on the man in front of him, watching the eyes for the flickering change of expression that would mean an attack.

If he let the seaman get in too close, then he was done for. The dagger would be so much more maneuverable that it would be in and out between his ribs before he could counter with the cleaver.

"Sec men come by around this time!" Rodriguez called from behind the bar.

Ryan hardly heard him.

Everything around him was fading into the crimson mist that fogged his mind. In all the world there was only Jonas Clegg and himself. And the two steel blades.

Nothing more.

Sparks danced in the smoky air as the knife and the panga clashed, Clegg thrusting and Ryan managing to parry.

The sailor was grinning with the tension, lips pulled back wolfishly off his teeth. His breath panted harshly as he moved around. The man was good. Better than Ryan had guessed.

Clegg nearly knocked over a table as he pivoted away from his opponent. Pewter tankards rattled and he reached for one with his free hand, throwing it at Ryan in a shower of ale, hoping to take him off balance. The seaman came in after it, ducking in anticipation of Ryan cutting at his head.

Ryan second-guessed him.

Knocking away the spinning mug he immediately swung the long blade back, ready for a deadly, hissing cut. He aimed low, knowing that Clegg would try to dive in at him, aiming for his stomach.

There was the unforgettable jarring thunk that ran clear up Ryan's arm from wrist to shoulder.

A blind man would have heard a strange sequence of sounds in the barroom of the Rising Flukes Inn that night—the faint hiss of honed metal through the air; a clunk, like a butcher separating a row of chops from a carcass; a gasp of pain or shock or surprise; the tinkling of steel falling to the wooden floor. And something else falling. Heavier. Sounding like one of the meat chops. From all around came the gasp of released tension from the horde of spectators.

And then there was the odd pattering, like heavy rain, or a leaking faucet, pattering on the sawdust that covered the wooden floor.

The blood jetted from the severed stump of the right arm, spraying high in the air as the crippled man waved it helplessly, backing away from the inexorable figure of doom.

Words of the Trader came to Ryan's mind as he advanced grimly after Clegg, careful to avoid the slippery puddles of blood. "Get a man going... Chill him quick an' best you can."

It was the best of advice. Ryan could still recall a young man from War Wag Two—must have been four years ago—whose name had been Rocco Papini. He'd put down a mutie girl with two rounds from his little Czech-made blaster. Instead of putting a third bullet into the young woman's head, he'd drawn his knife and knelt down to cut her throat, thinking she was helpless. The fight had revealed one perfectly formed breast through a tear in the mutie's jerkin, and Rocco had turned, grinning to draw his friends' attention to it.

She'd opened him from groin to throat with a straight-edge razor, spilling his guts all over herself.

It had been Ryan, with his 9 mm SIG-Sauer, who had blown the mutie girl's skull apart, which hadn't been much consolation to the dying Rocco Papini.

Clegg tried to parry the next blow from the panga, expecting it to come at his face or throat.

Ryan feinted high, and then struck low, taking care not to put all his strength into the cut. The one fault of the cleaver was that its heavy blade sometimes hacked so deeply that it got lodged in bone and wouldn't come free.

This time it hit the staggering sailor near the top of the thigh. A reflex made Clegg half turn, saving his genitals from being sliced through. But the panga hit him across the leg, cutting muscle and snapping the femur. He cried out, thin and feeble, like a rabbit in front of a rattler. The man staggered, but didn't fall down.

Automatically his arms dropped and Ryan was able to take a half step in and open up the front of Clegg's neck with a steady cut that drew the edge of the panga across the taut skin. More blood gushed and the seaman fell at last, kicking and jerking, breath bubbling pink from the severed windpipe.

"Neat," J.B. said.

Nobody else spoke as the body finally ceased moving and became, undeniably, a corpse.

At that moment the front door of the tavern swung open, banging on its hinges, allowing in a shudderingly cold wind, carrying tendrils of fog upon its shoulders. Ryan was kneeling by the body of Jonas Clegg, wiping the blood-slick blade of the panga on its coat. He knew the others would be watching his back, so he didn't bother to turn around.

He heard the noise of heavy boots and the tapping of the ferrule of a walking stick. His mind went to the figure that he and Krysty had spotted through the creeping fog the night before.

The voice was harsh, the words grating one against the other like the broken edges of river ice as it broke up in the spring.

"Is he chilled?"

Ryan answered without looking behind him. "Try waking him if you think he's just sleeping."

"Who's done for Jonas? The one-eyed outlander? I don't hear thee, landlord! Speak up, Rodriguez, or I'll have thee flayed."

"It was...Captain Quadde...it was..." the landlord stammered.

The panga wiped free of blood, Ryan sheathed it at his belt and straightened. And turned to face the ugliest woman he'd ever seen in his life.

Chapter Fifteen

CAPTAIN PYRA QUADDE was forty-seven years old. She was five feet ten inches tall and weighed in at a muscular one-seventy. Her hair was a wonderful deep auburn, spoiled by being filthy and greasy. She wore knee-length boots in stained black leather, cracked and dulled with salt. Her black skirt reached below her knees, and she was swaddled in several layers of thick sweaters. Over all was a dark blue pea coat with tarnished brass buttons. A belaying pin, its end gleaming from use, was stuck in the broad leather belt. Her right hand gripped a stout walking stick, its end gray iron and the handle a smooth piece of ivory.

From behind, Ryan guessed that she could have been mistaken for a middleweight male wrestler, run to fat.

From the front she was nothing but an astoundingly ugly woman.

Her complexion was sallow, the skin oddly tight in places, slack in others. The furrows and wrinkles were seamed with dirt. Spots and boils decorated her cheeks and chin. A bristling mustache clung as tenaciously to her upper lip as a beggar to his last ten cents. The eyes were sunken in rolls of fat, like raisins in dough, and they glittered like chips of jet, fixing themselves to Ryan's face. When she smiled, Captain Quadde revealed a most peculiar set of false teeth. Ryan realized with a shudder of revulsion that they had been carved from some kind of animal bone.

"Thou butchered goodman Jonas? Thou, with a single starboard glim to peek through? Is that true, Rodriguez? The truth, thou sniveling bastard."

The landlord couldn't meet her eyes. Glancing toward Ryan Cawdor, he decided he couldn't face him, either.

"Yeah," he muttered into the stillness.

"What?" She spoke softly, the way a cougar will snarl deep in its throat.

"Good evening, Captain Quadde," Ryan said. "I chilled your man."

"Thy name?"

"Ryan Cawdor."

"Why didst thou slaughter poor mild Jonas? He would not have harmed a sleeping babe." There was a snigger of laughter from someone near the piano, quickly muffled as the woman turned and stared in that direction.

"I didn't like the way he looked and spoke." The surging anger that had pushed him into the fight with the seaman still moved within Ryan. Gentler, like the waves on a beach after the eye of the storm had passed on, but still strong enough to fuel his instinctive dislike of the hoggish woman.

She moved closer, and he noticed that she limped on her right leg. His eye was caught by Krysty, who was looking at Captain Quadde with an expression of almost religious horror. Her lips were moving, and Ryan guessed she was whispering an invocation to Gaia, the Earth Mother. Her long crimson hair, sentient to the moods of its mistress, was coiled tightly and protectively about her skull.

"Didst thou not like the way Jonas spoke and looked?" the woman said musingly. "For that he was slain. Lies here leaking out his red, red roses."

Ryan allowed his right hand to drop to the butt of his blaster. "Don't come any closer," he warned her.

Pyra Quadde halted, a scant six feet from him. *Very* slowly she lifted the cane in her hand, until, as cold as death, the ferrule touched Ryan's throat. He made no move to stop it, knowing that she couldn't manage enough leverage from where she stood to harm him.

"Thou dost threaten me, outlander?" she growled. "Thou hast no love for living. Knowest thou not that no man in Claggartville would dare to life a hand 'gainst me?"

"Then Claggartville doesn't contain many men, does it?"

The walking cane was lowered slowly, until it tapped on the boards. The woman moved back a step, seeing that the spreading pool of blood from Clegg's corpse was oozing stickily closer to the toes of her boots.

"I'd give a rum keg filled with jack to have thee 'board the *Salvation* when we sail the day after the morrow. To go hunt the great whales across the gray ocean."

Her eyes roamed around the silent tavern as she spoke, and Ryan felt a faint prickling of something that was almost fear between the blades of his shoulders. The way this stocky woman seemed to hold the entire ville in thrall was frightening. He'd seen enough barons running frontier pest-villes who had less presence than Captain Pyra Quadde.

"What dost thou want done with...?" the landlord stammered, pointing at the corpse and not knowing quite what to call it.

"Garbage! Heave it off the dock and let the eels take it."

"Aye, Captain."

The woman fixed Ryan again with her stare. "Thou hast had a day, outlander. Times pass. List, and thou canst hear it sliding by. Three days without work and thou must leave or work'll be found. Think on that, Ryan Cawdor."

"Get out into the fog and blackness where you belong, or stay and get yourself chilled like that piece of dead meat there."

"Big words, outlander." She spun around and stepped to the door, the stick tapping smartly. She paused for a moment, hand on the latch, and Ryan half drew the pistol, expecting her to turn holding a hideaway blaster.

But she opened the heavy door, her dark shape silhouetted a moment against the white fog beyond. Then she was gone, with only the rapping of her stick fading away down the alley.

"Up to the room," Ryan ordered, collecting the others with his eye. It wasn't the time to linger in the cramped bar, among so many threatening strangers.

DONFIL WAS LAST into their room, shutting the door gently and leaning his shoulder against it. "Lot of sour badness in that woman," he said.

Krysty nodded. "Right. I could hardly breathe with her in the same room, Ryan. Why did you have to push the fight with...?"

"Because I had to. I did it, he's chilled and we move on."

"If I may venture a small suggestion," Doc said. "I think we would do well to consider the possibility of moving on from...from...from whatever this dreary place is called. Ah, Claggartville. It came back to me."

"I hate this place!" Lori said vehemently. "It's fulled of badness. We shall...should get out and back to the gateway and go someplace else."

Ryan looked at Jak and J.B., the only two in the group who hadn't spoken. "How about it?"

"Don't see any point staying," Jak mumbled, head down. "No work. No jack. I say go."

The Armorer still stayed silent. He walked across to the low window and peered out, wiping at the condensation with his sleeve.

"J.B.?"

"Trader used to say something about the man who doesn't get into a firefight but runs away, lives to run away on another day."

Ryan had heard it before, but the old joke still amused him. "Sure, but what do we do? I agree with Jak, in a way. Can't see much to keep us in this ville. Woman like that Pyra Quadde looks like she could pull a lot of strings in Claggartville. If someone mebbe plans to coldcock me, I'd rather not stick around for them."

"So we go?" Krysty said, the relief heavy in her voice.

"When should we plan our departure?" Doc asked, sitting on one of the beds, cracking the knuckles of his right hand with a sound like distant musket fire.

"Tonight?" Donfil suggested, also sitting down to avoid being stooped almost double under the low ceiling.

"Old bitch watch for us," Jak said, joining the Armorer at the window, looking across the fog-shrouded roofs toward the masts of the ships. Now that they knew the layout of the quay, it was possible to work out which was the *Salvation*. Farthest to the right, as they saw it.

"Mebbe," Ryan agreed.

"Lot of sec patrols on the roads. Might have to blast our way out."

J.B. was right. From what they'd seen of the ville, it was tightly run. The seven companions would have the firepower and could certainly get clear of the outskirts of the place. But that didn't guarantee that they could get back to the beach where they'd left their raft and make it across the treacherous waters of the sound. The ville was full of ships of all sizes. The sec men might simply shadow them from the sea and then pick them off like ants in a sugar bowl.

"First light? No. Dark's better." Ryan scratched the side of his nose with his index finger. "Can't wait until the three days are up. Too much pressure on us. Too many eyes. Too many mouths flapping about us. Best if we sit out the day tomorrow. Let them think we're ready to take anything on the third day. Early meal at evening."

The Apache smiled. "Truly but the Anglos are the masters of cunning and deceit that our fathers warned us against."

Krysty grinned. "Up here and out the window. Over the flat roof into the alley. Up through the fog, if it rises every night. We can circle around and the patrols won't be alerted like tonight."

"That's the plan. Anyone got anything to say? Things we should do? Mebbe things we shouldn't do? Anything?"

J.B. coughed. "Only usual things. Dark clothes and greased weapons. Lori to cover her hair and muffle the bells on her spurs. Doc to grease his knees to stop them creaking."

Everyone laughed. A joke from the Armorer was more rare than a necktie on a chicken.

"That's it, then." Ryan looked at his friends again. "Around this time tomorrow night. We go. Tomorrow we keep moving and stick together and try to keep a low profile. Let's not attract too much attention to ourselves."

Everyone agreed.

"AGAIN, OUTLANDER! Again, again!"

It seemed as if every inhabitant of Claggartville was gathered around Ryan and the others on the side of the main dock, close by a weathered clipper ship with a falcon for a figurehead.

"Smite the mark with the iron again, outlander! Thou hast nine scores from nine casts. Not a harpooneer in all New England could do better."

Donfil smiled courteously at the skinny old man who was handing him the long harpoon. "I'll try it for you."

"Not *too* much attention, Man Whose Eyes See More," Ryan whispered.

"Relax, One Eye Chills. The more they like me, the less they'll worry about us running from them." He turned away from Ryan to look among the open expanse of spray-slick cobbles, between the rows of eager faces, all of them looking at the heavy oak door that stood propped up against a pile of empty oil barrels. The white-bearded elder had paced it out, counting aloud, so that everyone there could ooh and aah.

It was a full forty paces. At the center of the door was a doubled circle of whitewash, not as large as the head of a child. The wood around it was chipped and scarred where it had been used as a target or test of skill for several years.

The seven friends had been walking through the ville in the bright morning sunshine, all the night's fog burned away. Whereas there had been mainly curiosity on their first walk around the streets and alleys, there was now suspicion, tainted with fear. It was obvious to Ryan that the shadow of Pyra Quadde lay heavy over Claggartville. The news had spread that he had fallen out with the *Salvation*'s skipper.

But they had been welcomed at the quay. Several men, some of them with bronzed complexions and long sleek hair, had been competing with the long whaling spears. Innkeeper Rodriguez had mistaken the tall Mescalero for a top harpooneer and the word had scurried along the lanes. Now the crowd wanted to see Donfil in action, pitted against the local champions.

"You don't have to do it," J.B. had whispered to the shaman. "If they suss you aren't good with the spear, then they'll be even more watchful of us. Understand?"

The Indian had nodded. He understood.

He'd taken the peculiar spear with its single steel flue, and hefted it, feeling for the balance. The shaft was of stout elm, about four feet in length. The metal was roughly two feet long, of iron, the cutting point of harder steel set in it.

"There is thy mark, heathen," said the old man, who seemed to be in charge of the friendly competition.

"May thy gods strike firm," said one of the young local harpooneers. "A deep strike and a rich harvest to thee."

"And to thee, brother," the Apache replied, balancing himself carefully, fixing his eye on the small white blob upon the door.

Ryan was uncomfortable, surrounded by so many strangers, many of them hostile. But Donfil's eager participation had made it even more hazardous for them to try to pass on by.

Ryan was a reasonable hand at throwing a knife, as was J.B. Jak was the best with his concealed blades that Ryan had ever known, but none of them had ever thrown spears.

There was a blur of movement, the only sound the exhalation of breath from the Apache as he released the iron. Then the gasp from the onlookers as the harpoon struck trembling in the center of the paint mark on the oaken door.

"Four-ace lucky!" shouted one of the middle-aged men watching. "Do it again, outlander!

Donfil More did it again, five times from five casts.

Nine times out of nine throws.

The cheer nearly raised the steep-sloping roofs of the houses of Claggartville, the noise sending a flock of feeding gulls screeching from the calm waters of the harbor.

The watchers broke ranks and pressed in on the strangers, but Ryan and the rest were almost forgotten. It was only as friends of the Mescalero that they were slapped on the back, their hands pumped, grins shining in their direction.

"I'll give thee a twentieth part of a voyage if thou wilt ship with me as harpooneer!"

"An eighteenth!" a second captain yelled, jumping up and down in his anxiety to secure the services of this amazing giant who could thread the iron through the eye of a needle.

"No. No, thank you all. But I am here with my friends."

"Thou needest work. All of ye," warned a chubby man with a stovepipe hat, tarnished green with age. "I'll find labor for all seven of ye. E'en the snow-head mutie and the wenches, if thou signest on for a year's hunting the right whale."

"Aye, Boaz, but what lay dost thou offer the heathen ironman?"

"Enough, I'll warrant."

The sailor who'd pressed the question bellowed with laughter. "Best lay thou hast ever offered a harpooneer was one-seventieth." He paused to make his point stronger. "And that was for thy wife's sister's oldest son, was it not, Boaz?"

The plump captain was not in the least set back by the gibing. "Aye, that be so, neighbor. And the worst hand with an iron I ever did see. When he fell from the top foreyard ten days from harbor, it was for the best."

The crowd joined in the general merriment.

But beyond them all, at the farthest end of the crowded quay, Ryan could see the quarterdeck of the *Salvation*. And the dark-clothed figure of its sinister skipper was leaning on a rail, smoking a white clay pipe. When her glance met Ryan's the woman straightened and spit in the water, turned away and vanished down the nearest companionway.

It cast a chill over the cheeriness of the moment for Ryan, though he said nothing to any of his friends.

Back at the Rising Flukes, while they waited for Rodriguez to call them down to their supper, everyone congratulated Donfil on his uncanny skill with the unwieldy harpoon.

"I swear it was the most stunning example of skill I ever did see!" Doc exclaimed, trying to flatten his straggling gray locks over the planes of his skull with the palm of his hand.

"Bastard double-chiller," Jak said, sitting cross-legged on a bed, honing one of his knives on the sole of his boot.

"How'd you get that good, Donfil?" Krysty asked, leaning against the wall by the window, one arm across Ryan's shoulders.

"Hunting. The war spear is not as long as the whaling iron, but it requires much the same skill. I have always had a good eye."

"Ten out of ten," J.B. said quietly. "Most men couldn't do that with a handblaster."

"Wins the gentleman a ten-cent stogie or a Kewpie doll of his choice," Doc barked, banging on the floor of their room with his swordstick.

"What's a Kewpie doll, Doc?" Lori asked.

"I fear I . . . I don't recall, my dear child."

They were interrupted by the landlord of the Rising Flukes calling them down to eat.

Unless something went dreadfully wrong with their plans, it would be their last meal in Claggartville.

Chapter Sixteen

THE CLAM CHOWDER WAS SUPERB, rich and thick, steaming in the handmade pottery bowls. Rodriguez brought in a great pot of it, glowing from the fire, ladling it out in giant portions. A serving girl brought over a loaf of new-baked bread and a crock of salted butter.

The tavern was oddly empty, with the exception of a dozen hard-faced men who'd commandeered the two tables on either side of the main door into the Rising Flukes. They spoke little, concentrating on their tankards of ale. Ryan hadn't noticed them before and tugged Rodriguez by the sleeve.

"Outlanders?" he asked.

"Who, master?"

"Near the door."

The landlord glanced around, rather too casually, thought Ryan. "Oh, the lads. Just a few honest whaling men."

"From which vessel?"

"Which vessel?" Rodriguez repeated, trying to paste a smile more firmly in place on his pale face. And failing.

"Would it help your hearing if I cut off your damned ears?" J.B. asked in a penetrating whisper.

"No, no, masters. I'm not certain sure which sailer they hale from."

"But?" Krysty prompted, wiping a dribble of chowder from her chin with a linen napkin.

"I think it may be the..." His voice dropped so much that all they could hear was an indeterminate mumbling.

"I believe that our jovial host mentioned a name not unlike that of the *Salvation*," Doc said, tipping up his bowl to drain the last of the chowder.

"Is it that?" Donfil hissed. "They are all from the *Salvation*?"

Rodriguez nodded. "They be."

Ryan glanced around again, finding that every single man jack of them was looking at him. He raised his mug of beer to them with a half bow. "They look no worse or better than any other men around the ville."

Rodriguez couldn't wait to explain things to them, his tongue tripping over the words.

"Don't think that 'cause of Pyra Quadde bein' the sort of a...she's got the best record any skipper from Nantucket and beyond ever got. She can catch the scent of a whale across a hundred leagues of sweating ocean, and that's... Some men sails with her year in an' out. Taking all the goods like the jack she brings to...and the bad an' all an' there's plenty of that and some don't come back."

"There's a spar breaker of a hurricane from thy flapping gob, Rodriguez," said one of the men near the door.

"Aye, masters, aye. Don't rock the boat is what Jedediah Hernando Rodriguez always says and always does."

"You say some don't come back?" Doc asked. "Why would that be, my jovial host? Some accident of the seas?"

"Rodriguez," warned the man by the door.

"I cannot say, lords, masters..." the man muttered. Despite his pretty clothes, he suddenly looked old, tired and drab, like a guttered whore. "There's many returns and a few as doesn't. But that's the way with many a vessel out of Claggartville when the large seas rise and the creatures rage from the sweltering deeps."

He saw that the bowls of chowder were finished, and he made haste to clear the table himself, not bothering to call on any of his serving girls. He bustled out, reappearing almost immediately with the main course of the supper.

He was still nervous and avoided eye contact with Ryan or any of the others as he laid out clean plates, hand-decorated with blue patterns of shark fins and whales' tails. "Finest in the house. From before the long winters came. Only for special guests. Food's coming. More ale?"

Taking their lead from Ryan's shake of the head, everyone refused more of the cool beer.

The chicken had been cooked in a way that Ryan had never seen before, in tender portions covered in bread crumbs, with baked potatoes and turnips. But when Ryan poked his knife into the side of the chicken piece, hot butter, laced with herbs, came spurting scaldingly out.

"Fireblast!"

Rodriguez couldn't conceal his amusement as Ryan wiped molten grease off his hands and jerkin.

"You think that's rad-fire funny?" Ryan asked, readying himself to stand and reach for the landlord's throat.

"It's just that the dish is so well named, as thou has found out. It is a very old recipe, masters, very old."

"What's it called?" Lori asked, cutting more carefully into her own portion.

"Chicken surprise, mistress." Rodriguez giggled delightedly.

Once they managed to slice the pale meat apart, the meal was delicious, the butter delicately flavored. A second helping was offered and accepted by everyone at the table, though Ryan began to worry whether any of them would be capable of running away from sec patrols after such a heavy supper if the need arose.

"I think we'll all go up to our room now, Rodriguez," he finally said. "Good food."

"Pay your reckoning on the morrow, won't ye? Won't ye all?"

"Yeah. Give us the check in the morning and we'll make sure it's settled," Ryan replied, pushing back his chair, carefully watching the group from the *Salvation*, who sat quietly at their table near the door.

Jak led the way toward the stairs. Jedediah Rodriguez, mouth working nervously, suddenly called out to Ryan. "Master?"

"What?"

"A word in thy ear." He glanced over his shoulder toward the sailors.

"What is it?"

Only the seven-foot-tall Mescalero remained in the barroom. J.B. paused with one foot on the stairs, looking back at Ryan, who waved him on.

"It's only for thee," the landlord repeated to Ryan.

"I'll go up with the others," Donfil said, ducking beneath the low beams of the room.

"No, stay. Can't be that secret that it has to be kept from the ears of a good friend," Ryan insisted. "What is it?"

Rodriguez seemed thrown by someone else remaining behind. Ryan saw him look again at the table of whalers, and thought he caught a slight nod from one of them. But the light from the guttering oil lamps wasn't that strong, and he couldn't be sure.

"Over here." He beckoned Ryan and Donfil to a small round table, close to the piano. They both sat down, looking expectantly at Rodriguez.

"Yeah?" Ryan prompted.

"It's that I've heard of threats made 'gainst thee and thy fellow outlanders." His voice was low and confidential.

"Threats?"

"Aye. Now rocking the boat is not the way of Jedediah Hernando Rodriguez. But I cannot stand by and watch thee..."

Ryan sighed. "Will you get the trigger of the blaster and not step all around the muzzle? Who made threats?"

"Captain Quadde." The tone of his voice made it appear like a great surprise.

"I'm tired, and it's late. If that's all that...?"

"I can—" Rodriguez had a great coughing fit, doubled over the table, face buried in his hands. Ryan heard muffled laughter from near the door. He eased his chair around so that he could more comfortably keep an eye on the group, his hand falling by reflex to the butt of his pistol.

But most of his concentration was occupied in planning their escape from the ville. Out the window and over the roof, cutting through the damp alleyways into the open ground to the north. Move fast and in file, parallel to the road east. Watch for the patrols of sec men, and if possible avoid them. If not...chill them. It was vital that they get away to the island where the gateway was hidden before any pursuers got close to them.

Ryan was drawn from his thoughts by something the landlord was saying.

"What? I was thinking about something else. What did you say?"

"I said I felt a chill and was going to take a schooner of fine old port. The very best, Master Cawdor. Only a dozen bottles left now from the dead days beyond recall. Thou and thy harpooneer friend will join me, I trust?''

Ryan was still locked into the details of their escape, hardly even listening to the nervous chatter of Rodriguez. But Donfil *was* listening.

"Not port wine, thanks. Too sweet. Too sickly. Drink for soft women. Have you nothing sharper to offer us?"

"Sharper? I have... Oh, I believe I take thy meaning. Sharper for a hand with a sharp iron. Is that not the manner of it? I have some drink made in the hills close by.''

"In the hills?" Ryan asked, the thread of the conversation crossing with his own thoughts. "What of the hills?''

"A drink, Master Cawdor. Like to what is called 'whiskey' by some. Here it is made in stills in the old family ways. We call it 'usquebaugh.' It has the kick of a heart-struck whale.''

Ryan was anxious to get upstairs and join the others. But the insistence of Rodriguez that they share a drink with him meant that a refusal could be more troublesome than acceptance. Knock back the usquebaugh quickly and then up and away.

"Very well.''

"Something's not right," Donfil whispered, leaning across the table, covering his mouth with his hands. He watched Rodriguez mince away behind the bar, wringing his long, delicate fingers. The purple shirt seeming to glow in the half-light of the lamps.

The group of men from the *Salvation* was completely silent, sitting with the air of men waiting for some great event to take place before their eyes.

"What?"

"Landlord's sweating like a hog. Man's scared out of his flesh."

"Why?"

The Indian shook his head. "Can't tell. Wish Krysty was here. She'd 'see' it. I can't do that like she can."

Ryan looked at Rodriguez as the landlord came back in, carrying a metal tray with three small glasses. Two were plain, and one had a faded red flower painted on it. All three glasses were three-quarters filled with amber liquid. As he placed the tray on the table, the glasses chinked and rattled.

"The usquebaugh, my masters. The water of life is what it's called. Gives a man great strength."

Donfil took one of the two glasses, and Ryan reached for the one with the flower. But Rodriguez stayed his hand. "That's my own, if thou mindest not. My lucky glass, as it were. Drink the crystal-clear spirits and part as friends."

Ryan thought that the moonshine liquor was a way off being clear as crystal. Milky as a chem cloud, more like.

"A stern wind, a short chase, a clean strike and the try-pots brimming," toasted the tavern keeper, downing his shot in a single gulp.

"A clean shaft and a swift passing for my brother the deer," Donfil responded, sinking the glass in a long swallow.

"A better tomorrow," Ryan said quietly, draining the glass of spirit.

It was fiery and bitter, scorching as it scalded its way down his throat. There was also a slightly dull, unpleasant aftertaste, like the cold ashes of a dead fire.

"Another?" Rodriguez asked.

"No," Ryan replied, feeling the liquor eventually find its way into the pit of his stomach, where it lay in a sullen, curdled pool.

"Can't say I care for this water of life." Donfil pulled a face at the flavor. "Hot enough, I'll give you that. But a taste like a vulture's claws. No more for me. I'm for bed. You, Ryan?"

"Yeah."

Ryan started to rise, but he suddenly felt sick. He blinked, putting a hand to his forehead. The light from the flickering oil lamps was dimmer than earlier in the evening, and his first thought was that the clam chowder might have gone off. Then, out of the corner of his eye, he saw that the whaling hands at the far table were all standing up, drawing cudgels and belaying pins from their belts, grinning to one another.

"Ryan," Donfil warned, his voice vibrating from a long way off.

"Gently, Master Cawdor. Gently..." said Jedediah Rodriguez.

Then Ryan knew. Knew with the bitterness of cold iron. And he carried that raging knowledge with him into the careening deeps of a great blackness.

Chapter Seventeen

While I was yet all a-rush to encounter the whale, I could see naught in that brute but the deadliest ill.

Moby Dick, by Herman Melville

DARKNESS, PIERCED by the needle point of a slim silver dagger; noises, soft and muffled, like the distant beating of a slack-skinned drum; movement, pitching and regular, like being in some giant's cradle; the smell, cramping and sickly, overlaid with the unmistakable stench of death and the sea.

Consciousness was slowly coming back to Ryan Cawdor.

The dreams seemed to have lasted for all of a dismal, bleak eternity. Swaying, pitching dreams that carried Ryan across gray mountain passes where his breath smoked like fire, through featureless swamps of turgid brown water, broken only by the gnarled roots of dead trees. Occasionally a bubble of foul gas would plop to the surface, leaving a tiny circle of frozen ripples in the scum.

Ryan had fallen by the wayside, and he had watched a parade of the hopeless and damned file past him with scarcely a glance in his direction. There had been a tall man in black, white collared, riding a great raw-boned stallion whose head was a fiery-eyed skull.

A pair of women, both of them slender and bare-foot, swayed along the center of the dreary highway through a steady fall of drizzle. Their faces were covered in masks of black muslin, and they were singing in a foreign tongue. But Ryan could recognize the word "death" repeated again and again.

A child, with golden hair and the sweetest smile, was herding along a flock of bedraggled sheep, aided by two slavering hounds. If any of the bleating creatures attempted to delay, or go to the side of the track and nibble the rank grasses, the dogs would pounce on them, rip open their bellies and claw out greasy loops of intestines, letting them dangle in the dust.

And all the time, the little boy smiled innocently and whistled a merry tune.

"Ryan. You..."

Two ragged men, sitting on a slope, were both staring at Ryan as he swayed with exhaustion. They were in the shade of a stump of a tree bearing only a handful of curling leaves. One of the men had his boots unlaced, and the other was nibbling on the end of a scrawny carrot. Eventually they looked away from him and carried on with their own waiting.

"Come on, Ryan. Wake up... Come on.... Open your eye, brother."

In his shuddering nightmare, he was running along a darkened corridor in an old castle. Rotting tapes-tries hid gaping holes in the walls, which were covered in a shimmering veil of iridescent beetles. Behind him Ryan could hear the murmur of voices and the pounding of boots on stone flags. The tapestries blew across the passage in front of him, and he had to run through them, wincing as they slapped at his face.

"Ryan! By Ysun, giver of all life, wake up! If I slap you any harder my hand'll fall off the end of my arm."

Slowly and painfully, Ryan eased open his right eye.

The pain was so severe that he closed it again. Fighting against the desire to throw up, he drew in several deep, slow breaths, his head swimming. After a few moments he tried again, squinting around him.

He could see the mantis figure of Donfil crouched at his side. They were in a small room, no larger than a broom closet, with chinks of light peeking through slits around a door in the ceiling.

Ryan's brain was still utterly befuddled. "Why's the door in the ceiling?" he croaked, aware that his throat was painfully dry and his voice was feeble.

"Come on, Ryan," the Apache urged, chafing his friend's wrists, trying to bring him to full consciousness a little more quickly.

"No. Why's the door...and why are we moving, and what's that smell like tar and fish? The creaking noise is... Oh, fireblast! Now I know. I can remember it all, Donfil. That fucking bastard Rodriguez!"

He sat up, moaning as the side of his head came smartly into contact with a protruding oaken beam. Donfil leaned back, folding his legs under him. "Yeah. We're at sea. The rad scum sold us out."

"Who...? You don't think...?"

Ryan got the answer to his incomplete question. Overhead they both heard the hollow sound of something rapping wood at regular intervals. Something that could only be the iron ferrule on the end of a walking stick.

"Captain Pyra Quadde," Donfil said, his face a pale oblong blur in the dim light.

The Indian had only come around himself a handful of minutes before Ryan, so neither of them had any idea how long they'd been prisoners aboard the *Salvation*. Both of them felt appallingly sick, a condition not helped by the cramped, stuffy locker where they were being held and the tossing of the vessel. Ryan knew little about the ocean, but it seemed as though the ship were breasting long rollers, rather than the choppy, short waves encountered near the coast.

"What about the others?" Ryan asked.

"They didn't drink."

"If you'd gone up with them, then you'd have been safe. It was me that the old gaudy bitch wanted. Not you."

"Unless she wanted me for my skill with the whaling spear."

"Likely the others have been thrown out of the ville by now. Or set to forced slave work. Doubt they'll have been harmed."

"No. You reckon she'll chill us?"

Ryan nodded, finding that the nauseating swimming across his temples was easing. "Sure. Do stickies love fires? She'll mebbe work me first. No place to run on a ship, is there?"

"No. Not much hope in fighting. Must be twenty or more men riding here."

"Just keep quiet and do like we're told. That's about the best plan I can think of right now."

Locked away, Ryan was forced to take stock of his situation, and to try to find what hopes there might be for himself and his companion.

There wasn't much on the plus side. They'd both been stripped of their own clothes and roughly dressed in thick cotton breeches and dark blue woolen sweaters. Because of Donfil's inordinate height, his pants barely reached his knees and the sleeves of his sweater finished just below his elbows. Both men were barefoot and both had been relieved of their weapons.

There were coils of rope in the locker, stowed neatly away, and several small anchors, but nothing that could conceivably be used to fight with. Ryan felt his way around the darkness, on the off chance that someone might have dropped a knife. But there was nothing of any use. And every rope he touched felt slimy and slippery, from the whale oil that Doc had been talking about, he guessed.

"There's no point, Ryan. It's the way of my people to make the best of what is. And not to weep over what is not. We're trapped. If they want to chill us, then they'll chill us. We can maybe take a couple with us to the shadowland beyond. But they might not chill us. So, we'll live."

Ryan couldn't think of a smart answer, so he crawled to his corner and sat huddled on a coil of thick rope.

Every now and again a wave of the drug would come surging up in his throat, like an extrahigh wave on a sloping beach, and it would suck him back into the dimness of half sleep. As Donfil had said, there was little point in trying to speculate on what might happen to them in the next few hours.

When it happened, then it would happen. The only thing that worried him at all was what might have happened at the Rising Flukes, once he and the Apache had failed to join the others.

IT WAS KRYSTY who'd found out that life had dealt a hand filled with spades and clubs.

While waiting in the bedroom, watching condensation trickling down the cold panes of glass, she'd begun to worry about Ryan and the Indian taking so long in their private word with the landlord. Like many people in the Deathlands, Krysty carried mutie blood in her. One of the effects of this was that she could sense certain things—see the future in a limited way, sometimes be aware of the presence of good.

And evil.

She'd rolled over on her side and sat, still fully clothed, waiting for them to begin their planned escape. She could see J.B., sitting cross-legged on his own bed, staring at her.

"I'm thinking..." the girl began, but the Armorer interrupted her.

"Yeah. Me an' all. I reckon I heard men moving in the alley. You see anything?"

Krysty closed her eyes. "I felt real bad down in that drinker there. Men by the door were waiting for…and Rodriguez was nearly shitting his pretty, tight trousers. Only… Oh, Gaia! I can *see* it now! Come on!"

By the time she'd reached the top of the stairs, weapon in her hand, it was all over.

The bar was filled with sec men, all armed, muzzles of rifles and scatterguns pinning her in place. Rodriguez was behind the bar, wiping sweat from his face. Ryan's weapons and white silk scarf were on the bar, as were Donfil's Smith & Wesson Distinguished Combat .357 Magnum and mirrored sunglasses. Both men were gone.

"Don't move, outlander. Place is covered tighter than a sea gull's shit hole." The voice came from the sec man who'd first stopped them on the road into Claggartville. It was a calm, gentle voice, with no anger or arrogance. Just a man doing his job with a quiet efficiency. "Thou and thy friends had best come down and leave us your blasters. Then ye can all go back to your own quarters until morning. Nobody will harm ye."

"Ryan?" she said hesitantly, conscious of her four friends at her shoulder, frozen by the sec men's overwhelming force.

"Gone to seek the works of the Lord, outlander," intoned Rodriguez. "And His wonders in the deep." He paused. "And may the good Lord Jesus, our Redeemer, have mercy on his soul."

Chapter Eighteen

RYAN AND DONFIL both jerked awake at the grating sound of bolts being kicked open. The hatch was lifted, and they were blinded by a flood of bright sunshine.

Callused hands reached down and tugged them out of the rope locker. First the Apache, then Ryan Cawdor, were heaved into the sunlight, onto the scrubbed white planks of the deck.

Ryan stretched, drawing in deep breaths of the bitingly fresh air, feeling it clear away the last shreds of the knockout drug. There was a boisterous wind blowing, and he could see the gray-green waves as they rolled under the bow of the ship. There were men all around, but Ryan ignored them, looking beyond their heads, over the bulwarks, scanning the horizon slowly, checking out the vessel.

Donfil was doing the same, straining on the tips of his toes, using his extra foot of height, both of them reaching the same conclusion.

There wasn't even a blur of land to be seen anywhere. The sea stretched in all directions, marred only by an occasional white horse of tossed spray. From the angle of the sun, it was toward the evening side of the afternoon, the shadows spreading out from their bare feet.

Ryan's guess was that they must have sailed before the dawn, slipping their moorings and sliding, ghost-like, through the misty harbor of Claggartville.

"Seen enough?"

The speaker was one of the men who'd been sitting near the door of the Rising Flukes the previous evening. He held a short, knotted length of rope in his right hand, and he was swinging it against his left palm, eliciting a solid thwacking sound.

"Yeah," Ryan said.

"Thou didst take the life from Jonas Clegg, didst thou not?"

"Yeah," Ryan repeated, sizing up the quality of the opposition. It looked as if most of the crew had gathered to haul them out of their prison. There were more than twenty men there, with a fair mix of sizes, ages and races. The one thing they all had in common was they were tough, weathered men.

Ryan wouldn't really have expected any different. He guessed that a whaling ship, especially with Pyra Quadde as skipper, was probably about as hard as a war wag.

"Jonas had sailed many leagues with us."

"Way I heard it, he's still sailing. Around the harbor. Less he's sunk into the mud by now."

"Think that's funny?"

"No." Ryan shook his head. "I don't think a chilling's ever funny."

Donfil was staring up at the mast, watching its slow, pitching roll. His face was completely blank, almost as if he'd put himself into a kind of trance. Ryan had seen Krysty do something similar.

A short man with a white scar that tugged at the corner of his mouth poked Ryan in the back with the end of a belaying pin. "Know what thou'rt here for, outlander?"

"To give Pyra Quadde a chance of revenge."

It wasn't the reply that the sailor had expected, and his voice showed it. "Oh, yeah. That's right. But it's Captain Quadde, or ma'am, or you'll get chilled quicker than yesterday."

"Very dim, it be. Very dim," another man said in a tiny chattering voice. He was well over six feet in height, but his head seemed only the size of a large apple, so out of proportion was it. "The body'll rot, but the soul rolls along. Like the fifth wheel upon a wagon, shipmates."

"Ignore him," said the man with the rope's end in his fist. "Jehu has but one oar in the water, if thou takest my meaning."

There was a sudden silence, broken only by the tapping of a cane on the deck. Ryan could hear the far-off crying of gulls that trailed in the wake of the whaling ship. The whole vessel creaked as timber chafed against timber, spars moving, cords and cables tugging. The wind was whistling gently through the rigging of the *Salvation*.

Ryan wondered whether these might be the last sounds he would ever hear.

"Get 'bout thy guttin' business." The harsh croaking voice was memorably that of Pyra Quadde, invisible behind the row of men.

"What if they try on—"

"Thou hast fewer brains than Jehu! Why I made thee second mate after Clegg turned in his seaboots I swear I'll never know. Get the men moving, Mr. Walsh."

"Aye, ma'am," he said, turning and jostling the crew to move them off the deck, and out of the captain's way. Ryan noticed that none of the men showed any desire to hang around. In moments the planks were bare of other life. Only Donfil remained, still smiling at the limitless ocean, and Ryan.

And Pyra Quadde.

"Well, well, well. See how the wheel spins and the ship turns to the helm. Not so proud now, Ryan Cawdor?" She waited, but he said nothing. She laughed, showing her hideous, carved-bone teeth. "Well, aren't ye a fine pair? A ragged couple, and no mistake. I never asked for the harpooneer, thou knowest."

"Just me, huh?"

"Triple strike, cully. Just thee. And now I've got thee."

"An evil woman is a swollen boil in the armpit of the Almighty," Donfil said, finally unfixing his eyes from the horizon and staring intently at the captain of the whaler.

"What's that thou… Best keep thine oilskin closed, or there might be a squall to take thee away. If thou dost not take my meaning, I suggest thou talkest less.

Thou canst return to port a rich man, Donfil More. Think on that."

"What lay would you give me? A tenth?"

She laughed, turning away a moment, trying to ease the hatred from her eyes before she faced the Apache again. "A tenth, thou sayest? Not even the finest ironsman sailing from old Nantucket ever got such a lay."

"No ironsman from old Nantucket ever struck the mark ten casts from ten, Captain."

"Thou speakest truth there, my lofty harpooneer. Ten from ten I heard said. If thou works and earns thy biscuits and ale, then I'll give thee—" she pondered a moment, head on one side, looking like a gut-shot walrus "—one-fifteenth lay, Donfil More."

"It's not—"

Pyra Quadde rapped her cane on the deck angrily. "Don't push thy luck, Indian! I'm not just giving thee thy flensing fifteenth lay!"

Donfil turned to Ryan, puzzled. "What does she mean by..." he began.

Ryan grinned. "She means that you also get to live, brother. That's what she means."

The woman nodded slowly. "Ryan Cawdor is not the fool he seems, Indian. He marks well what I say. Thou shouldst do the same."

"What lay do I get, Captain?" Ryan asked, tugging mockingly at his forelock of curling black hair.

Once more the stick lifted and the ferrule touched him on the throat, pressing him two steps backward, until he felt the raised rail against his spine. Out of the corner of his eye he could see the surging waves hissing by just below him. The cold metal pushed harder, and he knew that his life could be snuffed out like a candle if Pyra Quadde chose that moment. The gamble was that she wouldn't.

Not yet.

She laughed in his face, and he could taste the sourness of her breath. The point of the cane moved from his throat, traced a line down his sternum, over the flat wall of muscle across his stomach. It brushed lightly across his groin, making him shrink back, which drew a delighted chuckle from the woman.

"All men fear for their cocks. Perhaps that might be my revenge, Ryan Cawdor—have thee gelded with a flensing knife. Cock and balls over the side for the gulls. Hot tar to check thy bleeding, then keep thee around for a servant."

"You know I'd kill you."

She nodded. "I know that, outlander. Course I know that. Is't not true that any man on board the *Salvation* would open me from gob to gut? Yet, I live. Why?"

"Fear," Donfil said from behind her.

"And greed," Ryan added.

"I'm the best, yes, the best. Every year I bring wealth to the town. And those fawning bastards fall over at my shadow and kiss my ass. But they'd all see me dead. I can find the whales. Scent 'em across the miles. Hunt and kill them. Every year. Ye'll see it. The Indian could even live and become rich. But to throw an iron at an old door on a cobbled quay..." She laughed again, banging her stick on the deck. The man at the wheel looked over his shoulder as though he feared something coming up behind them.

"Ten from ten," Donfil reminded.

"These frail boats that line the ship—" she pointed to the five-oared whaleboats on either side of the vessel "—they go in the wildest white water and chase the leviathan. Ye hear me, heathen? Thou must look the whale in his age-old eye and grin in his jaws. Drive the iron trough to the deeps of his soul and follow as he trails across the ocean. The whale can be a hundred feet in length and crush a boat with a waltzing touch of his tail. Blood laid over the seas, outlanders. Ten from ten against a door... This will be no sport."

"Why not have me chilled? Easier than this?" Ryan stared down the stocky, muscular woman.

"Cheaper, as well. Have thee gutted and dumped in the cut for a finger of jack. Not that I paid that puking brownholer Rodriguez much. Just said I wouldn't break all his fingers and slice off the lids of his eyes if he had thee black-sleeped. Heathen harpooneer comes as a surprise."

"Still doesn't answer the question. Why not have me chilled?"

She hawked up a mouthful of phlegm and spit it over the leeward side of the ship. "Why art thou here, outlander? Because thou didst strike at me by chilling that mindless fool, Clegg. He was of use. I found times to use him." To Ryan's disgust, the woman hiked her skirts up with her right hand, showing pallid, muscled thighs—showing as well that she wore no underwear. She rubbed her fingers into the tangled mat of curling hair, licking her lips greedily as she watched Ryan's face. "Aye, thou seest what I mean. I used him well, and he never failed to rise to me. No man fails me, outlander. Or he's hauled from bow to stern and the barnacles rip him to salted pork."

"You stinking, murderous slut." Ryan took a half step toward her. Instantly the tunnel mouth of her .44 Astra was drilling into the air between them.

"I stink because I don't bother washing. I murder because it gives me power and pleasure. And I'm a slut because I . . . That thou canst find out when I need to use thee, Ryan Cawdor."

"Never," he gritted.

"We sail for many a month. *Never* is a flensing long time, cully. Don't say 'never.'"

"I'd not—"

"No," Donfil warned.

"Pagan's right, outlander. Open thy mouth to me without being told, and thou couldst lose thy tongue." She stepped in close and reached out with her free hand to pinch his cheek hard. "I have the power—the total power—on this ship, Ryan Cawdor."

It was a close call whether he broke her neck with a single chopping blow of the side of his hand—and died within moments of her—or stood still, hands clenched, and took the pain and the humiliation from her.

Pyra Quadde hadn't lived as long as she had by making wrong judgments. She smiled at him, pinching, her breath coming faster. "Oh, this is good, outlander. Thou art not a weak piece of deck rag like so many of the others have been. Thou wouldst so like to kill me and thou canst not. Life is worth keeping, isn't it, Ryan Cawdor? Isn't it?''

"Yeah, it is.''

"Yeah, *ma'am*, it is.''

He could feel a warm trickle of blood on his cheek where her ragged nails had punctured his skin. "Yeah, ma'am, it is.'' Nothing in his voice betrayed his desire to tear the woman's face clean off her raw skull.

"Good.'' She closed her eyes a moment and swallowed hard, trying to calm her own obscene pleasure at his pain.

"You want us to work?'' Donfil asked. He was talking to Pyra Quadde, but his eyes were watching Ryan, trying to read if his friend was about to discard both their lives by attacking the woman.

"Yes, heathen. Thou canst go below and get seaboots. Watch thy pagan head on the low beams. Ye can both go in the whaleboat of the first mate. Name's Cyrus Ogg.''

"Ogg?'' Ryan said, trying to ignore the throbbing pain in his cheek, feeling the blood already beginning to crust and dry.

"Want thy backbone to twinkle at the noon sun, outlander? If not, no jests about Cyrus and his name. Kinda touchy, he is.''

"Am I harpooneer?'' Donfil asked.

"Thou gettest a fifteenth lay on the *Salvation*—oil, meat, bone and ambergris—and thou dost question whether thou art harpooneer? Fins over! I thought

thee not a fool. Thou shalt be lead with the irons and
Ryan Cawdor shall be a plain oarsman.''

She pointed toward the bow, where a hatch framed
a square of darkness and the top of a flight of stairs,
going belowdecks. Donfil led the way. It wasn't until
Ryan was out of sight of Pyra Quadde that he touched
the livid pain of his torn cheek. He wasn't about to
give her more pleasure by letting her know how much
she'd hurt him.

KRYSTY AND THE OTHERS were still locked in their attic bedroom, sweltering below the tiles of the roof of
the inn. There were sec men all around, inside and out,
and they'd seen no glimmer of a chance of escape.

J.B. was constantly on the move, restless at his in-
ability to do anything, staring out toward the quay and
the harbor beyond. ''Must have sailed with him by
first light. Offshore wind and they're probably close
on a hundred miles to sea by now.''

''Think he's still alive?'' Jak asked, lying on his bed
with his arm thrown across his eyes.

''Ryan? Probably. Bitch'll use Donfil. Ten from ten
with the spear. She'll know about that. Ryan? She
wanted him dead, then that's what he'd be by now.''

''We got a chance?'' Lori asked.

''While we live, we have hope, my dearest child,''
Doc told her.

Krysty couldn't speak. She felt too close to choking
on hopeless tears.

Chapter Nineteen

THE *SALVATION* WAS a typical whaling ship. If a skipper from Victorian times had been time-trawled along with Doc Tanner and dumped aboard her, he'd have felt completely at home.

She was one hundred and twenty feet long and just under thirty feet wide. The crew comprised thirty-two officers and men. Pyra Quadde had her cabin in the stern, beneath the afterhouse that held the ship's wheel. The two mates had their own tiny cabins under the midship shelter. Everyone else messed together in the forecastle, in the rounded bow of the vessel.

The *Salvation* shipped three masts. From the bow they were the fore, main and mizzen. She carried four whaleboats, each thirty feet long, slung on davits, two to a side. A few paces forward of the mainmast was the tryworks, the ovens that would render the flesh of the whales, providing the clear, valuable oil that would be stored in the hundreds of barrels that rested in the depths of the hold.

The only large space in the whole of the whaler was the blubber room. It ran more than two-thirds the length of the ship and was where the busiest and bloodiest work of the long cruise would take place. The carcasses of the slaughtered creatures would be hauled alongside and tied there. Men would scramble down onto them, using long-handled knives to strip away great chunks of blubber. This was heaved aboard and cut up in the open space to be boiled down in the brick-and-iron oven.

One of the sailors pointed out to Ryan during that first afternoon that the *Salvation* was bark-rigged. This meant that the stern mast, the mizzen, carried a fore-and-aft sail rather than being fully rigged like a normal sailing schooner, enabling the actual running of the vessel to be worked by fewer men. That left as many sailors as possible to man the fragile whale-boats once the prey was sighted.

To the surprise of both Ryan and Donfil, the crew seemed to accept them on board without any obvious hostility. It became clear that Clegg hadn't been the most popular of mates, too ready with his fists. Most of the men were happy to show them around, telling them what their duties would be in such and such a situation. But any attempts to press them about their captain met only sideways glances and a tightening of the lips.

After their confrontation with Pyra Quadde, Ryan and Donfil were kitted out with seaboots and mar-shaled along to meet the first mate of the ship, Cyrus Ogg.

Ryan had once witnessed the impaling of a child-killer in a frontier pesthole, near the old Idaho pan-handle. He had been the mildest, gentlest-looking man you could see in many a country mile: rimless glasses behind which merry eyes twinkled; a halo of silver hair, brushed back off a high academic's forehead; neat little hands and feet—hands that had rammed a full beer bottle down the throat of a pretty little girl of twelve summers. Feet that had kicked her upper body so hard the bottle had smashed within her. His even white teeth had bitten at the dying child and... Ryan preferred not to recall the rest of the revolting details.

But at a first meeting there was much about Cyrus Ogg that put him in mind of the Idaho butcher. He had the same fluffy white hair and round, benevolent face, the hint of a smile at the corner of the full, cherubic lips. No more than five and a half feet tall, Ogg looked as though he might just tip the scales at 120 pounds, sopping wet. He wore black pants and jacket, like a deacon out to bless a summer barn raising.

He had greeted the two new recruits to his whaleboat's crew with a nod of the head. "I have heard of both of ye," he said quietly. "Master Ten-from-Ten, the Indian, and Master Deadman, the one-eyed outlander."

"Deadman?" Ryan asked.

"Some come to the *Salvation* living and slip into the waters to feed the fishes with not even a prayer to their names. Some come as men already dead and live to walk down the gangplank into Claggartville town with jack in their pockets and a song in their hearts. Who knows which thou shalt be, Master Deadman. But it is no secret how Captain Quadde thinks of thee." He shook his head. "With a sorry lack of affection, I do fear."

"She'll chill me." Ryan was careful not to even hint at it being a question.

Ogg pondered a few moments, tugging at the lobe of his left ear. "She will, I think. Pyra Quadde is a mystery shrouded in a puzzle, Master Deadman. The finest skipper to sail these waters. Generous in the 'warding of lays to ironsmen and crew alike. Yet there is a shadow that sits 'cross her soul and cannot be denied. Step always to windward of her and jump when she speaks. And who knows what might await thee at journey's end."

It was to be some days before Ryan and Donfil had the opportunity to witness the skillful aspect of the woman's character. But they were treated to a glimpse of her dark side before that first day had run its course through to evening.

Ryan and Donfil had been sent to the workbench, just aft the tryworks, running the strong line between them that would set in the main-line and spare-line tubs in each of the dories.

They talked quietly as they worked, but not of escape or revenge. That was pointless. Unless they could rouse the crew to mutiny there was no chance at all of escape. And such things only happened in the old vids and stories.

The Apache spoke to Ryan of hunting trips as a young man, across the crimson and ocher wilderness of the Southwest, chasing a mutie cougar that had carried off a dozen young children from their rancheria. He told of how a bullet from his buffalo rifle had put the beast down as it darted for cover in a narrow arroyo.

"More than half of a mile," Donfil said, his hand describing the classic rainbow arch of the long .50-caliber bullet.

"Good shot."

"What is your best shot, brother?"

"Like asking me what's the best breath I ever drew. Can't recall. Been too many."

"Those that saved your life, or the life of a friend?"

Ryan straightened a kink in the coil of rope. "Still too many, Donfil."

They worked on in silence for several minutes, only looking up as the first mate walked slowly past, hands clasped in the small of his back.

"Man as quiet as that is either a saint or a demon," Donfil whispered.

"I see him as a dangerous son of a bastard that we gotta watch real careful, Donfil. That's what I see."

RYAN AND DONFIL WERE ORDERED aloft with the rest of the deckhands to shorten sail and reef back as the wind began to blow with a serious intent. Chem clouds, rolling banks of deep purple, lowered over the eastern horizon directly ahead of them. They could see the frail silver of lightning and hear the sonorous drumbeat of thunder, flat and menacing so far out to sea. The rigging was cold, and Ryan found his hands clumsy on the sodden cordage. He and Donfil had

begun to climb toward the mainmast when Ogg beckoned them back onto the streaming deck.

"Captain Quadde would not deal kindly with me if
I let ye drown on the first day of our voyage. Wear
those boots aloft and ye are both dead. Naked toes,
my lads. Naked toes."

It was wise advice. Ryan was able to hang on to the
loops of ninny-shrouds with his feet, battling the
flapping canvas, risking, at the least, broken nails as
he fought to give the wind less sail to bite upon. Rain
beat on his face, soaking his hair and clothes. A few
of the men wore waterproofed coats, but they caught
the gale and made the reefing even more dangerous.
One man slipped and would have fallen if Ryan hadn't
reached across and grabbed him by the wrist, steadying him until his scrabbling feet found a safe pur-
chase once more.

"Thanks!" he shouted, barely audible over the
bedlam of the rising storm.

Lighting was all around them as they plowed
through the remorseless rolling waves of the Lantic.
One burst was so close that Ryan felt his hair stand on
end, and his skin tingled with the static electricity all
about. The sun had disappeared, and it was pitch-
dark, so that Ryan could barely even make out the tiny
rectangle of the deck as it rolled far beneath him.

Blinking rain from his eye, feeling it running bitter
and salty into the other socket, Ryan could just make
out the stumpy figure of Pyra Quadde, stalking about
the deck, bellowing out orders to her crew.

The mast was swinging so far that it was like being attached to a wild pendulum that threatened to throw the men far off into the sea at the end of each savage roll.

Ryan couldn't believe the casual skill that the crew of the *Salvation* showed, moving across the rigging like ants on a peach tree, never losing a foothold, taking in the sail in armfuls of stubborn canvas. Farther along the spar he could see the skeletal figure of Donfil, arms and legs tangled in the ropes, eyes wide with fear, jaws clamped tight.

After what seemed a thousand years of screaming wind, blackness and stark white light, it was done. Ogg and Walsh called the men down off the frail spars to the solid deck, Walsh speeding the tardy with curses and his rope's end, Ogg, with his deceptively gentle words of encouragement.

While they waited, huddled together and soaking wet, the crew exchanged jokes. Ryan found himself standing between the shivering Donfil and the sailor whom he'd saved from a watery grave.

"Name's Johnny Flynn, outlander. Thou hast me hand an' me heart for that deed o' goodness."

The hand was offered and shaken surreptitiously in the darkness. Flynn was a short man, barely five foot six. His face had an alert, foxy brightness, his smile marred only by a total lack of teeth.

"Do the same for any man," Ryan responded, careful to speak out of the corner of his mouth, so as not to draw attention to himself.

"I'd have been fine and dandy but I broke this shifting barrels yesterday forenoon." He raised the middle finger of his left hand, the joint swollen and purple, the nail crusted with dried blood.

"Why not tell one of the mates?"

Johnny Flynn laughed bitterly. "Sure can tell thou'rt not from these parts. There's good and plenty jack to be made with Captain Quadde. Long as thou dost not rock the boat with her."

"But your finger..."

"It'll mend. My Sara and the wee ones can't eat stones and air, outlander. I lose this post, and there's a dozen wharf rats waiting to take me place. No. Long as skipper doesn't spot it for a few days I'll manage fine. I'd hoped we'd not be aloft so soon to test it. If she..." His voice faded as Pyra Quadde strode out from the aft companionway, standing with legs apart, braced against the roll of the ship, eyes raking the assembled crew.

"What would she have done?" Ryan whispered.

Flynn touched his finger to his lips. "Don't let her see thee blabber. First couple of days of voyage are worst. Hasn't had it in a long time. Restless and mean. Looks for a man she can..."

The wind whipped away the rest of the words. Since Flynn's lips hardly moved as he spoke, Ryan couldn't even be sure that there'd been any other words. But Pyra Quadde's words came ringing clear enough above the storm.

"Slow, ye salt-ducking dogs of yellow-hearted bastards. I'd have done better to get a dozen deaf and dumb pot girls from the taverns of Claggartville! Better babes in arms than ye sluggard crew of cockless bastards! Ye're fit only to lick out the gaudy privies, aren't ye?''

There was a high-pitched giggle from Ryan's right, where he saw the tall figure of crazed Jehu. Water streamed off his tiny cannonball of a head, running into his slack lips. "Good, Captain!" he squawked. "Better'n the traveling quack show! Give us more of't!"

"Shut the dullard up," the woman called, but there was no anger in her voice. The men on either side of Jehu nudged him in the ribs, and he closed his mouth again.

"I'll say no more," Captain Quadde continued. "Next time aloft and ye'll be kissing the whip. Or I'll find ye all better to kiss than that."

Cyrus Ogg took a hesitant step forward, raising a hand to attract her attention. She beckoned him to her and he stood close, whispering in her ear. She listened to him, face showing no emotion, though her eyes roamed along the line of men until they settled on Ryan Cawdor, where they stayed while the first mate continued talking to her.

"Someone's for it," Flynn hissed. Standing close to the sailor, Ryan could feel his body begin to tremble.

Ryan didn't dare to reply, with the woman's piggy eyes staring at him. Ogg glanced around and then spoke again, using his hands to gesture to something. Something that was down below? He smacked a clenched fist into the palm of his other hand, all the while Pyra Quadde's gaze never moving from Ryan's face.

The wind seemed to be easing, and the storm was blowing away toward the west. The chem clouds were shifting and breaking, and the spray no longer blew across the deck. A few stray beams of fiery sunlight, low on the horizon, were breaking through. The first day at sea was nearly over. As Ogg finished speaking to his captain, Ryan wondered whether it would also be his last day at sea.

The first mate resumed his position in the front row of men, and Pyra Quadde stood still a moment, tapping her cane pensively on the deck. Finally she nodded to herself as if she'd reached a decision.

"I'm told hard news," she grated. "News that is sad for one man of this crew." She took three steps forward, which brought her close to Ryan. "To one man," she repeated, cane darting out and pointing.

"Outlander Cawdor," she said, smiling.

Chapter Twenty

RYAN DIDN'T MOVE. There was nothing he could do, nowhere he could go. He felt the short hairs lift at the back of his neck at the chilling malevolence in the woman's crooked smile. The spears of crimson sun struck her face, making it seem as if the filed bone teeth were painted with fresh-spilled blood.

The tip of the stick pointed unwaveringly between his eyes.

"Outlander Cawdor," she repeated, "I have an order for thee."

"I'm listening, ma'am," he eventually managed to say, though his tongue was reluctant to free itself from the roof of his mouth.

"Good, good, cully. First mate here, Mr. Ogg, has been telling me of a step across the line. A man doing that which he should not do. And not doing that which he should do."

"And there is no health in us!" Jehu yelled. "Amen. Ah, women. Ah, there she blows. Hallelujah and praise the blessed Pyra Quadde!"

Nobody moved or spoke. Ryan could feel a trickle of sweat down the small of his back, though he was stone cold.

"Where is Kenny Hill?" the captain asked in a voice as cold as a flooded grave.

Everyone turned and looked along the lines. Ryan and Donfil didn't bother. Since they didn't know who Kenny Hill was or what he looked like, they wouldn't know if he was there or not.

"He is not here," she continued. "Mr. Ogg tells me that the sniveling coward hides in the fo'c'sle. Scared to take his place and work with us. A man might die so that Hill can live. I will not have this."

Ryan sensed a murmuring of approval among the crew, and having been aloft in a storm he realized how one man's desertion could cause the death of another among the singing spars and rigging.

"Bring him here, Outlander Cawdor," she ordered, the half smile back in place.

Ryan sensed both her power and her evil. She had deliberately tried to frighten him, and she had succeeded, knowing he would imagine that the warrant for death was his own. His hatred for her grew even stronger at that moment.

"Quickly, man, or it'll be the worse for thee."

"Aye, ma'am."

He walked quickly to the companionway leading to their living quarters, already finding it easy to balance automatically against the rolling of the vessel. The second mate, Walsh, called after him. "Take a knife, outlander. Kenny Hill's quick with a blade."

Ryan ignored him, ducking, boots clattering on the worn threads. The whole ship, though it was trim and clean, was extremely old, and exuded a sense of frailty.

Ryan guessed that parts of it certainly dated from well before the long winters.

Behind him, Ryan heard the splintering voice of Captain Quadde. "Thou hast just two minutes, outlander. Then I come down and ye're both done."

The low-ceilinged forecastle was cluttered with bedding and discarded clothes. A single oil lamp turned on gimbals in the middle of the room, and at first glance Ryan couldn't see anyone.

"Hill?"

No answer. Ryan took his feet off the bottom step and looked more carefully. If the sailor had really taken refuge down here, then there weren't many places for him to be hiding.

"Don't fuck me around, Hill. She'll use this to chill us both."

"Don't wanna die."

"Nobody does." Now that he'd heard the voice, he'd also spotted where the man was lurking—in the corner behind one of the tables. Ryan wasn't sure, but he thought he detected the gold gleam of light off the steel of a knife.

"She'll kill me. I was frightened. Been aloft too many times too many storms. Wanted to jump ship this time, but she wouldn't let me. Had me down there, chained, all the time in Claggartville. Help me. Thou art an outlander. She won't kill thee."

"No. I'm her friend, Hill. She said to tell you not to worry. Come up and she'll tell you herself."

"Liar!" Ryan heard the haunted tone of someone who knew the words were lies, but desperately wanted to think that they weren't.

"Double-truth."

"No."

Time was passing. Ryan could hear it, with the beating of the pulse in his own skull. "I'm telling you the truth. On my brother's life." Such as it had been. "Trust me, Hill. What do you have to lose? What? Nothing."

"I'll slit thy throat if thou liest to me, outlander. I swear I will."

"I got no blade." He held his arms spread out sideways, fingers wide.

Ryan's eyes were accustomed to the poor light, and he walked across the forecastle, reaching out with his right hand in a gesture that was transparently friendly. He stooped toward the crouched figure of Kenny Hill.

"Thou wilt not betray me, outlander? Not to that woman?"

"My word on it. Come on."

The sailor held a narrow-bladed dagger in his right hand, and he reached out trustingly with his other hand to grasp Ryan's fingers.

Immediately Ryan pulled him up, with a great burst of convulsive strength. Fending off the knife with his other hand, he dropped his face and butted Hill across the bridge of the nose.

There was the satisfyingly soft, rotten-apple sound of bone breaking. As Hill cried out, Ryan jerked his knee hard into the man's groin.

The knife tinkled to the floor and the sailor slumped after it, retching and barely conscious. He started to weep.

"Get up, you cowardly little bastard," Ryan snarled, heaving him to his feet, lifting him across his own shoulders. He carried him up the swaying ladder, ignoring the crack as Hill's head struck the ceiling. Blood was gushing from the broken nose, puddling on the steps. As he emerged onto the deck, Pyra Quadde was near the hatch.

"Thou hast a minute left and... Oh!" she shouted. The warning died in her throat as Ryan appeared with Hill slung over his back.

There was a smattering of talk from the crew, and Ryan thought he even heard someone start to clap. But it might have been mad Jehu.

"Dump the offal there and get in line, Outlander Cawdor," she ordered. Ryan genuinely couldn't tell whether the woman was pleased to see him alive or not.

He joined Donfil and Johnny. The Apache looked quizzically at him. "Got no choice," Ryan whispered.

Quadde had the semiconscious man stripped by a couple of the other hands, and bound to the foot of the mainmast. Ryan noticed that there was a couple of iron ringbolts set into the decking, in just the right positions to shackle a man's ankles, forcing his legs spread wide. Hill's arms were tied behind him, then a length of rope was wound clear around the mast and knotted. Another cord was pulled tight around his neck, keeping him upright, preventing him from wriggling free. Captain Quadde stood near the sailors who were tying Hill, but she didn't seem to give them any other orders. It was as though they knew how to tie the prisoner, because they'd done it often enough before. A cold thought.

The light was fading fast now, even though the skies had cleared. The *Salvation* was butting her way into the Lantic wastes, a white bone of foam under her stem.

The captain leaned over the helpless man, who was now recovering consciousness. She stood between his spread feet, swaying to the motion of the ship. The metal tip of her cane was behind her, mere inches from Hill's genitals.

''This puking pus-dog has been caught for deserting his post in poor weather!'' she shouted. ''His punishment is to be kept here, tied and bare, for all of the night and all of the next day. He is to have no food and only one pan of water at noon tomorrow. Any man speaks to him or goes near him shares his punishment. Hear that well.''

''Doesn't seem that fireblasted harsh,'' Ryan whispered to Johnny.

''What thou hearest and what happens ain't always the same, matey,'' the sailor replied. Ryan crooked an eyebrow at him, but he wouldn't explain further.

''Don't let her do it, friends!'' Hill shouted, shaking his head to clear his mouth of his own blood. ''You know what she'll do.''

"Gag him," Quadde ordered, not even looking at the man behind her.

"You know!" Hill screamed, voice ragged with stark terror. "Don't let her do—"

His words disappeared under a hank of cotton waste that was rammed into his mouth and knotted in place.

"Now, to your quarters. Watch on deck only. Eat well. Tot of rum to every hand, Mr. Ogg. Carry on, men."

She didn't move from where she stood, ignoring the mumbling prisoner at her heels. The men filed dutifully away, down the companionway into the shelter of the forecastle. The cooks trotted off to begin the meal, in their cramped galley by the steerage companionway. Ryan was last off the deck, and he hesitated a moment, glancing behind him at the woman's silhouette.

But she had turned away from him, her stout walking stick lifted to her shoulders. Even as he stared, she brought the metal tip down with a vengeful force. Ryan couldn't see where she struck Hill, but he heard only the wet sound of iron on flesh as he descended.

It didn't take any imagination to know where the vicious blow had been aimed.

The rest of the men gathered around Ryan, slapping him on the back for his bravery in going after the armed man. None of them seemed to worry about Kenny Hill's fate, and Ryan shared their lack of concern. Best coward was a chilled one, in his view. Hill might get a beating, but it wasn't as though Pyra Quadde was planning to butcher him.

THE FOOD WAS TERRIBLE. The stew was mainly gristle and splinters and bone, floating in a scummy pool of grease. Mealy carrots and a handful of overcooked beans completed the main course. It was followed by a rusting tin of sweet red jelly that didn't taste like any fruit that Ryan had ever eaten. The whole thing was accompanied with weeviled biscuits and washed down with watery beer.

"Why's the meal so terrible?" Ryan asked Johnny.

"Once we get to the hunting, then the captain allows good meat and all from the locked freezer. Reckons it makes us all the more eager to get out the dories and cast the irons. The better the catch, then the better the tucker we get."

Ryan and Donfil were spared being on deck duty for the night watch. Sailing in untroubled waters, there was normally no more than one man at the wheel and another in the crow's nest, swaying at the top of the mainmast.

Shortly after they'd finished the supper, the crew began to bed down for the night. One man played a mouth harp for a few minutes, a slow, mournful ballad that Ryan thought he vaguely recognized. One or two were patching clothes, bent over their work in the poor light.

Ryan and Donfil clambered into their adjoining bunks. Johnny Flynn was across the port side of the forecastle, just opposite, and he waved a cheery hand to Ryan, making sure it was the hand without the broken finger.

Surrounded by snoring strangers, Ryan eventually managed to get to sleep.

PRESSURE ON HIS BLADDER woke him. There was no light, but his body clock told him it was around one in the morning. The steady movement of the ship was now familiar to him. He swung his legs from his bunk, feeling the rough wood cold against his feet as he padded across to where he could make out the ghostly shape of the stairs to the hatch. Moving with no more sound than a snake's breath, Ryan picked his way up, easing the hatch silently open. He emerged into the darkness of the main deck, just forward of the foremast.

It had been explained to him and to Donfil that the bodily functions were normally performed over the side of the ship. Taking care to pick the leeward side.

Someone else moving on the deck made him check his movements, crouch behind the windlass that drew up the anchor. He glanced up, able to see the bottom of the crow's nest on the mainmast. Whatever happened on the deck immediately below the lookout would be totally invisible from there. And the movement was near the base of the mast, in the lake of shifting shadows, near the place where Kenny Hill was bound naked for his punishment.

Ryan began to catfoot nearer.

He could see the pale shape of Hill, then something moving in front of it. His first guess was that one of the crew was risking the captain's anger by bringing food or drink to the helpless man. But the punishment seemed mild for the crime, despite the odd feeling in the forecastle. A feeling that Ryan hadn't quite been able to pin down. A strange resignation that Hill no longer existed.

The wind had eased and it was a mild, gentle night. Above the movements of the sails, Ryan could hear someone singing. Not the gagged Hill. Not the man at the wheel, since he was snugly under cover.

" 'The first time ever I...' "

A woman's voice. Now he could see the stocky shape, kneeling near the man, doing something in the shadows that Ryan couldn't see.

" '...rose, in your eyes...' "

Pyra Quadde stood up, and Ryan saw the flash of white flesh as she lifted her skirt, tucking it into her belt.

Then, like a great vampire bat settling on its victim, she lowered herself, booted legs astride, onto Kenny Hill.

Rising and falling, faster. Ryan heard the distinctive sound of a hard hand slapping a face. Repeated two more times.

The song changed to a children's rhyme that he recalled from his own youth in the Shens.

"When they were *up* they were *up*, and when they were *down* they were *down*..."

The voice becoming harsher, the breath panting in the woman's throat.

Sickened to his stomach, Ryan turned away and left the woman to her perverted pleasures, realizing now that Hill's punishment was indeed more harsh than he'd suspected. He went back to his bunk, but found sleep difficult to reach.

Ryan was woken by Donfil's hand, gripping his shoulder. He blinked his eye open, seeing the lean face close to his.

"What?"

"On deck."

"What is?"

The Apache backed away, keeping his head bowed to avoid cracking his skull on the low timbers of the ceiling.

"Come and see. Just been up to relieve myself and I saw it."

Ryan pulled on the heavy seaboots. He glanced around the dimly lit room and saw that nobody else was stirring. There was a chink of light all around the hatch onto the deck, showing it was close to dawn.

"Show me," he directed.

The deck was deserted as they stepped out into the misty morning. Visibility around the *Salvation* was less than a hundred paces in any direction. There was a pallid, opalescent quality to the glowing false dawning.

"Where?"

The Indian hesitated a moment, before shooting out his long arm. "There. Bottom of the mast. Look at him."

"Kenny Hill, d'you mean, Donfil? I can see him. What about . . . ? Ah . . ."

Death, once seen, could never be mistaken. It was like a poor imitation of sleep. Even at a distance of several yards, Ryan knew that the bound and naked seaman was dead.

"Best report it to one of the mates," he said. "If we get caught with this, we might go over the side with him tied around our necks."

Donfil shook his head. "Mebbe best we don't say a word, Ryan. Just leave him. Let someone else find the corpse."

"Suppose the slut bitch is watching us? No! Don't look around. Suppose she sees us and wants us to sneak away?"

The Indian nodded. "Could be, brother. Could be. I guess he died of the cold during the night."

Ryan remembered the dark figure, folding itself over the helpless victim. But he kept his own counsel.

Their dilemma was solved by the noise of feet behind them. A couple of the crew emerged, yawning, onto the deck, behind the tryworks. Immediately both saw the lolling body, but neither of them seemed surprised. One called down to wake the rest of the men; the other wandered casually to stand by the spread feet of the dead man, spitting beyond the side of the vessel.

"Flukes over, matey," he said.

The body was pale, the marks of the ropes and the gagging livid on the skin. The eyes were wide open, staring intently into the far-off mystery of his own passing.

"Froze, likely," the sailor pronounced.

Donfil stooped, peered at the neck of the corpse and glanced up at Ryan, who quickly shook his head to prevent him from speaking.

"First mate's on his way," said the other sailor, reappearing from belowdecks. "Someone's gone to wake up Captain Quadde."

"Likely she's sleeping sound this morning." The first seaman grinned.

"Likely thou might be taking 'is place tonight if thou dost not watch thy tongue, Ned," said the other man, glaring.

While they waited for authority to arrive, Ryan pondered on the corpse—on the ragged scratches, edged with dried blood, around the genitals, and on the dark bruises around the neck, looking as though he'd been strangled by someone with iron fingers.

But Ryan kept silent.

Chapter Twenty-One

"LORD, LET THIS Thy seaman depart now in peace from this world."

As has always been the right of sea captains the world over, Pyra Quadde was reading the funeral service over Ordinary Seaman Kenneth Hill, before committing his tortured and mutilated body to the waiting deep waters.

"Though he has been a sinner, now are his sins washed whiter than snow and he is truly clad in the garments of the Lamb."

The gray dawn had finally broken, but the pale mist still lingered over the slate-dull Lantic. The crew was lined up on both sides of the main deck, bareheaded, to pay their last respects to their fallen companion.

The sails, still close-reefed, barely filled with enough wind to give the ship any forward way, and the sound of the water rippling under the stem was clearly audible.

"Now we render this body to Thy hands, in the sure and certain hope of eternal life to come. Ashes to ashes and dust to dust. If Jesus don't get thee then Satan must." The service was concluded on a throaty chuckle of spluttering laughter.

The body lay on a wide plank, wrists tied across the front of the chest, giving the false impression of someone at his devotions. Hill hadn't even been given the minimal dignity of a length of old canvas for a shroud. Not even a shackle of anchor chain to weight the corpse down. In the shimmering light, the dark bruises and scratches cried out from the pallid flesh, the marks of the throttling clear and unmistakable.

"Is he ready?" the captain asked, folding her arms across her bosom against the chill of the dawning. "Stand by."

Ryan was in the front row, and he studied the woman's face, seeing the smug lines of satisfied cruelty, like a spoiled cat that has caught itself a helpless sparrow. She licked her lips contentedly while he watched her.

"Tip the bastard in!" she called.

Four of the sailors stood steadying the funeral chute, two at each side. At Quadde's shouted command, they lifted the board, shaking it to shift the stubborn body, until it flipped loose and fell in a clumsy tangle of arms and legs. It hit the sea with an almost soundless splash.

The captain smiled. "Always a good diver, our Kenny. Used to love diving in . . . everywhere you can think of."

She turned on her heel and stamped off to her quarters, stick rattling a merry tattoo on the planks of the deck. Cyrus Ogg quietly dismissed the rest of the crew and ordered them about their business.

Jehu, the only man on the ship whose height approached Donfil's seven feet, was standing next to the Apache and Ryan.

"A maimed, unwilling sacrifice," he said, voice lower than the usual high-pitched babbling.

"What's that?" Ryan asked.

"We shall give, as need arise.... Once the first price be paid, then there needs be no other. Not until the hunger moves again."

"What're you talking about?"

"Always the way. Short straw for Kenny there. And his lay to be split 'mongst the rest of us. One man poorer an' all of us the richer. Always the way on the *Salvation*."

He moved away from the two outlanders.

Ryan shook his head and went to the very stern of the slow-moving ship. He leaned on the rail above the helmsman's shelter, staring out along the disintegrating wake.

"Fireblast!"

"What is it, brother?"

"Look!"

He pointed out behind them, only about fifty yards astern, where the corpse of Kenny Hill bobbed and danced, upright in the water, looking as though it were calmly watching them sail away. Even as the two companions stared, a large gull came circling down and perched neatly on the thinning, plastered hair. Peering down, it delicately plucked out both of the staring eyes, tossing its head back as it swallowed them.

"If I had my blaster I'd chill that stinking bird," Ryan swore.

"And what good would that do thee or poor, lamented Seaman Hill?" asked a familiar voice from just behind them.

Ryan half turned. "No good at all, ma'am. Not to him and not to me."

"No, outlander. Now, the pleasures of the first day at sea are over. And we must be to the business of catching the great whales. I think that ye both have keen sight?"

Donfil and Ryan nodded.

"The mist is lifting and the wind freshens from the north." She sniffed appreciatively. "I can taste it."

Even as she spoke, the ship heeled over, timbers creaking, as the morning breeze caught her sails. Both men balanced against the sudden movement, without staggering.

Quadde noticed that and managed a thin smile. "Got your sea legs, already, lubbers? Good enough. Now go test them. Up the masthead with ye both. Get your glims raking the seas for a sign of the whale. Shout down and burst your lungs. And point where away ye see 'em."

Ryan looked up, seeing the spidery-thin rigging almost vanishing in the tattered remnants of the mist, the twin barrels fixed to the very top of the mainmast for the two lookouts.

"Aye, ma'am," he said, beckoning for the Mescalero to climb with him.

"Quickly, outlanders. Ye see how a poor seaman can perish of the cold through disobeying my orders? It might be your turn next if ye don't jump, jump and jump!"

Ryan thought of the strangler's marks on the cold corpse. And began to climb toward the light.

KRYSTY WROTH STOOD with her face pressed against the cool glass of their attic room, staring out through the murk, toward the tops of the masts that peeked through the fog. She'd hardly slept at all, and her night had been racked with dreadful visions that jerked her awake in a shivering sweat.

Ryan had been at the center of all her black night dreams. He was walking through an echoing, deserted castle. A dank, ruined place, standing at the center of a dreary expanse of sedge and stunted willows. Broken glass daggered in every window, and the stairs were slippery with bright moss.

She'd watched him, hanging at his shoulder like a shade of pending death.

Ryan had moved slowly and painfully, like a man suddenly tired and old, his back stooped and his feet scraping along the worn stones. His head never turned from left to right as he trudged wearily through the dim passages.

But that had not been the worst.

There had been a shadow.

Insubstantial, like some blasphemous entity from beyond time and space, of all colors and of no color at all. It was following Ryan, floating like a ragged sheet carried on a strong wind. Though it didn't seem to move with any speed, it closed in on the stumbling figure, rising in the air and hovering, seeming, to Krysty, to be about to strike at him.

As it plummeted toward Ryan, Krysty had woken, mouth dry, palms sweating.

Now she looked across Claggartville, conscious of the others around her climbing out of sleep.

Jedediah Hernando Rodriguez brought their breakfast up the narrow stairs himself, passing the pair of lounging sec men, who were engrossed in a game of chess on an old plastic hand set. The tray contained a loaf and a half of new-baked bread, with a crock of butter and some oversweet blueberry jelly. A chipped enamel pot held a simmering brew of acorn coffee.

He laid the tray on the rickety table between two of the beds, turning to leave without sayir.g a word. But Krysty stopped him with a hand on his arm, making the innkeeper jump and become even more pale.

"What? There's guards that I shan cout for and...I mean I can shout for them and thee wilt..."

Krysty laid a finger to his lips, hushing him, managing a smile through her seething hatred of the traitor.

"Quietly. I'm not going to hurt you."

He licked his lips, whispering, "I had to do it. Thou knowest that. She'd have done... Thou knowest not what Pyra Quadde's like. She... I didn't mean harm. Thy tall friend'll be safe...long as he strikes truly with the irons. And ye will all be safe. Once ville council decides what work ye will be given."

"We know that," J.B. said.

Doc muttered something that sounded like "lickspittle," but nobody took any notice. Lori was sitting on one of the beds, sulkily picking at rough skin around her heels.

Krysty pulled the innkeeper toward the window. "Do other ships sail where the *Salvation* goes?"

"Aye, mistress. That they do. But they keep away from the waters where Pyra plows the furrow. No man wishes to rock that boat, thank 'ee very much."

"But could a good captain track down where she'd gone?"

"Pyra always goes to the Great Banks. Everyone knows that. There's a ship out there now from this ville. The *Bartleby*. Captain Delano at the helm."

"I saw men on that ship there." She pointed to the second set of masts along the quay.

Rodriguez squinted where she pointed. "My seeing's dim at such a distance. The one with the white jack flying at her masthead?"

"No. The red flag next to it."

"Red?"

"Yes," Krysty grated, fighting to keep the impatience from her voice.

"Your fingers are creasing my good satin shirt. It cost a deal of—"

"The ship, Rodriguez," the Armorer persisted, quietly and calmly. "It's name?"

"It be the *Phoenix*. Named so as it was built from the burned shells of three other vessels, in the cold years after the time of the darkening skies. Aye, the *Phoenix*. Captain Will Deacon.''

''I saw men busy about her. She is a whaling ship, like the *Salvation*?''

''She is. She sails on the first tide tomorrow. It'll be around three in the morning. But why do ye ask?''

''Just idle curiosity, Rodriguez, that's all,'' Krysty replied. ''Nothing else. And thanks for the food.''

The landlord of the Rising Flukes left the room, looking slightly puzzled.

Chapter Twenty-Two

AFTER TWO MORE DAYS at sea, the crew—including both involuntary members—had settled down into a regular regime. Each man was part of a watch that served eight hours on duty, then eight hours off, their duties rolling on day and night. The only occasion when this would change would be in the event of one of the lookouts spotting the telltale signs of a whale, broaching in a gren-burst of frothing white spray and foam.

But so far, there had been no such sighting. Pyra Quadde kept to her cabin, occasionally pacing the quarterdeck, stick beating out a discontented tattoo on the scrubbed and holystoned planks.

Ryan was surprised how he and Donfil had been so easily accepted. The whispered talents of the Indian with the harpoon had ensured he would be welcome. A good ironsman meant more dead whales and less risk to lives. And Ryan's going unarmed into the forecastle after Kenny Hill had brought him a similar measure of respect.

The food continued to be terrible, but the weather stayed fine—bright blue skies and the cleanest air Ryan had ever breathed, free of the bitter chem taint that still lay across so much of the Deathlands, marring its old beauty.

Though some of the seamen hated being mastheaded at lookout for its boredom, Ryan loved it, and would volunteer to the first mate when it wasn't his turn to scramble aloft. Ogg gave him clues to watch for.

"The leviathan is not like any other creature, Outlander Cawdor," he said. "He has a cunning beyond our knowledge. I have read old books in what was once the liberry of the ville, telling of the whales and sharks and their ways; of a great white that frightened a town, and of its hunting; of how the whales can call to one another across a hundred miles of teeming ocean; of their mating and of their killing. I have studied them."

"And you hunt them to their deaths?"

Cyrus Ogg nodded. "Their chilling is my living. Through me and the other ships of Claggartville, the town survives. There is food, heat and light. And goods to trade. If the whales deserted these waters, then the ville would die. Sure as rad death lives in hot spots."

He told Ryan to watch for seabirds. Where they gathered there was often a whale close by. The gulls would circle about, knowing that shoals of smaller fishes would be disturbed by the monsters and driven close to the surface.

"A whale that's dived deep, down to the belly of the black canyons, will come to the surface carrying the taint of wet earth and mud. In a fog or at night thou canst taste it on the air. And thou wilt hear the cries. Deep as a cathedral bell, my granddad used to tell me. And the noise of a whale as he leaps clear is something thou never loses from the memory. Keep all this in mind, outlander, and thou wilt not come amiss on it. And call down fit to rend thy bellows if thou seest anything of the whale. That is what we are all here for, Ryan Cawdor.''

As HE CLUNG to the cold metal ring that rimmed the top of the barrel, Ryan swayed easily to and fro, going with the butting motion of the ship, seeing the spreading wake that the ship trailed, and the V of foam that peeled open under her stern.

The sea was empty.

No circling, screeching gulls. No dash of spray to mark the rolling gray-green pastures. High above the deck, it was a world of stillness, with only the sighing wind for company.

The wind and a man's thoughts.

Ryan pondered on his talk the previous evening with Donfil.

The shaman had been in better spirits than almost any time since Ryan had first met him. He'd tapped the dry biscuit on the chipped table, ignoring the small curling weevils that came tumbling from it. His eyes were bright, and he leaned forward to speak quietly to Ryan.

"It is a good day, my brother. Ysun, Giver of all life, speaks to me out on these waters. I have never, even in my visions, seen such a teeming emptiness. I cannot wait to hunt my brother, the whale. To meet with him out in those small boxes of wood, and sport with the long spears . . . It will be such a good time. I have prayed to White Painted Woman that my heart shall not fail and that my hand shall be true in the fire of the hunting.''

Ryan listened, concentrating on forcing down another spoonful of some of the most disgusting soy stew he'd ever eaten. In among the rancid lumps were gobbets of stone-cold grease. But one of the first things a child learns in the Deathlands is to eat anything and everything put in front of it.

Who knew where the next meal might come from? Or when?

Donfil had carried on with his enthusiastic monologue about the delights of the whaler's life.

''I know that the woman's a blood-eyed gaudy slut, but she hasn't threatened either of us. If she does, we can stand close and do what we can. If we live through to the end of this sailing, then we can chill her and all will be well.''

Ryan had asked his friend what his plans might be if they did survive.

The Apache had turned his mind inward and not replied for some time. Finally he'd nodded. ''Yeah. I have a debt to you, Ryan, that can never be settled. There, in the deserts, I was barely half a man. Now, here, with the wind through my hair and the taste of cold and clean in my mouth and nose . . . here I am a whole man . . . here I am a living man.''

Ryan, alone at the masthead, knew in his heart that the Apache's time with them was running out. It didn't matter how the dice lay. But if they should live through it, he felt that Donfil would choose to stay in Claggartville.

But first, they had to live through.

Because of his destroyed left eye, Ryan could gain little benefit from binoculars. But the captain had rummaged in a sea chest in her cabin and emerged with a long, brassbound telescope, which she'd given to Ryan, warning him what might happen if he were to lose his grip and let it fall.

"Better *you* fall, cully," she'd said with something approaching a smile, a smile that sent the short hairs prickling at Ryan's nape.

Now he used the telescope to scan the sea around the ship, watching for any sign of the presence of their prey. From the way the crew had been talking, he knew they were closing in on the grounds where they would normally encounter the great leviathans of the ocean.

But there was nothing.

Breathing in time with the slow pendulum swing of the mainmast, Ryan again allowed his thoughts to wander.

He thought of the large house in the blue-muffled Shens where he'd been raised.

His running years, alone, friendless, until he fell in with the legendary Trader.

Fighting, running, loving, chilling. That had been the story of those days. Those years. Ryan remembered the evenings around camp fires, with the smell of wood smoke and meat roasting on the embers. Companions who traveled together and fought for one another. Men and women whom you could trust to stand at your back when the steel flashed.

Then Krysty Wroth had come into his life, around the same time that the Trader was readying himself to quit this world, in his own mysterious way. And then nothing had been the same.

Ryan recalled the first time he'd seen that brilliant flame-red hair, which had been around the same time he'd met up with poor, disoriented Doc Tanner. Then they'd found the first gateways and made the first of their mat-trans jumps.

Since then?

He lifted the scope to his right eye and slowly scanned the horizon, noticing a few gulls gathering and circling a mile or so ahead, off the starboard bow of the vessel. Even in his short time aboard the *Salvation*, Ryan had picked up enough of the correct nautical phrases to avoid trouble from either of the mates or his fellow seamen. He fumbled with the crude focusing system of the archaic instrument, trying to sharpen his view, battling against the regular rolling of the whaler to keep the image steady.

The sea looked unflurried, but there were certainly the gulls. More and more of them, mute at that distance.

Though Ryan watched carefully for three or four minutes, until his eye began to water and his vision blurred, nothing more seemed to be happening and he eventually lowered the telescope again and returned to his musings.

In the past year he and his friends had traveled thousands of miles. Many had gone, most chilled in sudden, shocking ways, their lives snuffed out in the blinking of an eye.

Ryan made a tentative attempt to count the number of people he'd called friends who'd gone to buy the farm. Names trickled past his mind like a jerky parade of stone-faced corpses. He counted to fifty without even having to pause. Another twenty faces came to him, and he had the certain knowledge that another forty or fifty acquaintances waited, gibbering, in the black wings of his memory.

There was the killing cloud in the Darks.

The Russians who had tried to invade and been driven back. The snow and the cascading flood of choking ice.

The mud and the heat when he'd first met the young killer with the hair like snow and eyes like molten rubies.

Triple-crazies, gibbering a thousand feet below a lake, surrounded by all the laboratory trivia of a new genocide.

The return down the twisted lanes of the past, to confront the old nightmares. And the trip past the ruins of—

"Aloft! Anything...? Aloft, there! What dost thou see?"

"No!" Ryan called, cupping his hands to his mouth, taking the greatest care to keep the telescope safely tucked beneath his arm.

"Keep thine eyes skinned or I'll have thy backbone!" Second Mate Walsh screamed.

Ryan took up the glass, ready to look once more across the pitching acres of glittering water.

But part of his mind wandered away to Krysty Wroth, wondering if she still lived, thinking back to their many conversations on what future they desired. She hoped for safety and stability. Ryan looked for a perfection that he hadn't found yet. And might never find.

Time, to Ryan Cawdor, swinging effortlessly between heaven and the deep, cold sea, had ceased to have any meaning. He knew that when enough minutes had ticked by on the ship's chron, then someone would climb up the rigging and relieve him of the lookout's task. But until then, there was no hurry.

It was pleasant to have, for once, leisure without any responsibility. There was nothing he could do, for the time being, to extricate himself from the danger of his position. There was a rare opportunity to think about his past, and even wonder a little about his future. If there was to be one.

Ryan thought back to the many places in the Deathlands that he'd passed through. So many of them seeming the same bleak pestholes.

One of Trader's favorite sayings came back to him at that moment. "One handful of ashes looks just like any other handful of ashes."

His eye was caught by a flurry of white spray ahead of the ship, on the starboard side. Ryan didn't need the telescope to recognize what was happening, though he'd never seen it before in his life.

"There she blows!" he shouted. "There! There she blows!"

Chapter Twenty-Three

IT WAS MADNESS. The most terrifying, leaping, heart-stopping madness that Ryan had ever known. He was soaked to the skin within seconds, hands blistered from the heavy oars, muscles in his shoulders cracking with the effort of pulling. His hair was flattened to his skull, and he gritted his teeth as the frail boat bounded over the long Lantic rollers in pursuit of the broaching whale that he'd sighted.

How long ago?

Eternities hurtled by, like grains of sand. But his common sense told Ryan that barely twenty minutes could have elapsed. He'd been ordered down immediately from the masthead, to be replaced as look-out by one of the Oriental cooks. He was needed in the lead whaleboat, skippered by Cyrus Ogg, with its ironsman, Donfil More, crouched in the bow.

The long, narrow boat had been lowered hastily into the sea alongside the *Salvation*, now running under a skeleton crew, most of her men eager to row after their prey.

Pyra Quadde had raged the decks like a woman possessed of demons, lashing out with her stick at any sailor unlucky enough to run within range. Froth clung to her fleshy lips, and her eyes rolled bloodshot in their sockets.

"Now we see him, ye shiftless lazy sons of gaudy whores! Get to the boats and after him. Row and row, cullies. Jack in plenty for a good hunt and a clean kill. No food for a week if he slips away from ye!"

"NAUGHT BUT EARS and arms, my brave lads," said Cyrus Ogg, encouraging the five men to pull for their lives toward the patch of disturbed, misty water where the whale had last been sighted. "Pull and pull and pull again. That's the word for the silver mug of fine oil and a rich lay for us all. Pull and pull and pull yet more."

Ryan had never traveled in such a bizarre way before—with his back to where they were going, unable to see what was happening. Only Donfil in the triangular bow section and Ogg at the tiller in the stern could judge what should be done.

Walsh in the second whaleboat and a grizzled veteran named Piper Fairman in the third were only a dozen yards behind them. Ryan had heard that Captain Quadde sometimes took an iron herself if a whole school of whales was spotted. But here, with only a single beast marked down for the hunt, she was content to remain on board the *Salvation* and shadow the trio of small dories.

Because of the height of the long ocean waves, it was often impossible for the oarsmen to even glimpse the *Salvation*. Most of the time Ryan could see the three masts, and occasionally the whole white and black hull. The lookout at the top of the mainmast was still pointing dead ahead of them, to where Ryan figured he could see the birds waiting for the reappearance of the monster.

"Steady and together, my stout boys, with an in and an out, an in and an out. Any man stops rowing, and he'll be tied to the grating and I'll flog the skin from his back. Next I'll flog the muscles and flesh away from his back. Then the gleaming ivory of his spine shall feel the kiss of the metal-tipped lash. I'll whip that man so hard his liver and lights'll be shredded and flensed and pulverized and torn so that they can be served over the side as bait for the sharks."

The world was shrinking around Ryan. Though there were few men fitter in all of the Deathlands, the endless heaving at the clumsy oar, sometimes deep in the water and sometimes kicking the empty air, was taking its toll on him. He fought for breath, feeling soreness across the tops of his thighs from the pressure and the movement against the seat.

"I'll press thine eyes *in* and then *out* of thy skull and drive a white-hot awl *in* and then *out* of thine ears and hammer hook-end nails *in* and then *out* of thy nostrils." Each repetition of "in" and "out" was accompanied by a barely audible change in the pitch of the mate's voice.

"She blows!" Donfil yelled from the bow.

Ryan wasn't able to stop himself from turning on the planking seat, seeing the most amazing sight, catching the scent of old, old earth, ripped from the belly of the Lantic.

It was as though someone had thrown up a great wall of wrinkled, blue-gray stone across their course. Rearing it, dripping and gleaming, streaked with shards of green weed, unimaginably huge.

"Turn thy face to me, outlander, and bend thy back. Or we all perish."

Cyrus Ogg nodded at him like a friendly schoolmaster, mentioning some tiny error in his tables of multiplication.

Ryan bent again to the oar, hearing a deep, sonorous roaring, which seemed as if it were vibrating the very marrow of his bones, shaking the core of his being.

"She blows, she blows!" the Apache repeated. Out of the corner of his eye, Ryan could see that his companion had taken up one of the long harpoons and was hefting it in his right hand, just as he'd done on the quayside of Claggartville, aeons ago.

But now his target was not a daub of white paint upon an old door. It was Behemoth itself, the lord over all deep waters.

"Hold oars," the first mate called, raising his voice for the first time, forced to raise it over the caldron of boiling foam and spray that seethed around them. "Now, Master Ten-from-Ten! Here be thy chance. Strike!"

Ryan was able, now they had no further need of rowing, to glance over his shoulder once more and witness the next—and most dramatic act—of the murderous play.

The towering bastion of living flesh had hardly moved. Its skin was dappled with small shellfish and crusted with strange cancerlike growths. Near the crest of the blunt head Ryan could see the tiny eye—not dead like that of the great shark that had attacked them on their raft. This eye twinkled with life and with curiosity. The jaws were only just ajar, the sea swilling in and out between the fronds of its teeth. They were nearly close enough to touch it.

"In with the lance, outlander!" one of the rowers yelled.

"Aye," called another, voice cracking with tension. "Before he sinks us with his fucking tail!"

"Thanks for the meeting!" Donfil cried, casting the harpoon with all of his power, driving it deep into the whale, by the great hump of muscle behind the head.

"Clear of the line, lads," Ogg ordered, keeping one hand on the tiller, using the other to fill a metal dipper with seawater.

The thin rope that was attached to the harpoon ran through a notch in the bow of the whaleboat, under the seats of the oarsmen and around the stubby wooden post, called the loggerhead, between the feet of the first mate. The line was controllable there, running back into one of the two kegs of coiled rope. Hundreds of feet in all, ready to be linked together if the whale should run and run. And in the bow, clipped to a bracket, was a small honed ax. The other task of Donfil was to cut the line if the wounded monster should suddenly decide to dive deep. The ocean thereabouts was of a depth that could lose a thousand whales.

Walsh's harpooneer also managed to strike his iron from the other side. Provoked by the stinging pain, the whale exhaled in a gust of noisome air and mist. It began to move, towing the two dories behind it. The third whaleboat hadn't managed to pull in close enough and was soon left behind.

"Ship your oars, or they'll go over the side," Ogg ordered. "Quick, Master Deadman, and hold on tight for the devil's surf ride."

The rope ran out unchecked for the first hundred feet, to give a safer distance between boat and whale. It hissed along, whining as it smoked around the loggerhead, so that Ogg had to cool it with a pan of water.

The vast tail of the creature waved in the air, darkening the day, coming down with a cracking sound that hurt the ears, casting a welter of green water over the pursuing boats.

Ryan laughed aloud for the sheer animal pleasure and exhilaration of the chase. The whale was gathering speed, and the *Salvation* was disappearing fast behind them. Spray danced, and the sun dazzled through it in a burst of prismed colors.

"How far will he run?" he shouted to Ogg.

"How's that, Master Deadman? How far will the beast pull us?"

"Yeah. What if dark comes before it tires?"

"We will have it afore night come, outlander. But I have known a chase with a truly big whale to take a day and a night and half of the following day. But there was many a barrel of fine oil in that one, I tell thee.''

"It dives!" Donfil yelled.

"Ready to cut. Not until my order or I'll have thy cock and balls for clock chimes."

As the whale plunged beneath the surface, the day was instantly silent. The rushing, roaring noise of their mad progress was stopped, and the two whaleboats floated serenely, only a few yards away from each other, while gulls cried out above their heads.

"How deep, Mr. Ogg?" the second mate called, standing in the stern, watching the line as it continued to race out over the bow.

"Our iron went deep and true, Mr. Walsh. How went thine?"

"Deep and true."

"Then I think we shall see him again shortly as he tries to rid himself of the pesty barbs that hold him to us."

Cyrus Ogg poured more water over the smoldering line as it continued to race out around the loggerhead and beneath the sea.

"He's diving more shallow," Donfil called, leaning far out, shading his eyes against the reflection of the sun on the water.

"Shows he'd tiring fast. Ready to haul in the line, lads, soon as he broaches again. Outlander, thou must coil it as it comes, to keep all neat and unclogged in the keg there."

"Aye," Ryan said.

"Quiet and silent. Soundless it is. No sound. No noise. Still as death. Still as snow. Still as sleep and still as dark."

"Still as Jehu," Cyrus Ogg warned the gibbering crazie, "or you can swim back to the ship."

"Here he comes..." said Walsh. "The birds know it."

"Haul in," the First Mate ordered, voice betraying the excitement. "Where away, Ten-from-Ten? Tell me that."

"Close," Donfil said. "The rope's gone slack, but I can't... Ysun! It's right—"

The world exploded.

Ryan was hanging on to the side of the boat and the whale surfaced so near that its skin grazed his knuckles. It erupted clear into the air, hanging for an unbelievable, impossible moment of frozen time. Then it crashed down, its tail catching the other whaleboat a glancing blow as it dived again. The frail little craft was overturned, spilling men and oars and line into the sea.

"Cut thy line and save the boat, Walsh!" Ogg shouted.

Once again they were off in a flurry of white spray. But this time Ryan could detect a slowing in the exertions of the great creature. Then their forward motion stopped once more, and Donfil again peered over the bow.

"Going back beneath us!" he yelled.

"Out oars and spin her on a nailhead," Ogg snapped. "Quick for our lives."

Ryan grabbed at his oar, fumbling it into position and obeying the order to back water while the men on the other side tugged with all their strength. The tiller went hard over and the cockleshell darted around like a mayfly. Once they were facing in the right direction, Ogg ordered them to ship oars again, and pull in the slack line, so that they would be close in to the whale when next it surfaced.

"Heading for the men in the water!" Ogg muttered.

The rolling mountain of the beast's hump broke the surface about fifty feet in front of them, jerking them onward. As the first mate had said, the whale was making for the other boat. Walsh and two other crewmen had clambered back into it and were now bailing it empty. But the other five men were still floundering some distance away.

The sun was bright, showing the streams of crimson blood that flowed down the sides of the whale, spouting from the two irons in its flanks.

And the *Salvation*, all sail crowded on, was bearing down on them.

Ryan watched as the beast came closer, picking Jacob Lusk, one of the fattest members of the crew, building up more speed. Its jaws were open, funneling the Lantic between the rows of teeth. Above the sound of the rushing waters, Ryan and the others heard with an awful clarity the last scream of despair from the sailor as he vanished into the gaping suction of the jaws.

"Widowed wife and fatherless children," Ogg said quietly.

As though its spasm of savage revenge had exhausted it, the whale slowed down once more, half turning so that it presented its side to Donfil's harpoon. The Indian had taken out a longer lance, ready for the killing lunge.

Once again, sitting still in the gently rocking boat, Ryan glimpsed the whale's little eye, rolling toward him. It was shot with blood, seeming both resigned and fearful. For a fraction of eternity it locked onto Ryan's own eye.

He couldn't say what it was that he saw in that eye, but it made him gasp and shudder.

"Deep as the deepest well," Cyrus Ogg said, his voice caressingly soft.

Donfil stood poised like a statue, the harpoon gripped in both hands. Then he drove it at the whale's skin. The razored head and the first 2½ feet of the shaft vanished, and more blood jetted out, pattering on the cold water. Some of it splashed on Ryan's arm and neck, startling him by its heat.

"Again, again, again, again," crooned the first mate.

Donfil, lips pulled off his strong white teeth in a ferocious vulpine snarl, stabbed the iron in again and again, twisting it around to deepen the wound.

Ryan saw the light go out in the whale's eye as its life slipped away. Suddenly it was no more than a floating carcass.

Chapter Twenty-Four

ALL RYAN WANTED TO DO was to claw his way up the rope ladder dangling from the side of the *Salvation*, stagger to his bunk, strip off his sodden clothes and climb between the thin, gray blankets and sleep for a week.

But there was much to be done, miles of work to put behind him before he could rest.

The survivors of Walsh's boat had to be helped to safety, and then lines had to be made fast to the body of the whale. Johnny Flynn had told Ryan that speed was essential after the kill had been completed, for two reasons. The body would not float for very long, so it had to be tied alongside the mother ship. Also, the voracious predators that roamed the deep oceans would scent blood at a dozen miles or more, catch the sound signals of distress from the dying leviathan at ten times that range. They'd come to try to rend their own share of the spoils before the seamen could break down the carcass to blubber and oil.

"What of Jacob Lusk?" Walsh shouted.

"Flense it open and the wretch might still be living," Ogg replied. "I've heard of such happening. Years back in Nantucket, so they used to say."

"He could be alive!" Ryan exclaimed.

"If we're right quick in gutting the beast, then he might yet live."

The *Salvation* was heaving to, only a stone's cast away from the boats. Captain Quadde was leaning over the bow, the telescope in her fist.

"It took a man!" she bellowed.

"Seaman Jacob Lusk," Ogg replied warily.

"Clean swallowed?"

"Aye, ma'am."

"Fix lines and we'll haul it alongside. Got a man on the windlass. Sling the boats to the davits sharp as new paint, Mr. Ogg. Then all hands to flense and render down."

"Aye, ma'am." The first mate turned to his crew. "I'll drive a spike through your knees if ye dawdle and lollygag around, my hearties. Let's to it."

IT WAS CHAOS on a grandly, bloodily organized scale.

Ryan had been on hunts before, after the mutie deer and moose in the foothills of the ranging snow-tipped Darks. He'd seen the excitement of the ville when the carcasses were brought home on the backs of the cat wags, but he'd never seen anything like the activity on board the *Salvation*.

As soon as the whaleboats were hoisted on the deck, the men tumbled out and ran to their appointed places. Ryan and Donfil hadn't received any orders and stood, confused amid the scurrying, bellowing bedlam.

Ryan never heard the woman come up behind him. Most of the time the rapping of the cane located her position on the ship. But when she wanted, Pyra Quadde could move as quietly as a tracking tiger.

The first warning Ryan Cawdor had was a cracking buffet to the side of his head that deafened him and made him stagger, nearly falling into the scuppers from the shock and force of the blow. Donfil began to turn, but he was too slow. The woman grabbed him by the front of his soaking shirt with one hand, then tugged his head lower so that she could slap him across the face with the other hand. The Apache was unable to move with surprise.

"Get with Mr. Ogg's crew and do what thou art blazing told, thou scum ballast!"

She raised her stick as though she were going to lash out at the tall Mescalero, but hesitated a wary moment at the look of scarlet murder that blazed in his eyes. With a gruff laugh she turned away from them and walked to the port side of the ship, to watch the attempts to rescue the vanished seaman from the belly of the whale.

"By Ysun," said Donfil softly, rubbing at his face with a wondering hand. "No woman born of man has ever...can ever... If any of the people of my...my tribe had seen that, then the shame would mean I'd need to chill her. Tear the heart still beating from her body and devour it. Then—and only then—I could take my own life with some shred of honor."

"Thought you wanted to stick around and give the life of a whaler a tryout?" Ryan said, leading the way to where Johnny Flynn and the others from their boat's crew were working.

"It was a good day for the hunt, my brother. And as I took the life of that monster of dark water I felt his spirit flow to mine. Yeah, Ryan Cawdor. The job of harpooneer could be wonderful. But only when that daughter of cold fire has quit life."

Captain Pyra Quadde was back on the quarter-deck, watching as the two mates led the rest of the men. Once the dead whale was tied alongside, a half dozen of the most experienced and nimble hands swarmed down lines and began to hack their way into the creature. Blood flooded out, crimsoning the sea for a hundred paces around. Captain Quadde had ordered the yards backed so that the *Salvation* only crept forward slowly, avoiding too much pitching and rolling. The men worked with special butchering tools, such as knives with blades three feet long, lethally sharp, fixed into wooden hafts another four feet in length. They cut great hunks of meat from the animal, attaching iron hooks to it, while the men on board ran and scurried like monkeys, pulling and stacking the blubber, slicing it into smaller pieces ready for the try-pots. The cooks were loading hunks of the meat into the smoking ovens, ready to begin the stinking process of rendering it down to fine oil.

"Cut deep for Jacob Lusk's sake!" the skipper called, cupping her hands to her mouth to make sure her orders were heard.

Ryan and Donfil took their places on the lines, pulling up the dripping haunches of meat and carrying them to the growing pile on the main deck, then throwing the hooked cords down to the furiously hacking men. Ryan found himself standing next to Jehu, both of them waiting a moment for more blubber to be attached to their ropes.

"Can that poor bastard live?" Ryan asked.

"Jacob?"

"Yeah."

The round little head shook and nodded at the same time, so that Ryan couldn't tell whether he was saying yes or no. Other than the clatter of the cleated seaboots and the screaming of a flock of gulls, the only sound was the clean thunking of steel blades biting into the quivering flesh of the harpooned whale.

"Well, Jehu? Can he still be alive? He'll have choked to death!"

"Jacob might have climbed the ladder to the peace that passeth all understanding. Now he sitteth at the right hand of all good…and bad and different and all for rent and rent his garments on the road to Bozra where…"

"Forget it, you double-crazy stupe," Ryan said disgustedly.

But Jehu, little eyes fixed on Pyra Quadde, who stood to their left, plucked at his sleeve.

"What is it?"

"Master Ten-from-Ten, thy pagan friend."

"What about him?"

"Do his people butcher the double-crazies? Do they, huh?"

"No, they treat them well."

"So it is on the *Salvation*. Sailed on her for eleven years, has Jehu. Not many on board this trip can say that. Too many chilled by…the dark sea eagle, if thou dost take my meaning?" He nudged Ryan in the ribs to make his words more clear.

"I get you, Jehu. There's nobody so sane as the crazie who isn't."

"Near through the ribs, Captain!" called one of the men with the long flensing tools.

"All hands cease work and stand by. Listen well, lads, for a word from Jacob!"

Everyone obeyed Captain Quadde's order immediately, glad of the chance for a brief break in the spine-cracking labor.

"Two more trips and mad Jehu will have the lays to buy a fine chandler's store near the quay. And be a man of leisure and pleasure and treasure."

"Still haven't said if that poor bastard could be alive."

"Been stories of it happening. They comes out much changed, so they says. With their mind set to wandering and their skin all—"

"Hold thy noise, thou pinheaded loon!" the captain yelled.

"Aye, Captain. I'll hold my tongue so thrtth ognluur…" Jehu gripped himself literally by the end of his tongue so that his words became instant garbled gibberish.

The ship fell silent.

Ryan was joined at the rail by the rest of the crew, peering down at the ruined carcass. The head re-

mained untouched, but much of the meat of the sides
and back and belly had already been hewed from the
pale bones. Each of the flensers had a safety rope tied
around his waist, to help him keep his balance on the
slick flesh.

"I hear something!" called one of the men, from
down below, standing with head on one side, as
though that might somehow help his hearing.

Then they all heard it, soaring above the banshee
wailing of the gulls, silencing them and sending them
wheeling away to the north like etched shadows on the
blue sky.

The sound was muffled, but distinct. A human
voice crying for help.

"Quickly, my lads." Cyrus Ogg broke the spell of
stillness that fell upon every man on the ship.

The two hands standing deepest in the bloody
wreckage began to cut and slice with a renewed vigor,
opening up more of the noisome stomach of the
whale.

"Watch ye do not fucking cut him apart with the
lances!" Walsh yelled.

"Something's moving!" shouted one of the men,
clambering clumsily away from where a glistening expanse of pale yellow intestine could be seen rippling
like a polecat trapped inside a silken bag.

Ryan watched with the others, seeing that the swallowed seaman still lived and fought to tear himself free
of the sack of guts that held him a squealing, mewl-
ing prisoner.

Like the birth of some mutie lizard, the stomach wall tore open.

And Jacob Lusk emerged... What had once been Jacob Lusk.

Now it was as white as Jak Lauren's hair, bleached by the powerful acids in the stomach of the whale, acids that had already eaten away the shirt and pants from the seaman's body, and left his skin wrinkled and partly raw. The face seemed worst afflicted as Jacob Lusk turned it toward where he sensed the sun still shone.

He could only sense it, for his eyes had been seared from their sockets, leaving raw, weeping holes in the scoured bone. The lips had been eaten away, and the tongue and soft flesh of the inside of the mouth, so that all that came out was a gargling scream of horror.

"Virgin save us!"

There was a collective indrawing of sighing breath from every person there.

The creature stood, balanced, waving its peeled arms, fingers spread and oozing blood, crying out in its terrible choked voice. It was like seeing some dreadful embryo born, full grown, yet not properly complete.

"Fireblast!" Ryan called to the flensers on the carcass. "Chill the poor bastard. Cut him down, someone. Chill him!"

The cry was picked up by Jehu and by Donfil, by Johnny Flynn and a dozen more, until every man of the *Salvation* was calling out for Jacob to be set free from his misery.

Only Pyra Quadde said nothing, watching the nightmare scene from the rail of the quarterdeck.

But Jacob Lusk was quicker.

Some tattered shreds of consciousness remained in the dark skull, and he flung his arms together above his head with a damp, clinging, slapping sound. Without another cry he dived neatly off the dead whale into the welcoming waters of the Lantic.

They watched his whitened body as it sank into the gray-green deeps. It seemed to go down forever, until the rippling waves finally wiped the image clear away.

Ryan lifted his eyes to the horizon, seeing the first triangular fins of the hunting sharks that had taken over possession and lordship of so many of the oceans of the world.

Pyra Quadde had also seen them.

"No use watching him sink. Take him an hour or more to reach the mud around these deeps. Sharks coming after the blubber. After *our* blubber. Set to, cullies. Set to!"

Ryan shook his head. More gut-wrenching labor before they could rest. It crossed his mind at that moment to wonder where Krysty might be and what she might be doing.

"No sun dreams, Outlander Deadman," Cyrus Ogg said at his elbow. "Unless thou dost want to face some punishment from our captain."

"No, thanks," Ryan replied, readying himself to pull on the hooked cords.

Then he heard the shout from the lookout in the crow's nest, high above the blood-slick deck. "Sail ho! Sail on the larboard beam! A ship!"

Chapter Twenty-Five

DARKNESS HAD ONCE AGAIN come upon Claggart-ville. J.B., Krysty, Jak, Doc and Lori had been model prisoners, causing no trouble for the sec men who'd captured them. It seemed as if the outlanders were clearly resigned to their fate, eating the food provided and only leaving the narrow room when one of them wanted to go down the wooden stairs to the row of white-painted earth privies in the rear yard. And when they did that there was always a pair of armed men to take them and bring them back.

Within the group, the only note of discord had been struck by Lori Quint.

The tall blond teenager had started to become restive halfway through the first morning of their captivity, moaning on the bed, blaming Doc for having gotten her into such a threatening situation.

"Let's do what they wants us to do," she kept repeating. "Don't mind work. Just hate being stuffed up in this fuck-place."

Lori knew well enough how much Doc hated to hear her using obscenities, and he rose to the bait she offered.

"Please try to remain calm, my dainty pearl of the far Orient. Every cloud has a silver lining of threads amongst the gold." He hesitated a moment, passing a weary hand over his brow. "I fear that I have made some error in the recollection of the old saying, my most lovely angel of—"

Lori pulled a sulky face at him. "Shut up, you silly old crumbly! That's what you is."

"Are," he corrected automatically, his eyes showing his hurt.

"You are, are, are!" she yelled. "Old and no use for anything."

Krysty had stopped the fight, walking past Doc and staring at Lori. "Just one more word, girl, and I'll slap your eyes sideways. Shut up."

Lori had done as she was told, shutting up to the extent that she hardly spoke a word to any of them for the next two days. She slept alone and only picked at the food offered.

The girl was so withdrawn that J.B. took Krysty and Jak to one side on the last day in the ville.

"Think she'll whistle on us?" he asked, the afternoon sunlight bouncing off the polished lenses of his round, wire-rimmed glasses. His fedora was pushed to the back of his head, and he looked more worried than usual.

"No," Krysty said.

"Mebbe," was Jak Lauren's answer.

"Could chill her," the Armorer suggested, as calm and taciturn as ever.

"No," Krysty vetoed. "Doc might actually double-freak and crazy out on us. That'd bring the sec men on us like a thresher on wheat. I say leave her. Watch her."

"Could be time of month," Jak said with all the wisdom of his years, ducking as Krysty aimed a blow at him, only half joking. "What I say?"

J.B. HAD WANTED to be the one to set the killing ball rolling, but he'd been overruled by the others in their intense, whispered discussions.

"Has to be woman," Jak said. "Watch me, you and Doc like gators watch ducks. Get chilled straight off."

"Don't like it much, but I guess you're right. Try during the day if they'll let you two, Krysty and Lori, go to relieve yourselves together. My guess is that they will. If they do, then that's the way we'll do it when it's time."

The sec men never questioned the need of the two attractive young women to go down to the privy together. The armed pair simply escorted them down the stairs and waited outside for them, blasters still stuck negligently in their broad leather belts.

"Ready, Lori?" Krysty asked, feeling the latent power of the Earth Mother trembling through her body. On occasions when desperate measures were needed, she could lock herself into the power source, calling on Gaia to aid her. But it left her totally weakened for some time after. Also, she had been drilled constantly by her own mother, Sonja, back in the ville of Harmony, that the power was something so special that only life or death merited its being used.

The sec men were something she felt confident she could handle on her own.

With a little help from Lori.

"You ready?" she repeated.

"Yeah, course. Don't keep on at me. I know what I'm got to do."

It was late, full dark, with the usual mist that sidled along the alleys and hung around in the cobbled courtyards. It was particularly thick near the river, where the *Phoenix*, under her skipper, Captain Will Deacon, was making ready to go to sea on a whaling voyage that would take them close by the waters where the *Salvation* was known to sail.

Krysty had gone into the privy, intending to simply sit there for a couple of minutes and then come out into the shadowy patio area to confront the guards. But the tension brought pressure on her and she eventually dropped her pants and squatted on the wooden seat. Once she'd finished she peeked through the heart-shaped hole carved in the oak door, making sure nobody else had come out to join the sec men. Lori's door swung noisily open and Krysty came out to join the blonde.

"Have ye done, ladies?" asked the taller of the sentries.

"Yeah."

"Then let us escort ye both back to your quarters, if we may?"

He made a mocking half bow, echoed by his short companion.

"Thank thee," Krysty replied, locking her fingers together and clubbing the man on the back of the neck, a ferocious, chopping blow that laid him out, instantly unconscious, on the damp stones of the yard.

Lori took a half step in closer to the other sec man, driving her knee into his groin with all her strength. The air exploded from his lungs, followed by most of the contents of his stomach, splattering noisily on the stones. He fell to his knees, mouth open, both hands clutching his genitals. Though he was crippled and out of the action, Krysty knew that it wouldn't be good enough. Half measures meant half failures.

"Put him down," she whispered.

Her own victim lay on his face, arms outstretched. He was breathing slowly but regularly. He could recover any time in the next half hour.

Krysty judged her aim carefully in the dim half-light. If she miscalculated she could cripple herself. She dropped with all her force on her right knee, all her weight striking the unconscious sentry on the exposed neck, snapping it like a dry branch. His body convulsed and he gave a very small cry. And died.

The other guard's mind was tucked away, trying to cope with the sickening pain that paralyzed his legs and stomach. Lori slapped him contemptuously across the face, sending him sliding into the cold dirt. He moaned, and threads of vomit straggled from his pale lips.

"You fuck!" the girl gritted, putting all her seething resentment into the vicious kick to the base of his skull, just below and behind the right ear.

Krysty heard a sound like a large orange being violently squeezed. Soft and wet. The sec man's legs kicked out like a brain-hit rabbit, then he, too, lay still in the swirling mist.

"Walk the road alone." Krysty stopped by the nearer corpse, taking the weapons from the belt.

Lori hadn't finished. She swung her leg back and kicked at the man's head again, the toe of her boot splitting open the skin of his cheek.

"Leave him! He's chilled. Can't feel anymore, Lori. Get his blaster and knife and let's go. Time's sliding."

"Sure," the girl muttered. "Why can't we stopping running some day? I'm tired, Krysty. Real tired, tired, tired."

"We all are. Gaia! This isn't the time or the place for this, Lori. Get his weapons and let's move."

The taller of the dead sec men was carrying a chromium-plated Smith & Wesson .38, which had a rare Wichita winged rib sight assembly on top of the barrel. The man wasn't carrying any kind of knife in his belt. Krysty rolled the dead corpse deeper into the shadows near the rear wall of the yard and straightened up. She could see that Lori had plucked a pair of small pistols from the other body. The light was poor and Krysty wasn't any kind of expert on blasters, but she guessed that the little guns were Beretta .22s. Lori also hefted a long knife. More like a small sword, broad bladed with an ornate brass hilt.

"There." The girl grinned, her blond hair gleaming like spun golden wire, condensation from the drifting fog glistening in the long strands like thousands of tiny diamonds. Now that they'd successfully achieved the first part of the plan, the teenager's good humor had been restored.

THE BACK STAIRS of the tavern were quiet and deserted. It was late enough for most of the inn's drinking customers to have already gone home to their own beds. And the crew of the *Phoenix* would be busy down on the docks, readying the whaler for her voyage. From the kitchens of the Rising Flukes they could hear the melodious voice of one of the serving girls, singing as she finished the evening's washing up.

"Up to the attic," Krysty whispered, waving for Lori to go ahead of her. The pair of sec men had been alone on the top floor, but there were at least three more men, generally lounging around in the taproom or kitchens.

Then someone entered the kitchen through the far door and the singing stopped.

Lori, halfway up the first flight of stairs, hesitated and looked behind her.

"Someone's—"

"Get the others. I'll deal...go on, Lori. Go, now!"

The blonde picked her way up the stairs, vanishing just as the door into the hallway opened. And Jedediah Hernando Rodriguez walked out.

He was wearing the same purple shirt as when they'd first met, jewelry chinking on his hands. The little pistol was in his belt with the pretty stiletto. His limpid brown eyes clicked wide as he saw Krysty standing there alone.

"What art thou...? Where's the sec men? Thou wilt find trouble if thou dost rock the boat by—"

The big .38 filled the woman's hand, the chrome gleaming in the soft light of the oil lamps lining the wall.

"How did...? Where...?" His face went white as linen, and for a moment Krysty thought he was going to fall over in a faint. But he recovered, leaning one hand on the closed door to steady himself. The girl began to sing again, a different, older song.

Krysty raised the gun toward the landlord's throat. If she pulled the trigger he'd be blown apart. But the chilling would bring the other sec men rushing in on them.

"A word, and you're dead. Like the two double-stiffs out there." She gestured to the yard.

"What dost thou want, mistress?" Rodriguez whispered, his mouth working like a man stricken with an ague.

"Your toy blaster and the knife." She held out her hand, taking the derringer and slipping it in a pocket of her coat, feeling the cold metal of the dagger's hilt in her left palm. She beckoned the man closer, keeping the blaster under his chin to force his head back.

"Sec men? How many and where?"

"Three in the snug. Sleeping, two of 'em. Two at the front and one by the back gate. But the roads out of the ville swarm with 'em, mistress. Best give up now and take the judgment. Or be cut down as thou runnest."

Krysty nodded. The landlord could taste the scent of excitement on her skin, like a feral musk. The scarlet hair seemed to his terrified eyes to be moving gently around her shoulders, as if it had a life of its own. But that wasn't possible. Her closeness aroused him, and he could feel the tentative beginnings of an erection nudging at his breeches.

"Art thou breaking out? I'll help thee. I can show thee paths out of the ville. Secret. Nobody knows."

Krysty's preternaturally sharp hearing picked up the sound of steps moving cautiously down the creaking stairs from the high attic. Time was slipping by perilously fast. She took the knife and delicately placed the point an inch within Rodriguez's right nostril.

His head jerked back farther, neck sinews straining, trying to get away from the sharp steel. A tiny, frail worm of blood inched from his nose over the broad, sensuous lips.

"Please, please," he whispered. "Spare me, mistress. I had to do it. She'd have killed me."

It was time.

"So will I," Krysty said quietly.

She drove the long-bladed stiletto deep into the innkeeper's head, through the top of his nose, tearing the web of cartilage apart, the thin point sliding into the forepart of the brain. Krysty angled the knife, twisting her wrist to make the wound more devastatingly final.

The man's weight slid off his feet, almost tearing the dagger from her hand. The blade cut through the side of his nose as he fell to the floor, hands reaching up and clutching her knees. A dark patch of damp spread across his trousers as death loosed his bladder.

Blood frothed over his mouth and he struggled to speak. To her right, Krysty saw J.B. leading the others, pausing on the steps, watching the tableau of death and life.

"I never sold the ring my...mother gave me," Rodriguez mumbled. "She died thinking I had, but I never wanted. Wanted her..." He coughed and more blood came from the cavern of his throat. "Didn't want to rock...rock..."

"The boat," the girl completed, straightening and wiping the stiletto on the dead man's bright, shiny shirt.

CAPTAIN DEACON WAS in his fifties, a tall, straight-backed man with neatly trimmed white hair, framing a face of ruddy honesty and good humor. He liked smartness and insisted that his crew all wear scarlet sweaters and black pants while on board the *Phoenix*.

Everything had gone well, with supplies loaded and the water barrels filled on time. The entire crew was aboard and all were sober. The tide was filling, and within the half hour Captain Deacon was ready to give the order to cast off the shore lines and set sail for the whaling grounds of the Lantic.

The outlanders came ghosting up the gangplank, like creatures from a nightmare, armed to the teeth, with blasters that totally outgunned anything he had on his ship.

It was no contest.

KRYSTY HAD EXPLAINED it very simply and very quickly, so there wouldn't be any misunderstandings between them.

"Pyra Quadde's lifted a friend of mine. Two friends. You heard?"

"I heard. One-eyed outlander and the Indian harpooneer as scored ten from ten, casting the iron. Yeah, I heard about it. And I heard about ye five."

"We're taking you and your ship, and we're going after Ryan and Donfil. And we'll get them and chill the woman. You get the ship back after you bring us safe to land here."

"If I don't?" the skipper drawled.

J.B. shook his head and came close to half smiling. "I wasn't raised to waste time on people *pretending* to be stupid, Captain Deacon," he said. "You know what happens. Everyone knows."

Jak spelled it out for the listening crew. "Too few us to fuck 'round. We chill captain. Next man refuses, we chill him. Keep chilling until someone says 'Yeah.' Won't take long."

Doc stepped closer, his trusty Le Mat .36 in his gnarled fist, its scattergun barrel yawning like a war wag's exhaust. "I trust you will believe me, Captain Deacon, when I tell you that we truly wish you no harm at all. But our dear friend, Ryan, and the Apache wise man, have fallen into the hands of the wicked woman of the seven seas. We wish to rescue them and ensure that she does not live to stain the good name of womanhood for another day. If you assist us in this, then there will be no trouble and no man harmed. If you do not..." Doc shrugged his shoulders expressively.

"Can ye promise to chill the witch queen of the Lantic?"

"Yes," Krysty said.

"Sure an' certain? If I help ye and Pyra Quadde wins out, then I'm dead meat. I'll be walking around, but I'll be deader'n a sharkskin hat."

Krysty didn't dare to look back. It could only be a matter of minutes before someone found the corpses of Rodriguez and the two sec men. Then the hue and cry would begin, and it wouldn't take long for the hunt to lead to the docks.

It would be a bloody firefight.

J.B. was thinking the same. "You got ten seconds, Captain. Set sails and go after the woman now. Or I chill you. Now."

The captain sniffed, glancing at the sky. Stars peeked through the ragged curtain of cold, salt mist. "Never liked the bitch, anyways.

"Loose lines, Mr. Mate! Bow line and hold one stern line. Set t'gallants. Main sails when we reach the channel. Let go forward and aft on my command! Lively, now!"

So the whaling ship *Phoenix* moved slowly away from the quay of Claggartville, into the dark waters of the Lantic Ocean—hunting not her usual prey, but going after something far more deadly.

Krysty and the others took over the captain's quarters, making sure that they kept it secure with their blasters. But Deacon didn't seem concerned about the way they had hijacked his vessel, going about his business with a calm, unflustered efficiency.

And the crew took their lead from him.

The weather was kind, and Deacon knew from experience where Pyra Quadde was likely to have gone.

It wasn't many days out from port before they heard the shout from the lookout in the crow's nest, high above the deck. "Sail ho! Sail on the port beam! A ship!"

Chapter Twenty-Six

"CANST THOU MAKE HER?" Captain Quadde shouted, standing with legs spread against the pitching of the short westerly sea.

"No, ma'am. Dark hull. Can't make her ensign at this distance."

She bellowed him down, glancing around, her eyes falling on Ryan. Her face lightened, her smile showing the hideous false teeth, which were worse than any plas-dents he'd ever seen.

"Outlander Cawdor. Thou hast more seeing in thy one good glim than these offal with their brace. Take the spyglass and get aloft. Tell me what thou seest there."

Ryan slipped off his seaboots, taking the telescope with a muttered word of assent. The ship was rolling in the swell, with an uncomfortable, chopping motion. But he knew well enough what a refusal would mean. As he had no desire to be tied naked to the mast for the woman to use for her pleasure, he climbed as nimbly as he could into the spidery rigging. He drew a deep breath of relief as he reached the relative safety of the crosstrees, swinging across to the narrow barrel of the crow's nest.

"Quickly or I'll have thee flogged for it. What ship is she? What flag does she fly, outlander? I can't hear thee!"

The shout rose almost to a scream. Ryan had heard the crew say that other captains from the region took good care to steer well wide of Pyra Quadde. One or two that didn't had been found floating belly-down among the fish guts of Claggartville harbor. So another ship coming close to them meant something out of the ordinary.

He steadied the glass on the flag that fluttered from the masthead of the approaching ship, trying to make it out, fumbling with the brass focusing screw.

"Fireblast! Can't ... Ah, there it is."

From the earliest days, every ship out of New England had her own pennant, so that she could easily be recognized at a distance by any of her fellows. Even now, in the heart of the Deathlands, a hundred years after the skydark, the practice was maintained by everyone.

Even by Pyra Quadde.

Her flag cracked and snapped in the wind, only a few feet from Ryan's head.

It was a circle of crimson upon a rectangle of plain white. But as the wind tugged at the ensign it distorted the circle, elongating the bottom half, so that it sometimes resembled a bloody skull.

The oncoming vessel sported a flag of blue, with two horizontal white stripes on it. Ryan hallooed that information down to the woman on the deck, cupping his hands against the wind.

"Two slant whites on blue, thou sayest?" came the reply.

"Aye, ma'am."

"That be the *Bartleby* under Delano. Old Preaching Biddy hisself. Does she show any signal?"

Ryan could hardly hear the woman's words, but he leaned half out of the iron-hooped barrel and managed to catch them.

"No signal. But she's heading straight for us, ma'am."

Captain Quadde beckoned him back from the masthead, sending up another member of the crew to replace him as lookout. Ryan sat on the deck and gratefully pulled on his seaboots again. Though he had a good enough head for heights, the rolling crow's nest wasn't the best place in the world to be.

The whole of the crew came out to watch the approaching vessel. Ryan recalled again that such an encounter was very rare, particularly as most of the skippers along the New England coast knew Quadde's reputation and kept plenty of sea room between themselves and the ill-starred *Salvation*.

Slowly, tacking her way against the breeze, the *Bartleby* drew closer. As she did, the wind fell away to a mild zephyr, barely breathing enough air to enable the two whaling ships to maintain their forward momentum through the flattened waves.

Captain Quadde took her place at the port side of her ship. Ryan noticed that she had buckled on the Spanish Astra short-muzzle .44 and wondered whether she was anticipating trouble.

The ships would pass port side to port side. The crew of the *Bartleby* was also lined up along the rail, staring in silence at the *Salvation* and her crew. A short, skinny man in a bottle-green tailcoat stood alone near the stern. He had a mane of white hair that made him look like pictures of Old Testament prophets that Ryan had seen in some of the many Bibles that still survived in the Deathlands. It was an odd fact that around half of the books he'd ever seen in his life had been Bibles from before the long winters. Yet he'd never read anything to confirm that the old United States had been such a profoundly religious country.

"Captain Quadde!" the man hailed, using a battered tin megaphone.

"Good day to thee, Captain Delano. What bringest thee to my waters?"

"The waters are not thine, Captain Quadde, and it be blasphemous to claim them."

"When the Almighty comes sailing and whaling across these banks with a brace of big fish hauled tight to his flanks, then I shall allow him to share of *my* waters, Captain."

"Thou art...!" The man controlled himself with what was an obvious effort of will. The ships were still nearly a hundred paces apart, their courses meaning they'd pass within about ten feet of each other on their parallel ways.

"Make thy speech quickly, Preaching Biddy!" Quadde shouted, beaming at the ripple of laughter from her own crew.

"If I did not . . ." Delano began. "I will not quarrel with thee or damn thee, Pyra Quadde. The savior sees all, and he will judge at the ending of thy life. I seek thine aid."

The request sounded as though it had been torn from the man's soul with white-hot pincers.

"What aid, man? Wouldst thou know where the great whales sport? I slew one within the day, and he be the first of a bounteous harvest in rich lays for my lads here."

"I have hunted well. Too well," Delano replied. Now the ships were closer, the figureheads barely thirty yards apart.

"Then what . . . ?"

"Both my brothers are lost, Captain Quadde. Dearest to my heart."

"Lost? Both?"

"Aye." The man was on the verge of tears, and Ryan could see the whiteness of his knuckles gripping the carved rail.

"To lose one brother is unfortunate, Captain Delano. To lose both seems like foolishness."

"Thou flint-heart! One was tillerman and one the harpooneer in the lead whaleboat. They had struck a massive right whale, bonnet calked thick with barnacles. We had lost a sail from a broken halliard jammed in a block. A sudden fog came down, as it often does upon these waters. . . ."

Now the ships were fully alongside, the crews staring curiously at one another. Ryan found it odd that all these seamen came from the same ville, yet not a word was exchanged. Captain Delano was leaning out over the rail, hands reaching imploringly toward the impassive figure of Captain Quadde.

"And thou hast seen nothing since?"

"Nothing. But the whale was bearing this way. When the fogs..."

"I have seen nothing."

The words were cold and flat. Dismissive.

"The two of us, together... We could quarter the sea and find my brothers."

"We could, but we will not. I am here to hunt the whales. Not to scour the waves for dimwit orphans who know not their trade. Good day to thee, Captain Delano."

Now the sterns of the two vessels were level, the two skippers scant feet apart, gazing into each other's eyes.

"Turn and let us talk longer, Captain Quadde. I beg thee, in the name of thy savior."

"These are my waters, but he is not my savior, Preaching Biddy. Get to thy search."

"One day? But give up one day's hunt. I'll pay thee for thy time."

"Fare thee well!" Pyra Quadde shouted across the widening gap. She turned to her crew. "I can find work for any idle hand I see skylarking out here. Mr. Ogg! Set them to it."

"Aye, ma'am."

Ryan joined the others, scurrying away belowdecks to lend a hand at the noisome task of boiling down the chunks of blubber.

He heard the last, fading words of Captain Delano of the *Bartleby*, torn away by the wind.

"May thy stone soul sink thee to hell, Pyra Quadde. And may any man who sails with thee join thee in everlasting torment!"

The next time Ryan Cawdor came out on deck, the other ship was a tiny black speck, hull down, on the horizon.

For the next two days they pressed on, sailing deeper into the whaling grounds, but without a single sighting of their prey. And with each hour that passed, Pyra Quadde became more and more ill-tempered, with a curse and blow for any man who came within her reach.

"She's getting hungry again," Johnny Flynn whispered, mumbling through his toothless gums, as he and Ryan worked together on splicing a length of rope.

"Hungry for what?"

Jehu was also busy nearby and he heard the muttered conversation.

"Hungry for meat, shipmates. The meat that grows from the loins of a man. The meat that grows and shrinks and rises and falls. That's the fine red meat for our captain's tastes."

THE *BARTLEBY* WAS homeward bound, her voyage ended prematurely by the loss of Captain Delano's two brothers. Her search across the vastness had been a fruitless one, and she was headed back to Claggart-ville to mourn her dead. She passed by the *Phoenix*, close-hauled on a starboard reach, and the captains were able to pass on their hurried news.

Krysty and Jak stood by Captain Deacon, to make sure he resisted the temptation to reveal his plight. But he kept silent about his unwelcome quintet of passengers.

The men of the *Bartleby* gazed with naked curiosity at the white-haired boy and the fire-haired young woman. But there was no time for questions. Just the one vital question, answered by the wild-eyed Delano, shaking a fist toward the heavens.

"Less than a hundred leagues ahead. On the southern edge of the whaling banks. If ye seek her for some vengeance, go with my blessing. If to aid her, then may ye sink with my curse."

Then the whaler plunged astern of them, vanishing swiftly. Deacon turned to Krysty, tapping at his teeth with a forefinger. "Closing. The *Salvation* is not the swiftest vessel from the ville. With a good wind we can claw a couple of knots from her. More if Pyra Quadde is quartering the Lantic for the whales. Delano has seen few in a week or more. We could come within sight of her in another couple of days or less. Maybe less."

"Be good," J.B. said, joining them.

Deacon looked at the Armorer, unsmiling. "Yeah, mister. It'd be good. Good to see the backs of ye outland chillers, and get on with our job."

"When we get our friends safe, you won't see us for dust. Or for spray," Krysty replied.

Deacon, hands locked in the small of his back, walked away from them to the other side of the deck.

ANOTHER DAY on the *Salvation* without the sighting of a whale. Toward evening Captain Quadde beckoned Ryan to where she stood on the main deck.

"Figured I'd tell thee that I'm set on having thee, Outlander Cawdor. Soon. Settle the score 'twixt us. Well set-up man like thee." Her long tongue peeked out between the filed ivory teeth and licked her chapped lips. In an attractive woman it would have been a stimulating and coquettish gesture. In Pyra Quadde it was simply frightening. And disgusting.

That night, while the rest of the crew slept around them in the forecastle, Ryan told Donfil about the threat from Pyra Quadde.

Coiled uncomfortably in his too short bunk, the shaman asked him what he intended to do.

"Got no choice. I'll do a lot to stay alive. Trader used to say a man who died of pride was a fool. A corpse can't get any revenge. But her idea of fucking ends in death. We know that."

"You'll chill her first?"

In the rolling darkness, Ryan nodded. "Yeah. Guess so. If I can do it right. Then see if we can take out enough of the crew to win the ship. Not much of a hope, I guess."

"I got nothing better. Maybe we'll catch some whales tomorrow. Take her mind off...off other things."

"Yeah. Maybe."

Chapter Twenty-Seven

FOLLOWING A HUNTER'S instinct, Pyra Quadde set her course back toward land, moving northerly, hoping to pick up one of the mighty schools of whales that broached and sunned themselves off the deserted coves.

The sun shone brightly, and the last of the blubber was finally rendered in the ovens and stored in sealed barrels below the main deck. The whaleboats were cleaned, lowered and raised again, the men on the davits chanting an old whaling capstan song to lighten the chore.

Though the sun shone brilliantly, Ryan noticed that dark clouds were building up, far away ahead of them, thunderheads that rolled and bubbled, filled with venomous lightning, streaked with white splashes across the violet sky.

"Yeah," said one of the other sailors, when he mentioned it to him. "Over the land, that is. Wind rips it apart and pushes it our way. Could be bad from the height of them chem clouds."

"How come the sea's so flat?" Donfil asked.

It was true. The waves had flattened out and disappeared, and even the long ocean swell had almost gone. The ship sailed gently on, as if it were a child's toy, placed upon a painted, mirrored sea. The sails flapped idly on the yards and the helmsman spun the wheel, looking for a breath of a breeze to help them on their way.

Captain Quadde had a canvas chair brought out and placed on the quarterdeck, where she sat and watched her crew with a baleful eye. It was warm, and she'd changed out of her heavy sweaters.

Now she wore a white blouse, with torn, dirty lace at collar and cuffs. One sleeve was ripped from elbow to wrist. The material was thin, and it was possible to see that the woman wore nothing beneath it. The dark circles of her nipples pushed at the tight blouse.

Her skirt was cotton, pale blue, covered with food and drink stains down the front. It was too tight for her around the waist, and she'd tried to pin it shut. But it revealed a gap of rolling fat. Her wide belt carried the belaying pin on one side and the .44 on the other. Her legs and feet were bare, the toenails crooked and jagged.

She had a bottle of the usquebaugh at her side, as well as a chipped tankard of clouded glass. By late afternoon she was visibly, and audibly, drunk.

"No fugging whales in the whole fugging sea. She was only a fishmonger's daughter, but she knew how to lie on the fragging slab and say fill it! Fillet! Where's the pigging whales gone? Must be the outlander with his one fucking eye and all bad luck. Like whistling on deck. Brings lucking bad fuck, it does. Yeah, it does."

Around noon the lookout from the masthead had called down that he could see the top spars of another ship. Shadowing them, so he said. But he couldn't make out enough of the cut of the jib to be certain that it was still the *Bartleby*, searching for her missing children.

"Course it's them," Quadde shouted. "Preaching Biddy Delano! May his balls rot and his cock wither and his ass leak his brains all over his clean frogging decks."

Each change of lookout reported the same sight. Just on the edge of seeing, only the top spars visible, keeping her distance, beating in toward the stormy land at the same speed as the *Salvation*. Maybe just a knot or two faster.

"Don't keep telling me the same, or I'll have thee bunking 'stead of th'outlander."

So, after that, none of the crew mentioned to their captain that the whaling ship on the horizon was steadily creeping in closer. Cyrus Ogg ventured to mention to Second Mate Walsh that in his humble opinion the other vessel wasn't necessarily the *Bartleby* under Captain Delano. He certainly wasn't about to hazard his lay on whose ship it was. But the set of the mizzenmast reminded him very much of the *Phoenix*, Captain Deacon in command.

DUSK WAS BEGINNING to ease itself across the mirrored sea. The wind had just begun to freshen again, bringing the threat of the storm clouds even closer. Now, from the crow's nest, it was possible to make out a gray smudge away to the north, beneath the dancing daggers of the lightning.

"Shore, right enough," Johnny Flynn confirmed, sitting behind the tryworks, exercising the joints of his broken finger.

"How far off?" Ryan asked.

"Good many sea miles, yet, cully," the sailor replied.

"The chem storm looks closer."

Flynn spit over the side of the ship, nodding his agreement. "Aye, outlander, it is that. Me da's da spoke of the years after the long winters and the red fires. Said they had storms then as a man would die in. Off the sea it'd rain purest acid and strip the flesh off of thy bones faster than a pack of mutie sharks. Lightning spears so thick and fast a man couldn't hope to dodge 'em. But . . . we still get good blows now and again. Best beat away from 'em."

The wind was freshening, growing stronger with every minute that passed. Already the sea was patterned with lacy cat's-paws, and the sails were straining at the yards.

Pyra Quadde got up from her comfortable chair and vanished below, reappearing a minute later in her more familiar garb of seaboots, sweater and longer skirt. But the gun and the belaying pin were still at her belt.

"Be all hands to reef soon enough," Flynn muttered.

But the voice, cracking with excitement from the masthead, altered that.

"They blow! Three...five...a dozen or more! A great school of right whales."

"Where away?" the captain shouted, squinting aloft, as was most of the crew.

"Port bow, ma'am. Large a school as ever I seen! There!" An outstretched arm, like a hunting dog, pointed to the whales.

"Helm over!" she yelled to the helmsman in his shelter. "Mr. Ogg! Mr. Walsh! Boats' crews at the ready. Hands to the davits! We've struck lucky at last."

Ryan was one of the men nearest to Pyra Quadde. Cyrus Ogg was standing right by him, and he walked up to his captain. His face was worried, mouth working nervously as he peered out over the bow, toward the maelstrom of spray where the whales were broaching, visible now from the deck.

In the direction of the looming menace of the storm.

"Captain," he began.

"What is it, Mr. Mate?"

"There's a bad squall yonder."

"I see it."

"We lower and hunt, then the whaleboats will be in peril."

"Aye, Mr. Ogg. What of it?" Ryan noticed her right hand was creeping down to touch the shining wood of the heavy belaying pin. But her face was solid, betraying no emotion.

"Dost thou not think it a danger, Captain?"

"Aye. Our lives are danger, Cyrus Ogg. Who knows when infinity will strike us down and pluck us to the bosom of Abraham?"

"Truly. But I think it would be safer and better to haul off for three hours or so. The whales will not move far."

"Ah, *thou* dost think, dost thou? It would be safer *and* better! I think not."

The mate didn't move, balanced against the increased rocking of the ship, hands at his side, licking his lips. Jehu stood next to Ryan, and he began to patter a kind of a prayer beneath his breath.

"Save him, brave him, grave him. Shut up his mouth and seal his eyes and fill his mouth with oysters and tell him lies, lies, lies."

"Thou still dost stands to argue with me, Cyrus Ogg? Dost thou?"

"The storm will take the dories under."

"That storm?" She pointed with her left hand, ahead of the ship. The mate followed her finger, staring toward the silver-slashed murk.

And Pyra Quadde hit him.

The belaying pin was more than a foot long, tapering down from the thickness of a child's wrist, and was made of ironwood. She smashed the heavy end into Ogg's mouth, knocking him clean off his feet. There was the unmistakable sound of teeth splintering. Blood poured from the crushed lips, and the man rolled over, struggling to rise, spitting out shards of crimsoned bone, shaking his head like a steer under the poleax.

Captain Quadde stood and looked down at him. "Get blood on my boots, Mr. Ogg, and thou shalt lick it off. Go forrard and obey my orders. Now!"

The last word cracked like a bullwhip. With a great effort the first mate managed to stand, eyes glazed with shock. He tugged a dark blue kerchief from his pocket and stuffed it against his smashed mouth.

At that moment Second Mate Walsh came running aft, pausing as he saw the tableau. And the spreading pool of blood.

"What's been...?" he began, words faltering and dying.

"What's thy business, mister?" the captain growled, caressing the long, blunt club. She frowned down at it, then picked away a jagged piece of one of Ogg's front teeth from the tough wood.

"I was—"

"Thou hast not come to tell me that the sea is rough and the skies dark, or some other milksop toss-water whining, hast thou?"

"No. I was..." Words failed him and he stood, miserably, head down.

"Next man crosses me takes the place of Outlander Cawdor tonight," she said, grinning wolfishly at Ryan. "Think on that. Mr. Walsh, I think thou had come to tell me thy boat should be first into the water for the chase. Didst thou not?"

"No." He was shocked at her words.

"What?" She lifted the club to her shoulder, making the man step hurriedly away from her. "Wouldst thou kiss the bottom of this ship from side to side and stern to stern, Mr. Walsh?''

"No, ma'am. I mean that I wanted to get thee to allow my whaleboat to be first to the water."

She smiled at that, her little eyes glinting with a perverse pleasure at the range of her powers over the crew. "Then thou shalt. And Outlander Cawdor's place tonight to pleasure with me is still snug and safe."

The crew was sent to reef. Flynn explained to Ryan that the greatest danger to a sailer was to get caught by such a storm on a lee coast, trapped there without enough sea room to work her way clear. The sighting of the school of whales had been less than a half mile from the rocky shore, near the heart of the raging chem squall.

"I swear it will be a close-run thing," he said. "The clouds stoop and kiss the waves. They race upon us. It was always said that Pyra Quadde would chase a right whale into the very jaws of Satan himself. Now she will prove that. And take every man of the *Salvation* with her."

"Why not stop her?" Donfil suggested, blinking spray from his deep-set eyes.

Flynn grinned. "Why not place thy pagan head between the jaws of a great white and bid it to be gentle with thee?"

The lookout reported that the great school of whales had vanished in the shifting murk of the chem storm, but that news did nothing to check the woman in her wild lust to hunt and to butcher. Whatever the cost.

Groping claws of blackness stretched clear across the sky, with a few shreds of vivid cobalt-blue trapped and shrinking between them.

"Man the davits. Mr. Walsh to lower away first!" the captain yelled, her voice fading under the eldritch cry of the storm.

Ryan stood, hands on the ropes, ready to begin the launching of the whaleboat. Each wave snarled higher, white-topped. He glanced around, but his horizon was limited by the waves of the raging ocean, a gray-green, obliterating the land, hiding the tumbling whales ahead of them, hiding the masts of the ship that had been shadowing them. That ship had been completely forgotten in the thrill of the gale and the excitement of the chase to come.

Ogg—kerchief still held to his bleeding mouth—was at Ryan's side, ready to give the orders. Walsh, face pale as a winding-sheet, was already at the tiller, his crew climbing slowly and fearfully to their places.

"I fear it will mean good sailors going to a chilling," Ogg said very quietly.

The wind tore at Ryan's clothes, and the salt spray soaked him clear to the skin. The ocean boiled with the fury of the storm. Yet so great was the fear of Pyra Quadde, that not a single man raised a voice against her orders to launch the frail whaleboat into the howling inferno.

"We'll be on the lee shore in minutes at this rate," Flynn screamed, mouth inches from Ryan's ears.

Ryan had rarely seen such a ferocious chem storm. Up in the Darks there were winds that would tear through the steep valleys and rip the land away from the bedrock. Some of the hot spots in the West and Southwest of the Deathlands were the birthing places for dreadful hurricanes, whipping up nuke-fire from the missile pits, bringing the bone-sick death to anyone unlucky enough to be caught out in them. He'd been locked safe in a massive war wag and felt it rock and vibrate with the force of winds, had found its painted metal wiped clear by the shredding sands.

But he'd never faced such a storm with only a single layer of fragile wood between him and a plunging death.

"Lower!" Pyra Quadde yelled.

THE *PHOENIX* HAD LAID off from the shore, avoiding the worst of the storm. But even on the fringes it was a terrifying experience. Jak was hanging onto the shrouds, throwing up over the side. His other hand clutched the butt of his heavy Magnum pistol.

Captain Deacon had taken the wheel himself, with Doc standing in the steering cabin with him. There were two lookouts in the crosstrees, lashed there for safety, and two extra men in the eyes of the ship, peering through the murk.

"She is crazed," the skipper said, teeth gritted. "They say she goes after the school of whales we sighted. They were within a league or less of the rocks, and she goes grinning to perdition. I fear thy friends are likely doomed, Dr. Tanner."

The old man clung to the rail around the shelter, as though his life and his reason depended upon it. His voice was cracked and low. "And the second of the angels poured out his vial upon the sea, and it became as the blood of a dead man. And every living soul died in the sea."

"Book of the Revelations, Doctor. Know it right well."

"It spoke truly of the day of judgement," Doc said. "Day of sky dark and long winter. The Good Book talks about that. A mighty earthquake and the sun became as black as sackcloth of hair and the moon became blood. The stars of heaven fell to earth. The great men, the captains, the kings, the rich, the successful, the military, the powerful and the poor...all of them departed. That was a great cleansing, Captain Deacon. A great cleansing."

The whaling skipper said nothing, concentrating on holding his course, keeping sea room. Away from the eye of the storm where he knew the *Salvation* had vanished.

THE ROPE STRAINED in the blocks as the crew lowered the first of the whaleboats to the sea. Normally each crew would lower for itself, but the water was far too rough for that. Long before they actually reached the end of the rope, the tops of the waves were snarling around the flanks of the dory.

"Faster, ye cockless scum!" Pyra Quadde yelled.

The davits squeaked as the boat was dropped in a rush. The moment it splashed down, it was swamped by a huge wave, tearing it from the mother ship, snapping the retaining ropes like thin cotton. Every man aboard was immediately tipped out into the turbulent ocean.

Walsh and one other member of the boat's crew were saved. The rest vanished utterly into the raging waves and were never seen again.

The *Salvation* was less than two hundred paces from the surf pounding on the jagged boulders of the shore.

Chapter Twenty-Eight

THE SHIP WAS HIT HARD by the chem squall, suffering damage to both foremast and mizzenmast, as well as to much of her canvas and rigging. Planks had been started around the bow where she'd plowed into the butting rollers, and fifteen feet of rail had been torn away. It was a grudging tribute to Pyra Quadde that the ship didn't founder, or carry upon the rocks of the bleak shore.

As it was, it took all of her skill, culminating in her bludgeoning the helmsman to the deck with her belaying pin and taking the wheel herself, battling the head of the ship around, toward open water. None of the crew stayed below; they huddled together behind the tryworks, while the waves broke over them.

Ryan had made his plans. Though he thought death was nearly inevitable, he would never lie back and give in to the dark-masked creature with the glittering scythe. He had found some rope and decided to bind himself to any drifting wood, when the vessel eventually shuddered upon the headland that loomed over them.

The noise of the waves on the shore was deafening, the banshee wail of ten thousand drowned sailors.

Captain Quadde laid out a trailing anchor to keep the bow of the ship turned toward the wind, running under bare spars.

Chem storms obey no natural order. They can come howling from a clear sky; they can vanish as swiftly as a traitor's smile.

A scant hour after five men had gulped their last desperate breaths, the waves flattened and the clouds scudded away to the northeast. For a few brief minutes the day brightened, the sun managing to break through. But its light was sullen, like fouled brass, and it gave little warmth to the soaked seamen.

In less than an hour, the fog appeared.

Pyra Quadde hadn't had time to get a thorough damage report from the first mate. The sea anchor still trailed out, line limp, across the expanse of painted ocean. Tatters of canvas hung from the spars, and the splintered wood of damaged bulwarks was unmoved. Whatever happened, the *Salvation* wasn't in any fit shape to hunt whales for several hours.

And by then it would be night.

"Mist off the shore, Captain!" shouted mad Jehu, who was the lookout. "Land's vanished clear away. Coming out from east and west, like the horns of a bull, Captain."

She waved a hand to acknowledge the weather warning, calling back to ask if he could see any sign of the whales.

"Gone to the bosom of the deep, where they be hunted by bold Olaf, Sammy, Diego and George. Eyes rotted, finger bones holding the oars, they pitch and toss in the canyons of the deepest waters. Irons fast in the spirit whales. Their lay a seat in paradise, Captain!''

"Shut thy noise, madman!"

"They smell land where there be none. Taste blood where there be none. See light where there be none. Breathe in the good air…where there be…where there be none!''

"No more, thou double-crazy stupe bastard, or I'll puddle thy brains on the deck.''

"Shall I not tell thee of the ship I spy a'sailing by on Chrissimus Day in the morning? Shall I not tell thee, ma'am?''

"Rot thy blabbering lips, Jehu! I know of that sainted imbecile Delano and his endless quest for his fucking brothers. Less of the Delano! Let them sail the seas for eternity and a day for all I care.''

Only a few miles away from the *Salvation*, J.B. Dix perched uncomfortably in the crosstrees of the *Phoenix*, binoculars steadied on the distant whaler, noting the obvious signs of storm damage to her masts, spars and sails. Noting, too, the fog that was creeping silently across the water from the visible shore.

"DROP ANCHOR. What's the deep here?''

Johnny Flynn took the loop of line, marked at intervals with knots of colored canvas and cord, to mark off the readings. He steadied himself on the protruding cathead, just to starboard of the bowsprit, and swung the lead in a humming circle, dropping it forty yards ahead of the stationary ship. He called out the readings as the line slipped through his fingers. "No bottom at ten fathoms, ma'am! None at twenty. And five. Thirty and five. No bottom at forty fathoms."

"Haul in the sea anchor, Mr. Ogg. Work her in and keep Flynn on the lead. Drop anchor when it reaches twenty fathoms. In this triple-shit fog we must take care not to run her aground. The Seven Virgins guard one of the bays near here. They'd tear the keel out of the ship before a lookout could see his hand in front of his face."

"Aye, aye, ma'am."

"Is Walsh dried out? Then I want him on his duty. No skulkers on this ship."

Cyrus Ogg knuckled his forehead and walked off, passing Ryan.

"Let's go below," Donfil suggested.

"Storm not put your mind off the idea of becoming an ironsman, brother?" Ryan grinned.

"No. We float safe. It was only her madness that drowned those poor dogs. There is a risk, but there is always a risk, brother. For them it was a good day to die."

"Not for you?"

"Who knows?"

Flynn joined them on the deck, near the top of the companionway that led down into their quarters.

"Pyra's fit to piss steam, friends. Keep well clear of her in this mood. It bodes ill for some poor devil that she—"

The voice interrupted him.

"This has been the worst of days, Outlander Cawdor. Truly the worst. I have lost time. Lost a school of whales. Lost one of my boats that will cost more jack than I can spare." She hesitated. "And five men gone to the long swimming on a single day. Now the *Salvation* is damaged. She will take time to put to rights." The voice continued calm, but she was inching closer to Ryan, her boots shuffling along the scrubbed deck toward him. Her eyes glittered and her tongue danced out to moisten her lips. The woman's hand tightened and loosened convulsively on the belaying pin, whitening the skin at her knuckles. Her other hand hovered by the butt of the Astra pistol.

"Permission to go below, ma'am?" Johnny Flynn asked, trying to break the woman's mood.

"Go, double-stupe. Go on, thou toothless piece of hulk meat."

"Come on, outlander," the little man urged, tugging at Ryan's wet sleeve.

"I said thou couldst go, Flynn. *Not* the outlander."

"Leave it lie, Johnny," Ryan said quietly. He sensed that the woman's mood was on the far edge of sanity and wanted to avoid pushing her to the last, crumbling step.

"Aye, sailor," Quadde agreed. "This bad, bad day can yet be saved. This cursed fog that blinds us about means no hunting until the morrow. Every man has work to do, readying us for the Lantic once more. But I can rest this night. Rest and take myself some pleasure."

The last word was hissed between clenched teeth, stretched out, finally fading into a frighteningly gentle stillness.

"But . . ." Flynn persisted.

"Leave it," Ryan warned. "No point."

"No point," the woman repeated, slowly drawing the .44 and leveling it at Johnny Flynn's chest. "No point. Thou dost get the point, Flynn. Outlander here gets the point. *I'll* get the point. And plenty more. Come here, right close, Cawdor. Hear what I plan for thee. And if thou playest thy part as a man . . . aye, manfully. Thou *might* live."

Ryan had lived long enough on the razor cut of violence to know what that meant. Whatever happened, Pyra Quadde was going to have him chilled. During the night. Either during or after she'd compelled him to ease her savage temper.

He moved in closer, wondering whether to chop her across the throat now and break her neck. The fog had come around them so thick that he could hardly see from one side of the deck to the other. Very faintly he could hear the sound of surf on rocks, which meant that the shore wasn't that far off.

Ryan wasn't the strongest swimmer in the Deathlands, but he reckoned he could hold his own with most men. The sea was velvet flat. The only threat was the creatures in the water. Compared with Pyra Quadde, they were probably kinder.

Now he could smell her sweat. She was breathing faster, her oilskin jacket thrown open to show the cotton shirt.

"Let me tell thee what we shall do, Outlander Cawdor," she whispered.

Using techniques taught to him by Krysty Wroth, he tried to blank out his hearing and his mind, so that the sweet, bubbling threnody of obscenities dribbled by him.

It worked.

Partly worked.

But it didn't shut out the fingers that crabbed at the front of his breeches, spidering inside and reaching him, fondling him as she breathed her sick desires to him. The muzzle of the Astra was pressed like a small, cold mouth against the side of his neck, holding him still.

Eternities gathered on his brain, layering it in dust. Eventually the voice stopped, and he blinked himself awake.

She laughed throatily. "I know what thou thinkest, outlander. But thy body dost betray thee, does it not?" The muzzle of the blaster was removed from his throat. Without meeting her glance, Ryan reached down and zipped up his pants.

"Leave him be, you bitch!"

Johnny Flynn lost control, pushing Ryan aside to face Pyra Quadde, his fingers knotted into angry fists.

"Fool," she said calmly, clubbing him across the side of the head with her pistol. She dragged him to her by the hair and crushed her knee into his groin, sending him to his knees. She gave him a coldly savage beating, never hitting him hard enough to bring the relief of unconsciousness.

Knowing that a move would bring a .44 slug in the guts, Ryan stepped away, breathing long and slow to keep his own self-control. He knew that if he was going to plunge into the ocean and swim for his life, he would first butcher this bloody-eyed slut.

Flynn swayed from side to side, hands clamped between his thighs. Crimson threads trickled from both ears, masking his face from a dozen swollen cuts. Quadde stepped back a moment to admire her handiwork, measuring the distance. Then she swung her muscular leg in a sweeping arc and cracked open Flynn's nose. More blood gushed out, over his shirt and pants, spilling across the deck. Two more casual backhand swipes with the heavy pistol closed one eye and opened a deep cut at a corner of his mouth.

"There, Flynn," she panted. "A lesson well given and well learned." She raised her voice. "Mr. Ogg? Be thou there?"

"Aye, ma'am."

"This seaman has fouled the clean decks of the *Salvation*. Have him clean it. I'll be back within the half hour. If I spy a stain on the planking, then I'll have him flogged to death."

"Aye, ma'am." Ogg's voice was gray and gentle, lacking any emotion.

She turned to face Ryan again, half smiling. "I am well in the mood for thee, Outlander Cawdor. Report to my cabin immediately after the evening meal. Do not be late."

She stomped off, leaning on her stick, its tapping vanishing with her into the swirls of fog. Behind her, the tableau remained unchanged: Flynn, sobbing quietly, snuffling blood through his crushed nose and mouth; Ogg, silent, looking out into the wall of mist.

And Ryan Cawdor, busy with his thoughts.

Chapter Twenty-Nine

THE *SALVATION* SAT quietly, enveloped in the fog. It cut her off from the world beyond, shrouding her from the sea and the sky. Water dripped in heavy lumps off the canvas and spars. Apart from the work of repairing the storm damage, the hands had been set to lowering two of the remaining whaleboats, leaving them sitting quietly on the flat sea. Donfil told Ryan that he'd heard Walsh say that the great whales sometimes came to the surface in such a fog and could be easily harpooned if a ship had her boats ready.

Once the word spread that Pyra Quadde had picked Ryan Cawdor as her victim, he became an invisible man. Nobody spoke to him. The silence screamed out that he was a dead man. Walking, but dead.

Johnny Flynn washed down the deck, clearing the blood off the white wood before the captain came back to inspect it. He refused Ryan's offer of help with a mute shake of the head, and went below to wash the crusted blood from his bruised face. One eye was completely closed, his nose and one cheekbone obviously broken. He was also concussed.

Ryan and Donfil talked together with a great intensity. The Apache felt that Quadde would use other crew members to enforce Ryan's compliance in her sexually perverse lusts, that they should kill the woman now and make for the shore.

Though the fog would give them an excellent chance of slipping over the side, it also raised an insurmountable problem—it *hid* the shore. The shaman had tried to find out from the crew how far away they were and what kind of landing they might have. Opinions ranged from one mile to three, and from sheer cliffs to a sloping beach. The only interesting thing Donfil had learned was that they had sailed along the coast until they were roughly in the area where the redoubt had been. In their quest for the whales they had quartered the ocean, coming in closer to land.

"I could swim a mile if it stayed calm and there weren't any currents. Just about, I reckon. You?"

The Apache shook his head. "I can taste the earth. I think it may be closer than a mile. But even so...it would be beyond me. Better stay here for me."

Ryan nodded. "I see that. The way I see it the bitch would prefer me more willing. If she has me tied or a blaster at my neck—or anywhere else—she can't enjoy the funning so much. I'll go, reluctantly. But I'll go. Then I'll wait till we're alone and throttle the slut. And be in the water."

Donfil sighed. "Doesn't sound too great a plan to me. Too many maybes and ifs to it."

Ryan managed a grin. "Yeah, my brother. But it's the best damned plan I got."

DOC HAD BEEN SINGING a half-remembered whaling song. "An uncle of mine sailed from Nantucket. I was married the year Herman Melville passed away. Eighteen ninety-one, as I recall. He wrote a book about whaling that—"

"Called *Moby Dick*. Know it. Read it."

"I had a niece, Catherine, born on his birthday. Melville's, that is. The first day of August, I recall it well."

Deacon ignored him, concentrating on allowing the *Phoenix* to creep slowly forward through the banks of fog. He'd managed to take a bearing on the maintop of the *Salvation* before the weather closed right in. Now he was inching along on blind navigation, closing in on Pyra Quadde's vessel. Seeing that his conversation didn't interest the captain, Doc returned to his singing.

It's advertised in Claggartville, Missouri, Ohio,
A thousand brave young sailors, a'whaling for to go.
Singing, blow ye winds of darkness,
Blow ye winds hi-ho,
Sharpen up your laces now and blow, boys, blow.

The mist was darkening as evening crept over the quiet ocean. A very long way off both men heard the mournful belling of a school of whales, eerie in the isolation.

"Best tell the men to keep quiet," Deacon suggested. "Wouldn't want little Pyra knowing we were crawly-creeping up on her like this. She might lose her calm, and then ye can watch for squalls. Aye, Dr. Tanner. When Pyra Quadde finds fault with life, then it's time to up anchor and run for the shelter of a safe harbor. Believe me.''

''I believe you.''

''GO OVER THE SIDE, matey.''

Ryan had walked alone into the bow of the whaler, leaning on the rail, feeling its cold slickness under his hands. He looked down into the water, which was barely visible in the mist. The voice behind him made him start.

''Slay her quick, cully.''

The mumbling, toothless voice could only be that of Johnny Flynn, who was lurking behind the windlass, invisible in the clinging fog.

''Thanks for trying to help,'' Ryan said quietly. ''Appreciated it. Sorry you got yourself—''

''Not the first time.''

''Over the side or chill the bitch? You're giving me two bits of advice, Johnny. Which would you take, if you were me?''

''Can't swim, matey. Hardly a man on the *Salvation* has that skill.''

Despite the peril of his situation, Ryan was intrigued at this piece of news. ''Sailors and you can't swim! How can...?''

The voice was slurred, indistinct. ''Thou goest over into the Lantic...'less thou dost get a rope thrown to thee as she goes on by, then by the time the ship's turned around thou hast been in the water for an hour. Likely more. Chance of finding a fingernail in a ton of manure's better than getting thyself picked up. So the cold or the sharks get thee. And it's better that thou dost go down fast and stay down. Less pain, outlander. I can't take that much more of the paining.''

"So you'd chill Pyra Quadde?''

"No."

"Why not? You told me that I should—''

"Thou still knowest her not. She's faster and stronger than nearly any man on board. Harder. More cruel. Ruthless and all. She'd kill me.''

Ryan grinned into the mist. "Likely she'll kill me, Johnny.''

The answer was a long while coming. "Yeah. Likely she will, outlander. But if thou dost want a chance, thou must to strike quick and straight. Like a snake. Or else.''

"Or else?''

"Or she'll draw the blaster. Cuff thee in chains to her bed. Frame's cold iron, bolted to the bulkheads and deck. Once that's happened, thou art deader than salt pig.''

"I get it. Hadn't figured she'd ... I'll think on it, Johnny Flynn. Sharks or the bitch? Fine choice.''

But there was no answer. And when he turned on his heel and walked aft along the deck, the space behind the windlass was filled only with the suffocating wall of fog.

"TOO THICK.''

"Too thick," J.B. repeated.

"Aye. I can no longer hazard my vessel and my men."

"You know we aren't in danger from the shore. You told us. There's no more land out there for a thousand miles."

"There's Pyra Quadde," the captain said stubbornly.

"Captain," Jak interrupted, coming into the cabin to join the others. "We come out sea to catch her. No other reason. Must be close. No?"

"Yeah, sure. But all thou hast said is that we get to her and tie alongside. Ye will take those cannons ye got and blast the living savior out of anything and anybody that gets in your way. Simple as that? Have I got it right?"

The Armorer nodded. "Sure did, Captain. All you got to do is put a man way out on the pointed thing at the front. Bowsprit, would it be called?" Deacon sucked at his teeth and said nothing. J.B. continued. "Out there. Sharpest man you . . . wait. Krysty, think you can do it?"

She shook her head. "Don't know. This fog distorts so much. But if we keep death-quiet, we gotta hear them before they hear us. Can have a half dozen men relaying the bearing and distance back to Captain Deacon here at the stern. How's that sound?"

Deacon's expression didn't change. Finally he held out his hand to the girl, who shook it with a smile that brightened the poorly lit cabin. "I'll do it, little lady. Truth is, when thou shanghaied the *Phoenix* and held

a blaster to my head...well, darnation! I could have
seen thee all over the side and I'd have been smiling as
I sailed on. Now...? Now's different. I'll help thee.
We'll do as thou sayest. Thou hast mutie hearing,
lady?''

"Sort of. And I can 'see,' you know. Like a doomie
but not as clear."

The skipper looked at the flame-haired young
woman. "What dost thou *see* of thy friends on the
Salvation?''

Krysty closed her eyes. "Nothing plain. I think the
fog's clouding everything down. And it feels like
Ryan's in danger, but he's got choices that confuse
things.''

"So. All of ye wish us to go on in now? Not wait?''

Dix looked the silver-haired man in the eyes. "We
go in. Soon as we get to her, we go alongside and hit
her hard. Maybe try and hole her with the blasters.
They won't fight so hard if their ship's going down
under 'em.''

Deacon laughed. "I thank the Lord that I am on
your side. Who has need of any enemies when friends
include ye five?''

THEY CAME FOR RYAN.

Four members of the crew escorted Donfil away,
keeping him under guard. "Captain wouldn't want
thee harmed, Outlander Ten-from-Ten," Cyrus Ogg
told him, hefting a well-preserved Webley revolver.

Ryan's foursome were Second Mate Walsh, Jehu, a pockmarked seaman named Brandt and Johnny Flynn.

Walsh was armed with a rusting Glock 9 mm pistol, while Brandt held a sawed-off scattergun, bracing himself against it as though he were terrified the weapon would go off without warning. The other two men wielded belaying pins. Johnny Flynn caught Ryan's eye and shrugged his shoulders helplessly, struggling to convey the message through body language that this was none of his choosing.

Ryan hadn't expected such a heavily armed escort to Pyra Quadde's bed of sexual delights.

The fog seemed even thicker, the vessel blanketed in a damp silence. There wasn't a breath of wind to tug at the bellying canvas, not a ripple on the gray glass of the Lantic.

Brandt led the way along the deck, shuffling sideways, stumbling over ringbolts and coiled rope. Walsh snarled at him. "Keep thy finger off that nuke-withered trigger, thou triple-fish-gutter! One fall and thou would blast us all to red spray and bone."

The mate was behind Ryan, with Jehu and Flynn bringing up the rear. The crazie was smiling, his grin filling his tiny face, and as they walked aft he kept up a ceaseless chatter of nonsense.

"Cheese and water and bread and wine and chalk. Sacrament for us all. Drink at the fount of youth and life and death. Bury thy hands in blood to the wrists. Enter the temple of the ear of corn and allow that dominion of death shall be short, short, short."

Ryan said nothing, concentrating on readying himself for what was to come. The shotgun had been an unpleasant surprise. If he made a move to go over the side now, the nervous seaman would probably blow him in two.

"Here," Walsh said, knocking on the door of the cabin. The five men were crowded together in the narrow corridor at the bottom of the short flight of steps down from the quarterdeck.

"Bring him in," the woman barked, and the second mate turned the brass handle and opened the heavy door.

Pyra Quadde was lying on her double-size bunk. She'd washed and curled her hair, which was coiled tight around her angular skull. Her face was heavily made up, with eyes ringed in mascara and lips slashed scarlet.

Her dress was amazing.

Occasionally, in parts of the Deathlands, you might find an old magazine from before the bright heat. Ryan had seen dozens in his time, and some of them had carried features on what the well-dressed lady of the town should wear for an evening's entertainment.

Captain Quadde's dress seemed to date from that era. It was strapless, cut low at the front, allowing most of her breasts to surge upward. Then it tapered to the waist and flounced out again until it reached her feet in a tumble of material. It was covered in glittery, shimmery patches of sequin and diamanté. There were layers of different colors, one over the other, giving an impression of a great richness of texture. Green predominated, with fiery orange and red, covering deeper tones of blue and purple. Lace and chiffon puffed its way to the surface of the dress in several places.

Yet, despite the ornate finery and elegance of the dress, Ryan's overwhelming impression was of decay. He could almost taste the dry flavor of the tomb and the winding-cloth about the rotting splendor of Pyra Quadde's gown. It was as though she'd risen from some underground catafalque, burst open the bronze doors of an ancient sarcophagus.

"Come in, outlander. I've been waiting for thee." The room carried the heavy smell of homebrew usquebaugh.

On the table near the bed was an assortment of Pyra Quadde's toys: three whips of varying length, one with tips made from tiny steel nails; an open razor, its edge dulled with old, dried blood; a broad-bladed cleaver and a slim dagger; several coils of silken cord, one with knots all along its length; a mask of supple leather, with what looked like an inflatable phallus-shaped gag attached. A dirty hypodermic needle rested in a stained metal kidney-dish over a small spirit lamp.

"What dost thou want us to do with him, ma'am?" Walsh asked.

"Strip and cuff him, o'course. Didn't think thou wouldst need telling, Mr. Walsh."

Ryan saw then that the bed had a frame of solid iron, painted black, with several sturdy metal rings set into it at both top and bottom. Once a man was chained there, his life would be done.

"No!" Johnny Flynn shouted, backing up against the door of the cabin.

"How's this, madman?" The captain stood up slowly.

"No. This must stop. Thou dost bring this on thyself by thy..." His voice trembled into stillness, but the pistol in his hand remained steady.

Ryan recognized it as a Polish blaster from the middle of the twentieth century. Called a Duo, it was a pocket-sized 6.35 mm handgun. Not of much use above twenty paces, but sufficient in a small, cribbed room.

"Thought I heard a rat sneaking around the ship's gun chest an hour or so back," the woman said gently. "And it was little Johnny, all along."

"Let him be," Flynn said. "Come, outlander. Move cautious, and we'll go over the side. The boats are in the water, ready. Two men can manage 'em. Pull for the shore, eh? Never find us in the fog out yonder. Come on."

Something was wrong. Ryan's fighting sense told him that. Brandt and Walsh were both scared of the blaster. Jehu didn't seem as if he'd even noticed it. But Pyra Quadde acted as though it weren't even there. She was either mad or...

The woman picked up her own blaster from the bureau under the stern window, keeping it pointed at the deck.

"I'll chill thee..." Flynn shrilled, leveling the Duo at her face.

"Not with an empty blaster, cully." She smiled. "Try it." She walked toward him, lifting her own, much larger pistol.

Ryan hissed between his teeth. That was it! She'd known all along there was no danger. The trigger snapped, the action of the blaster clicking, the noise thin and feeble. Flynn tried again. And again.

"Open thy mouth, cully," Quadde ordered, standing right against the quivering man. "Open it now."

The cut-down twin muzzle of the scattergun pressed hard into Ryan's back, keeping him very still.

Flynn turned his eyes to Ryan, tears gathering in the swollen corners, trickling down his stubbled cheeks. The useless, empty blaster was still in his hand.

"I'm sorry, Johnny. Real sorry. Thanks for trying."

"Yeah," the captain said, ramming the short barrel of the handgun between Flynn's toothless gums, making him gag. "Yeah, thanks from me, too. Been meaning to rid the ship of thee for some time, cully. And this'll give me a special taste for the main course of my meal, will it not?"

"SHE'S THERE," came the word, carried in whispers along the deck of the *Phoenix*.

J.B. had relayed his orders to Deacon and his redsweatered crew.

"Our fight, not yours. Lay alongside and hold there. That's all. We'll go in. We want the woman and to free our friends. But I guess it'll mean breaking a few heads. If all goes well, she'll be ours within fifteen minutes." He turned to Deacon. "Got your word not to cut free and run?"

"Thou hast my word."

"Then let's do it. Jak. You and Krysty with me to the stern. The back. Find the woman. Watch out for Donfil and Ryan. Lori and Doc, take the front. Chill anyone who even looks like resisting. Let's get to it now."

Deacon had persuaded him not to try to hole the *Salvation*, pointing out there was little point in scuttling such a valuable vessel.

Now, the five champions stole out onto the damp deck, blasters cocked and ready, seeing for the first time the spectral masts of their prey, only feet away from them.

In the enveloping stillness they all heard the sudden, unmistakable noise of a blaster, the explosion oddly muffled.

Chapter Thirty

A LARGE CHUNK OF BONE was raised from the crown of Johnny Flynn's skull, as a gentleman would lift his hat to a lady.

A brief eruption of blood and brains came puffing out through the crack, leaking down across the forehead and the pale skin of the seaman's face. The force of the .44 slug punched Flynn's head against the paneling with a solid thumping noise. The actual sound of the Astra firing was muffled by the barrel's being jammed inside the wretch's open mouth. But it was still sufficiently loud to be heard throughout the length of the ship.

Pyra Quadde held Johnny upright, gripped by the throat, as his heels drummed against the cabin door. The Duo dropped from the dead man's fingers, rattling on the floor. Smiling broadly, she removed the pistol from Flynn's mouth, tugging it from where he'd clamped his jaws on it in a dying spasm of pain and shock.

As she released him, the corpse clattered to the deck, twitching. She pushed at it with her foot, her smile now directed at Ryan.

"We'll have this removed and tossed over the side,
I think. Unless we leave it here to spice our pleasure.
What thinkest thou, Outlander Cawdor?"

Ryan thought that the pressure of the shotgun had
eased a little. But still not enough for him to make the
play that his life would totally depend on.

The *Salvation* shuddered gently, as if some great
undersea creature had scraped itself beneath her keel.
The captain turned immediately, sensitive to every
shift and movement of her beloved vessel.

"What was . . . ?" she began.

Now they could hear feet pattering on the deck—the
heels of combat boots—shouts and the unmistakable
chattering sound of an Uzi submachine gun.

The captain swung around to face Ryan, her ornate
finery rustling. Her heavy features were convulsed
with an almost insensate anger, and a worm of spittle
inched down her chin. "By all the gods!" she spit.
"Thou bastard . . . bastard! We are done!"

Walsh was heading for the door, but his boots
slipped in the spreading puddle of Johnny Flynn's
blood, sending him careening sideways. He clutched
at the arm of Brandt, who held the scattergun, finger
on the slim trigger.

The jolting shock was all that it took. The sawed-off
blaster boomed, both barrels firing in a single convulsive explosion.

Brandt had been half turning, eager to get out of the
confines of the cabin and onto the deck. Walsh had
been less than a foot away from him. At that range,
the double shock of the 10-gauge lifted him clear off

his feet and threw him across the cabin, where he knocked into Quadde, sending her tumbling backward. Her pistol rattled into the corner beneath the long stern window. The second mate thrashed on the floor, his blood and guts adding to Flynn's. The entrance hole in Walsh's stomach was smaller than the fist of a woman, but the buckshot had ripped him apart, the exit wound large enough to hold an iron bucket. Fragments of splintered bone were embedded in the far wall, along with the clotted pellets of distorted lead.

Brandt staggered, holding the empty, smoking blaster, his face slack with shock. Jehu had fallen to his knees in the slippery scarlet lake, still gripping the belaying pin. Ryan could see no sign of Walsh's battered Glock. The floor was so deep in blood and intestines that the blaster could have fallen anywhere.

Above his head, he could hear yelling and more blasters going off. He hadn't the least doubt that a rescue party had emerged from out of the fog.

Pyra Quadde was struggling to rise, reaching for her gun. Brandt was between Ryan and the door, and Jehu was weeping loudly, seemingly out of it.

Ryan tried for the razor with his left hand, missing at first grab. Brandt punched him across the top of the leg, numbing the muscle, then grappled with him. Ryan's right hand, flat on the cluttered tabletop, brushed against the hypodermic syringe. He grabbed it in desperation, driving it without a moment's hesitation into the man's right eye.

Brandt screamed and let go of him, putting a hand to his own blinded eye. It gave Ryan the chance to pick up the open razor and slash it against the sailor's exposed throat.

A crimson mouth gaped open, revealing the whiteness of bone in its maw. Brandt tried to scream, choking in his own frothing blood. He fell away from Ryan, onto the bed, patterning the pale sheets with gouts of arterial red.

"Basssstard!" the woman hissed, still unable to get up, her dress now sodden with blood. For a moment her fingertips had the butt of the Astra, then it slithered away from her.

Without a way of getting his hands on another weapon, Ryan decided to join his friends on deck.

Jehu had other ideas.

"Outlanders must all perish!" he screeched, shuffling on his knees to block off Ryan's exit.

"Fireblast!" Ryan swore, still holding the blood-slick razor in his right hand, aware that the captain might snatch up her fallen blaster at any moment.

"Repent, repent," the madman moaned, his little round mouth working and twitching, his hands clawing toward the outlander.

"Get out of the bastard way!" Ryan snarled, raising the honed steel.

"Nay, for I know the world, and the world..."

In midsentence Jehu grabbed suddenly at the razor, nearly catching Ryan off guard. The crazie's fingers actually grasped the single-edged steel. Ryan, holding the handle, jerked it back with even greater violence.

Out of the corner of his eye he saw Pyra Quadde finally grasp her blaster, fumbling with hands made slippery by blood.

Jehu screamed like a scalded baby, as the singing edge of the razor was drawn through his palm, across the inside of the knuckles. Ryan felt the steel grate against bone and yet more blood flowed from the horrendous cuts.

Now Ryan was at the door, pulling at the handle, his own fingers slick with hot crimson, knowing that he could expect a .44 round between the shoulders at any second.

Jehu was dancing, boots slopping on the deck, trying to hold his cut hand to his chest, yet wanting to attack Ryan at the same time.

"Get out the poxing way!" Captain Quadde shouted from behind the iron bed.

"Hurt me, he has, he's hurt me!" Jehu moaned.

At last, after an eternity of sluggish seconds, the handle turned and Ryan faced the corridor and the companionway that led to the deck. He caught the sound of Doc Tanner's voice, bellowing a warning to someone, which was followed by the echoing boom of the big Le Mat pistol.

He felt someone clawing at him from behind, and heard the plaintive shrilling voice of Jehu in his ear. Nails tore at his jacket, holding him helpless in the doorway. Ryan tried to reach around with the razor and cut at the sailor's face, but the constricting space trapped him.

"Let me go!" he raged.

The flat bang of the short-muzzle .44 interrupted him, and he felt Jehu thrust hard against him, propel him into the corridor. The door slammed shut behind them.

"Done me," the seaman gasped in a small, frail voice, slipping to his knees like a lad at his first communion, hands clasped in front of him. Blood dripped steadily from his hands and mouth. As he toppled at Ryan's feet, the dark hole in the back of Jehu's sweater showed where Pyra Quadde's bullet had hit.

There was an eerie screech of frustrated rage from behind the cabin door. Ryan heard three more shots as he dodged toward the steps, and three chunks of white, splintered oak flew across the passage.

He glanced to the rear, saw the absurdly tiny head of Jehu roll. "Done me, she has. Oh, dear, dear."

It wasn't a time to hesitate. Ryan leaped up to the top of the steps, seeing from the open hatch that the mist wasn't quite as thick. Alongside the *Salvation*— coming up on her port quarter—was another tall-masted sailing vessel, with cables already hooked to the rigging of the *Salvation*. Several men, faces only blurs in the dim light, lined the bulwarks of the stranger, though none of them seemed to be taking any part in the fight. A tall, grizzled man stood on the other ship's quarterdeck, watching the scenes on board the *Salvation*.

Ryan cautiously stuck his head above the coaming, scanning the deck, seeing that the battle—such as it was—seemed nearly over. The evidence of a short and bitter firefight was all around him.

He counted nine bodies—two still moving—crumpled in the coiling mist. As he looked on, he saw a slim boy with a mane of stark-white hair, bound from left to right, holding a gun that looked too big for him.

"Jak!"

"Ryan?"

"Here."

The teenager appeared alongside the hatch, kneeling on the deck. There was a bruise on the boy's left cheek, and his camouflage jacket was torn across the shoulders. But he was grinning like a hunting wolf, eyes glowing like lasered rubies.

"You well?"

Ryan nodded. "You all here? Krysty? Nobody been hurt?"

"Far's I know. Donfil's up front. J.B. an' Lori chilled his sec guards."

"Got my blasters with you?"

"On *Phoenix*."

"What?"

Jak gestured with his thumb to the whaling ship that was moored alongside them. "That's *Phoenix* there. Stole it. Captain's okay. Said he'd help if we chilled bitch-woman."

J.B. spotted them and darted along the deck. His mini-Uzi was in his right hand, and the fedora was pushed to the back of his head. His glasses were rimmed with tiny beads of condensation.

He nodded to Ryan. There wasn't any need for anything more. They'd known each other too long for wasted words.

"Ship's taken," he said. "None of us hurt. Some chilled. Rest gone into the room up the bow there. Like living quarters."

"Fo'c'sle," said Ryan.

"How's that?"

"It's called the fo'c'sle."

"Sure. That's where they are. Can't get out under our feet, can they?"

Ryan shook his head. "No. There's no way out. Once we get everything safe we can offer them terms. I'm sure they'll accept once they know we got the queen bee of the bastard hive."

"Where is she?" Jak asked.

Ryan jerked a thumb over his shoulder. "Down there with an Astra .44 and a lot of real bad temper."

"Best we move some," J.B. suggested.

They crept quickly through the fog, just a few yards, to take shelter behind the bulk of the mizzenmast, close to the stern.

Krysty's figure loomed out of the mist, holding Ryan's SIG-Sauer P-226, her long red hair cascading behind her like a torrent of purest fire.

"Hi, lover," she said, showing no surprise at finding Ryan crouched behind the mast. "Want your own blaster?"

"Yeah. Be good to have something. I feel kind of undressed."

"We got everything on the *Phoenix*. Donfil's stuff, too."

He leaned across and kissed her quickly and gently on the cheek, feeling how cold her skin was. "Good to see you, lover," he whispered.

"You, too," she replied with a hint of a catch in her voice.

"Who's minding the store up front?"

"Lori. She's got your Heckler & Koch. Blown away four of the crew with it already. Don't think they'll try and rush her."

"Seen a short guy? Fluffy white hair and a charming smile? Quiet-spoken. Looks like everyone's favorite uncle?"

"Yeah," Jak said. "I seen him, Ryan. Was going blast him. Patted me on head and wished luck. Went down hatch."

"That's Cyrus Ogg. First mate. After the woman, he's the one we want. Watch for him."

The *Salvation* was quiet now, only the gentle lapping of the sea under her stem breaking the fog-muffled stillness. Still snug behind the mizzen, the reunited friends heard boots on the deck and the creaking of knee joints.

"Upon my soul, Ryan, my dear chum. I am so delighted once again to renew our acquaintance."

They shook hands. Doc had his Le Mat strapped to his belt, and he carried his sword stick in his right fist.

"These rogues have taken to their lair. Dear Lori guards them and will vent her spleen upon any that attempts escape." Adding, a little ruefully, "And it must be said, my dear fellow, that the child has been exhibiting a touch more spleen toward my good self than is tolerable. But let that pass."

"Need a hand?" shouted the white-haired man from the quarterdeck of the other ship. "We can make out little through this murk."

"We have the *Salvation*, Captain!" Krysty answered. "A few minutes more and we can take the rest of the crew prisoner. But they aren't a threat anymore."

"What of Captain Pyra Quadde? Where be she?"

"In her cabin," Ryan replied, "awash with blood and corpses."

"Is she injured? Or chilled? Or held close as a prisoner?"

The note of caution was unmistakable. It reminded Ryan of the time the Trader had wiped out a small ville of cutthroats in a wooded valley near the wide Mississippi. Their leader had been a giant, more than eight feet tall, and blind in one eye. He'd so terrified the locals that they wouldn't even come and look at his dead body. In the end they'd used some of their valuable gas from the store wag and burned the baron's massive corpse.

It was the same with Pyra Quadde.

The same terror that would only end when she, too, was safely chilled.

Chapter Thirty-One

WHEN THEY SEARCHED the *Salvation* they discovered that one of the whaleboats was missing. Cyrus Ogg was no longer on board the ship. Nor was Pyra Quadde.

"Slipped the cable and away in the fog," Deacon concluded. "Be damned to it! There's scant hope of picking her up by the dawn. The mist clears but slowly."

"Which way will she have gone?" Ryan asked. "To shore?"

"Aye."

"Can the two of them handle the boat on their own?" Donfil asked.

"On such a sea!" Deacon laughed bitterly. "My eight-year-old nephew and his pet rabbit could scull to the shore in such a calm."

"Can we man the other boats and go after her? We've got enough men, surely?" Krysty suggested.

"No, mistress," Deacon said. "Pyra Quadde's cunning as a butter keg of polecats. She'll wriggle, twist and hide and, save us all, come grinning back to Claggartville."

"Are we near the...old redoubt?" J.B. asked cautiously.

"The fortress? Aye. By true reckoning we lie off that lee shore, no more than a couple of miles. If that."

"To row in that far? She could land safely, could she?"

"Neither she nor Cyrus were wounded? No? Then by now they are probably safe and snug. Beached the boat and beginning to strike inland for the old coast blacktop. She could be home before us and have her reception waiting. We can have little hope of the wind rising 'ere noon on the morrow."

Ryan sucked at a back tooth. "I guess your helping us won't make the slut love you. Mebbe we should come back to the ville with you and face her down?"

Deacon sighed. "Bad business. I dearly wish that ye had not chosen the *Phoenix* as the agent of your relief."

"Price you pay for being the Good Samaritan, Captain," Doc observed.

"I recall nothing in the Good Book, Doctor, about the Good Samaritan finding his help enforced with a large-bore blaster pressed to his temples."

"Ah, yes. Point taken, Captain," the old man muttered.

"But what do we do now?" Donfil asked, now in his own clothes, eyes hidden once more behind his mirrored sunglasses.

J.B. was reloading his Steyr AUG pistol with rounds dug from the capacious pockets of his coat. "We got the crew quiet. Put the chills over the side. And that's brought us a fair crop of sharks to the feeding. I say we take a boat and pull for shore. Make for the redoubt and then go from there. Just like we usually do."

"And Pyra Quadde?" Lori asked. "What are done about her?"

Nobody answered the blond girl. Finally Ryan spoke.

"Chances are we'll never see her again. She'd lost her ship and half her crew. Depends on her power base back at the ville." He looked at Captain Deacon.

"Can't say. If I can persuade the remnants of her men that her authority is done, then she will find it hard to win back her place."

"Figure trouble with her seamen?" J.B. asked.

The sailor shook his head. "No. Pyra Quadde ruled with her fists and with fear. As long as she's not around, then the fear's gone as well. Course, it could return the moment she appears, hull up, over the horizon."

"Dawn's not far off," Doc said.

For several long seconds, nobody spoke. Ryan was struggling to make a decision. Over the past few months he'd almost begun to think of himself and his companions as being on a kind of a mission: they traveled through the Deathlands encountering wickedness, cleansed the land like a driving wind and then moved on.

They'd flirted with death and disaster with Pyra Quadde, and now they seemed to have broken her power. But if they went back to Claggartville with Deacon and the *Phoenix*, they might find a civil war in the township.

The harsh days at sea had taken their toll, even on Ryan Cawdor's great strength, and he felt tired.

"We'll go in with a whaleboat," he said, finally breaking the silence.

Captain Deacon nodded. "And go on thine own way, Outlander Cawdor?"

Ryan shook his head. "No."

"No?" Jak and Lori said in perfect unison.

"No," Ryan repeated. "We've got tracking skills and we outblast them. We row in now and try to pick up their trail. Can't be difficult. They'll be pressed to head for the ville. We should easily overtake them and chill them."

"Murder them!" the sea captain exclaimed.

"Try to shoot them from behind or from cover. Yeah," Ryan replied. "You'd want me to go and stand in front of them and challenge them to draw fastest? Like the old westie vids? Come on." He shook his head in disgust.

"But ye . . . Oh, I suppose that it's only justice for her. But ye can catch her?"

"Yeah. They've got no more than an hour or so's start. Two to their boat. We can close fast with seven of us at the oars."

"Six," Donfil said quietly.

"How's that?"

The Apache smiled gently at Krysty. "Ryan knows that...if we survived...I wanted to say farewell to you all. And remain."

"And do what?" Jak asked.

Captain Deacon answered for the shaman. "The whole ville was abuzz with talk of Outlander Ten-from-Ten. I hear from Pyra Quadde's crew that the Indian acquitted himself well and bravely against the monsters of the deep."

"I shall sail back with the *Phoenix*. When the *Salvation* is sold at public auction—unless the woman betters you, Ryan—then I may ship on her as first harpooneer. Or with Captain Deacon here." He smiled again, eyes glinting behind the polished lenses of his glasses. "It will all depend on who offers me the best lay of the profits."

"It will be me, I'll promise thee, my lofty friend," Deacon said, patting him on the shoulder. "And thou wilt look right handsome in one of my red sweaters, I'll warrant."

THE LAST GOODBYES and handclasps were, of necessity, very brief. Every minute that passed put Pyra Quadde and her taciturn first mate another hundred paces away from them.

Lori smiled at Donfil and turned her face to accept a kiss on the cheek.

Jak shook his hand. "Try and grow a little, Eyes of Wolf," the Apache said with a smile.

"Try and shrink bit," the boy retorted.

J.B. shook hands firmly. "Always watch your back," he advised. Donfil nodded.

Doc Tanner was next. Half bowing, he placed one hand over his heart. "I swear that I shall greatly miss your friendship and your wisdom. I truly will." He sniffed, wiping at his nose with his kerchief. "I fear that some specks of this damned mist have got into my eyes," he muttered, on the brink of weeping. Donfil stooped and clutched the old man to his chest, arms enfolding him.

"I have enjoyed being with you, Dr. Tanner," he said. "And I shall miss you. Miss you very much, I think."

"Gaia go with you, Donfil," Krysty said, kissing him on both cheeks.

"And Ysun ride always at your shoulder, Fire Hair Woman," he replied.

She held out the small black polished stone. "I shall keep this Apache tear with me forever, Donfil, and it will hold your memory for me."

Ryan was last. The whaleboat rocked gently below him, provisioned and watered by Captain Deacon's men. The whaling irons were still in their place, laid on the starboard side, close to the harpooneer's position in the bow.

"I do not think we shall ever meet again, Ryan Cawdor," Donfil said, taking off his reflecting shades, nodding solemnly. "This is a good day to part, I think. Good luck and may all your gods go with you."

"We might see you again in Claggartville if we don't hunt down the bitch queen before then."

"No. No, Ryan. I do not see that happening. I see you leaving and going into a darkness. But I do not see us meeting again."

"Fair enough, Donfil. Then, goodbye."

After a brief, firm handshake Ryan straddled the rail of the *Salvation*.

Captain Deacon lifted his hand to the peak of his cap in a salute, which Ryan returned, then swung easily down the rope, taking his place in the narrow bow of the whaleboat. J.B. was at the tiller, the other four manning the long oars.

"Sure ye know your course?" Deacon called. "Dawn'll be on the way in an hour. Keep it to your starboard hand and ye cannot go wrong."

Raggedly, they began to row, the rudder hard over to carry them away from the two ships, still tethered together. The red-sweatered crew of the *Phoenix* lined the side and gave them three hearty cheers to speed them on their way.

The fog was patchy, lying low on the dull gray surface of the Lantic. Ryan, in the bow, stared behind them, seeing the bulk of the *Phoenix* vanish, but the top spars of both vessels were still visible. There was clearly a light breeze springing up, and a bright moon peeked through the mist.

When they were a good two hundred yards off, Ryan took one last glance backward, over his friends' heads, and saw the very top of the *Salvation*'s mainmast, with the ensign fluttering in the pallid silver glow. As it folded on itself, he saw the crimson shape against the darkness. Once more he was struck by how much like a bloody skull was Pyra Quadde's chosen flag.

"In and out and in and out. Try and keep it together, Doc," the Armorer moaned. "You'll have us crabbing around in circles."

The next time that Ryan looked astern, both ships had totally disappeared in the shifting murk. He turned and looked only ahead, watching for the first sign of the distant shore.

Chapter Thirty-Two

IT WASN'T AS EASY as Ryan had thought. The tide was turning, ebbing away from the invisible coast, bringing with it a powerful offshore current. It tugged at the whaleboat with its inexperienced crew, making forward progress difficult. The mist was dissipating, but hanging in pockets here and there. Ryan could sometimes see clearly ahead for close to a quarter of a mile. Then, without warning, the fog descended once more and he could hardly make out the hunched figure of J.B., gripping the carved tiller.

"Are we still moving forward?" Krysty called, panting as she rowed on the port side of the narrow dory.

"Yeah. Bend your backs, my hearties, and pull and pull," Ryan said, parodying the cries of the mates of the *Salvation*.

"Shut fuck up and come row yourself," Jak gasped.

"Least it'll be even harder for Pyra Quadde and Cyrus Ogg," Ryan replied. "Just two of them to row and no hand to steer. I reckon we could be closing in real fast on them."

"Dawn's coming," J.B. called, keeping his voice pitched low. "Times of poor seeing they could come up on us unseen. Like we did on the *Phoenix*. Better if Krysty takes lookout, Jak steers and watches from back. They got the best eyes of anyone here."

"I can see well," Lori complained. "And I'm the tiredest. Why can't I have some rests and watched out? It isn't fucking fair!"

Doc was too exhausted to reproach her for the bad language.

"Don't shout out like that!" Krysty admonished the angry girl. "If that woman's near ahead of us you'll warn her we're closing in. Sound carries a long way over water. Uncle Tyas McCann taught me that, back at the ville of Harmony. So everyone try to keep real quiet."

DAWN CAME, but the last, lingering tendrils of fog didn't clear. Visibility still varied between ten and one hundred feet. The sea remained completely calm. Once Krysty asked everyone to stop rowing, which they were happy to do, while she listened intently.

"Yeah. I can hear waves on rocks. Or shingle, mebbe. Difficult to tell. I guess it's within a quarter mile or so."

"Anything else?" Ryan asked. "Nothing like rowing or voices?"

Krysty shook her head. "Sorry, lover. Nothing at all."

"There's something dragging at oar," Jak said from the seat in the stern. "Saw it on Doc's oar. Like thick rope."

"I can feel it, my young colleague," the old-timer replied, "pulling at the stroke. Could be weed of some sort, I imagine."

"It's stopping my moving the rower," Lori protested.

They could all feel it now.

Ryan lifted the blade from the sea, peering into the dismal, murky light. Fronds of shining brown cord were draped over the oar. They were about the thickness of a man's thumb, and one end vanished beneath the flat waves. As he looked, there was a distinct tug, and he gripped the oar more tightly.

"Fireblast! It's trying to—"

"Pulling it away from me," Lori said. "Can't hanging on!"

There was a small splash, and the girl's oar was plucked from her hand, sliding out of sight as neatly as a magician's illusion.

"Lift them, quick," Ryan ordered.

The weed had a strength and purpose of its own, coiling its tendrils around the rowers' blades and trying to draw them away. Ryan reached for his panga, dragging his oar in nearer to the boat and slashing at the loops of the weed. They parted easily enough, giving out a stinking ichor, the color and texture of molasses.

The others used their knives to cut free, the severed ends of the weed falling limply into the ocean. Ryan glanced over the side of the boat and saw that they were trapped in a veritable pasture of the sentient plant. If plant it was.

"Gotta get out of here!" he yelled, the possibility of Pyra Quadde's hearing them forgotten in the urgency of the moment.

"It's on rudder," Jak called, drawing one of his throwing knives and hacking furiously at the slowly writhing cords.

As Ryan lowered his oar cautiously into the sea again, one of the pieces of weed looped lazily up, resting across his forearm, stinging him like a thousand tiny, fiery needles. With a shout of pain he wrenched himself free, examining his skin and seeing there were rows of neat little punctures, each one proudly showing its own speck of bright blood.

"Keep away from it." If any of them went into the water, they were dead. The weed was thick and voracious enough to destroy any of them before they could be pulled back into the whaleboat. "Row for our lives!"

For nearly a quarter of an hour it was a touch-and-go battle, one of the hardest that Ryan had ever been involved in. His panga was the best weapon they had for hacking away at the brown fronds, and he shipped his oar, leaving it to the others to carry on with the rowing.

Lori started to cry, slumping in the bottom of the boat, oblivious to the struggle of the others. Jak left the tiller and double-banked an oar with Doc. Steering was no longer important. All they had to do was break clear of the patch of killing weed.

Eventually, having lost another oar, they were in clear water. Doc was doubled up, fighting for breath, finally managing to pant, "At my age to fall victim to an aquatic herbaceous border!"

"I can smell land," Krysty said a few minutes later. "Earth and growing things."

Above the layer of mist they could all hear the lonely cry of swooping gulls, cut off from their food in the invisible ocean.

Doc called out that his oar blade had struck something. "Must be a rock. Must be closer in than we thought." He stopped rowing and leaned over the side of the boat, recoiling with a gasp and shifting to the center of the thwart. His lined face was as pale as a laundered sheet.

"Doc?" Ryan said. "What's wrong? Are we running aground?"

The old man managed a nervous laugh. "Run aground, my dear fellow? I think not. A blessing, that would be. No, I believe . . . yes, I am certain of it, that we would do well to bend our backs and hasten for the shore yonder."

"Doc," Ryan repeated, fighting for patience. "Just tell us what you saw."

"You recall, shortly after our arrival in this part of old New England, that we had something of a difficulty with a mutated killer whale and great white shark?"

"Yeah. Fireblast! You mean there's—"

The boat shifted uneasily as something grated along its keel. Doc waved his hand in the air as he struggled for expression. "The great-grandfather of all mutie sharks. Upon my soul, but it's so. Fifty feet if it's . . .

I looked straight down into the grinning jaws and that devil's eye, empty and without soul. Oh, let us away, friends.''

Nobody needed any further encouragement, bending to the remaining oars, propelling the little boat forward in a series of great rushes, the whirlpools from the blades vanishing swiftly behind them.

Krysty, in the bow, kept careful watch for any sharp-fanged rocks that might suddenly tear the bottom from the whaleboat and dump them all in the treacherous chill water.

"Left, Jak, left," she called, hearing the sucking noise of the sea, tangling around the gray boulders that marked the mixing of land and ocean.

The fog was finally showing a willingness to clear away. Visibility improved, and the sun broke through above their heads in a vapid glow. Ryan twice spotted the great dorsal fins of the mutie carnivores as they skimmed toward the shore. The bodies of the chilled seamen from the *Salvation* had obviously attracted several of the whale-sharks, and the noise of the oars in the water had brought them in close to hand.

"I can see it!" Krysty called. "Bit to the right. There's a channel between rocks. Looks like it leads to a beach.''

Now they could all see land, the rowers squinting over their shoulders. There were cliffs above a strip of glistening shingle, and on either side of the boat they could make out numerous tiny islands, mostly peaks of rock sticking above the calm sea.

"Recognize it?" Ryan asked J.B.

"No. Once we get ashore I'll use the sextant to get a bearing. Deacon knows this coast and figured we were close to the redoubt. Fortress was what he called it. Got to be same place."

"Take it slow and easy," Krysty warned. "Lots of stuff just below the surface."

The narrowing channel twined between the fragments of the old reef. Ryan remembered now the state of the redoubt, with its sunken corridors and tidal damage from the old nukings—and wondered how easy they'd find it to get back inside and reach the gateway.

The final few yards to the shingle were between jaws of rocks less than a dozen feet across. Beyond them was a last stretch of water where tiny waves tumbled ceaselessly, one upon another, whispering to the smooth pebbles. Under the keel, Ryan could see through clearer water, to the bottom, perhaps twenty feet below. Even as he glanced over the side of the boat he saw the sinuous form of one of the lethal whale-sharks, white-bellied, move past them, teeth bared in its eternal smile.

"Put the oars in," he ordered. "Too narrow. Sea'll carry us in from here."

They floated in, silently, all of them staring up at the lowering cliffs, their shining flanks streaked with bright splashes of emerald moss. The last remnants of the mist still clung to the rock walls, like ghostly webs.

"Let me come in the bow," Ryan said, changing places with Krysty. He held his automatic rifle in his right hand. As he moved, his boots slipped on the long whaling spears that were tucked in near the bow, their hafts ready for the hand of the harpooneer. For a moment his mind flicked back to Donfil, and he thought how he'd miss the tall Apache.

As he'd missed so many good companions over the years.

"Hurry up, boat," Lori said crossly, shuffling on her seat.

Gradually, riding three feet forward and then two back, the boat came in closer. The rocks loomed on both sides of them, seamed with narrow caves and shadowed inlets. But their attention was on the beach, where the keel eventually grounded.

Ryan stood, ready to leap onto the shingle to haul them up higher when the familiar rasping voice froze him in place.

"Not a blink of an eye, cully, or it's fins over for everyone."

Chapter Thirty-Three

"BLASTERS AT YOUR FEET. Slow, slow and very slow."

Ryan lowered the Heckler & Koch, putting it on the thwart of the boat, seeing from the corner of his eye that the others were doing the same. Only Jak, in the stern, wasn't moving. The boy's mouth was set in a tight, etched line, and his fingers moved toward the butt of his Magnum.

"Snow-hair's about to meet his Maker," Pyra Quadde cackled. "Does he bleed white as a mutie or red as the roses?"

"Let it alone, Jak," Ryan snapped. "She'll chill you! Put the blaster down."

Reluctantly the boy did as he was told.

Moving like a scout through a trembler mine field, Ryan turned to face the woman, knowing that life and death were now a breath apart for all of them in the whaleboat.

She stood in the bow of the dory. He guessed that she must have heard their approach and chosen the tiny cove to hide. The boat was pulled in so that it could only be seen when one was past it. She wore the long dress, with seaboots beneath it, and the Spanish pistol was held steady in her hand. She was smiling.

Just behind her and a little to the side was Cyrus Ogg, holding his own blaster aimed at the six friends. They were only about twenty feet apart.

"Well, now, here's a thing, isn't it, Mr. Ogg?" Pyra Quadde sneered.

"Indeed, ma'am, here's a thing, indeed. As thou sayest, Captain Quadde, here's a thing indeed," he agreed.

"Rowing all this blighted way through fog and sharks to meet up again like the best of friends, wouldn't thou say, Mr. Ogg?"

"I would say that, ma'am. Indeed, I would surely say that."

"Now, easy to pick off as stabbing a legless roach in a tin basin, Mr. Ogg?"

"Even easier, Captain. Even easier than that, I'd say."

Ryan had rarely seen two people looking so smugly pleased with themselves.

Something moved near the edge of the rocks, darting toward the water with a fast, skittering gait. It caught everyone's eye, but neither Pyra Quadde nor Cyrus Ogg relaxed their vigilance, or let the muzzles of their blasters wander away from the whaleboat.

Ryan watched the creature, which looked like a cross between a small rabbit and a large rat, but with a skin that glistened in the dawning as if it were covered in scales. It ignored the two dories and paddled across the cove, quickly reaching deeper water. It passed only a few feet in front of Ryan, head held back, little eyes twinkling like polished buttons, whiskers perkily aloft, paws twitching up spray. Its teeth were bared with the effort of its exertions.

There was a swirl and a flash of dull white sandpaper skin, and teeth, row upon serrated row, as the shark rolled belly-up in its attack. The little animal vanished, and the water cleared once more. It was as though nothing had happened.

One single bubble of dark maroon blood came plopping to the surface and burst, the color spreading and dissipating.

"Not a good place for swimming, Mr. Ogg."

"Not a good place at all, Captain."

"Fucking get on!" Jak shouted.

"Language, laddie!" the woman reproved. "Mebbe thou should wash out thy mouth with good salt water. Ample under thy feet, cully."

"It's only me, you sick bitch! Let the others go."

"That an order to the captain, Outlander Deadman?" Ogg grinned at Ryan. "Well named, art thou not? Deadman. Outlander Deadman."

Ryan was trying to work out the odds. There wasn't much doubt that the first volley from the mate and the woman would put at least two and probably three of them over the side. And that meant death with the sharks cruising by, jaws gaping. One of the friends might snatch up a blaster and chill them both, but all the pointers were for a lot of dying.

A triangular fin broke the water near their boat, causing a wave to rock them from side to side.

Another appeared in the entrance from the open sea, and then a third. At a guess Ryan figured there were now at least a half dozen of the mutie monsters in the constricted waters of the narrow cove.

Their ceaseless swirling was raising a swell, water lapping at the jagged walls of the mollusk-covered rocks.

Ryan's boat, grounded in the shingle, only moved a little from the waves. The blasters rattled and jostled in the bottom. Near Ryan's hand, where he steadied himself on the thwart, was the shaft of one of the long killing harpoons, its curved end glittering in the dawn.

"Bastard belly-rippers," Pyra Quadde said. "Canst thou not make 'em hold still or go out into the open Lantic, Mr. Ogg?"

"Do better," he said, firing three spaced rounds at the nearest shark.

The weaving killer that Ogg had fired at disappeared for several seconds. Allowing for the deflection effect of the clear water, it wasn't likely that the first mate had harmed it.

But to everyone's shock and amazement, the shark surfaced, trailing a ribbon of blood behind it. The long tail thrashed at the water, kicking up a spray of blinding foam. Ryan saw two of the other creatures, tasting blood, sensitized to the faint electrical emanations of the wounded beast, dart in, the sound of their rending teeth clearly audible as they entered a feeding frenzy.

One lashed out with its tail as it rolled, teeth locked in the flesh of its comrade, throwing a huge wave across the cove.

Pyra Quadde's boat careened sideways, sending Cyrus Ogg tottering into his skipper, arms clasping her as he fought for balance. Petrified by the sudden hazard of toppling into the frothing sea, the woman also staggered, hands waving and pushing at her first mate.

For a crazed second, they were both helpless.

Ryan reacted first and fastest.

The blaster was too far off. By the time he'd stooped and risen again, a bullet from the Astra would be shredding his flesh. His fighting brain raced in overdrive as he dropped his hand to the narrow wooden shaft of the whaling iron, drawing it smoothly from the bow of the boat. He braced himself and aimed in a single, fluid movement.

Muscles exploded into action, the breath hissing through his teeth as he released the harpoon at Pyra Quadde's stocky figure. The woman had seen him go for the lance and was opening her mouth to scream at Ogg. Off balance, struggling in the bow of the pitching dory, she still managed to snap off two shots at Ryan before he'd let go of the harpoon.

One gouged a long splinter of curling wood from the seat, less than a foot from his leg, the other whistling past his right ear, close enough for him to feel the heat of its passing. It struck the boulders at the base of the cliff and howled off into the last fingers of mist.

But the iron was thrown.

It seemed to cross the space between the two whaleboats with agonizing slowness, the shaft vibrating with the power of the cast.

The point hit the woman below the breastbone, an inch to the right, piercing through her lungs and emerging under her right shoulder blade.

The Astra fell from her hand, splashing into the turbulent water. The long ugly shaft of the lance protruded from her chest, impaling her like a collector's specimen. Its weight tugged her forward, a few shambling, clumsy steps. Her eyes were wide open, showing the whites all around the dark pupils. They were fixed to Ryan Cawdor's face, as though she were seeking to memorize it. Her mouth opened and closed, but not a sound broke the heavy silence of the cove.

Pyra Quadde toppled into the frothing water without a single last word, falling among the flailing tails and teeth of the maddened great whites, bouncing off one of the creatures, her booted feet and the hem of the pretty dress the last to vanish.

"Gaia!" Krysty breathed.

With the exception of Lori, every one of the others had dived for their blasters, using the distraction of the sharks and the thrown harpoon to cover them. Four guns drilled in the direction of the hapless seaman, who was standing, utterly stricken, as he watched his captain go over the side. The Webley trailed at his side and his eyes were turned to the pitching water.

Pyra Quadde wasn't quite gone.

The huge mutie sharks were so crazed that they got in one another's way as they tried to tear at the body of the dying woman. She was tossed from side to side, rising and falling, the broken end of the lance appearing and vanishing repeatedly.

"Saints preserve us all," Doc muttered, as the slow and dreadful passing of Captain Pyra Quadde continued to its inexorable ending.

As she was drawn beneath the sea for the very last time, her desperate eyes were still fixed to the face of Ryan Cawdor, who turned to look across the bloodied waves to the motionless figure of Cyrus Ogg.

As Ryan picked up his own blaster, the first mate shrugged his shoulders expressively, letting his gun slide to join the mangled corpse of his captain.

"I named thee wrong, Outlander Deadman," he called. "I should have called thee Outlander One-from-One, for that's all it took to slay her."

Ryan looked steadily along the barrel of his pistol, the familiar weight and balance of the SIG-Sauer P-226 filling his hand.

The mate shrugged again, looking like a benevolent old uncle, the fringe of white hair pasted about the ruddy cheeks by the tossed spray. The sharks had left the tiny bay as suddenly and mysteriously as they'd come, leaving the white-bellied, raggled carcass of their fellow. Apart from the film of oily blood, there was not a single trace of Captain Quadde's body.

"I'm no threat to thee, Outlander," Cyrus Ogg said. "Not now. Go your ways and my blessings to with ye all."

The serrated grip of the pistol was cool and damp against Ryan's hand. He looked across the small space of water at the obsequious figure of the *Salvation*'s first mate. And shot him once, the 9 mm bullet hitting Ogg through the top of his nose. The sound of the blaster, with its built-in baffle silencer, was no louder than a muffled cough.

The sailor threw his arms wide, back over the side of the whaleboat, landing spread-eagled like a fallen star.

Ryan jumped from their boat, boots crunching in the tiny pebbles.

"Come on, people," he called. "Looks like we're done here."

Chapter Thirty-Four

CAPTAIN DEACON PROVED to have been correct in his guesstimate of their position.

Using the miniature folding sextant, J.B. was able to work out that they'd come ashore on one of the many little islands just off the mainland, and that the redoubt they'd left was only six miles to the west.

The fog had finally dissipated, and the morning sun rose on a most beautiful New England day. The sea was calm and the monsters of the deep, if they were close by, sailed past with their jaws sheathed.

The boat kept in close to the shore; no one wanted to risk another encounter with the hideous patches of sentient weed. The land rose above them in rolling hills, mostly covered with bright stands of maple, beech and oak.

They moved easily through the placid sea, and ahead Ryan could make out the outlines of the stone redoubt, could see the spidery outline of the rusting ladder that they'd climbed through the teeth of the screaming gale. Coming in by sea, they would be able to reach the jammed entrance gates without any trouble—once the setting of the tide was right for them. They would find out if Ryan had, indeed, remembered to lock shut the doors into the twin gateway chambers.

"Keep your dreams as clean as silver, this may be the last hurrah," Doc sang.

THE TIDE WAS HIGH, and they had to tie the boat to an enormous red iron mooring ring a few feet away from the doors. Ryan noticed that the gap hadn't altered and piles of loose sand, and mottled seaweed had collected around the dark opening.

Eventually the water fell far enough to reveal the worn concrete of the landing platform. The stone was rough and pitted, showing the rusted ends of iron.

Most of them had slept during the four-hour wait, but Ryan had stayed awake, as had Krysty. She had used the time to bring him up to date on what happened back in Claggartville and how they'd managed to escape on the *Phoenix*.

"I'll be happy to get out of here, lover," she said to Ryan.

"Long as the gateway's not flooded out."

Krysty smiled. "Sure. Always that chance, isn't there? What would you do if we couldn't make another jump from here?"

"Guess we'd have to try to make our way across to that redoubt in the Mohawks. Nearest we know about from here."

The girl hesitated. "You wouldn't want to stop around here if the gateway wasn't functioning?"

Ryan shook his head. "Claggartville? No, love. Not here."

"Anywhere?"

"Somewhere." He smiled at the look on her face. "Cheer up, Krysty. We've gotten away light this time around. You know I want to settle. I don't know when and I don't know where. One day. We'll just keep looking and one day we'll find it. And when we find it, lover, then I know we're going to know what it is."

Krysty leaned nearer, kissing him gently on the lips. "Whatever you want, lover, I'm with you. All the way." She pressed harder against him, her tongue sliding between his parted teeth, her hand fluttering across his muscular stomach, touching him....

"Tide's down." Jak's voice intruded, making them both jump and break apart, grinning like guilty children.

"One day, Ryan," she whispered. "I love you very much."

"Love you too, lady."

They left the whaleboat tied to the ring by a long painter, in case they needed to get out of the redoubt by the same route.

Ryan led the way, with J.B. bringing up the rear. Neither needed to say anything about how to work a patrol. It was second nature, as simple as breathing to them.

The stone was covered in a fine, slippery layer of sand and weed, making the footholds treacherous.

Doc helped Lori out with a courteous hand, receiving a wide smile from the teenager. "Sorry I've been a real bitch, Doc," she said. "Real sorry."

"Feel anything, lover?" Ryan asked Krysty. "No muties around?"

"Can't tell. Don't think so. Sure smells inside, though."

As Ryan pushed through the entrance he saw inside what was causing the appalling stench. A manta ray had been sucked into the gap in the doors by the tugging current and not been able to angle its way out again. Its rotting carcass lay in eighteen inches of salt water near the bottom of the flight of stairs that had earlier saved their lives.

"Best not hang around," Ryan told them. "If there's a problem near the gateway we want to get out of here before the next tide comes sweeping in. Let's go. Fast and careful."

The corridors were streaked with patches of seaweed, small colonies of shellfish already taking over corners, building one upon another. The lights still glowed in the ceiling, though the intruding ocean had put some out of commission. Ryan guessed that it wouldn't be long—days rather than weeks—before all of the lighting in that section of the redoubt failed.

It took them some time to find their way through the maze of passages and corridors, all of them scarred by the ocean.

In the hollows and dips there were deeper pools of water, many containing small fishes or scuttling crabs.

They finally reached the stretch of the corridor that led to the gateways. It curved around to the left and sloped a little. Ryan, out in front, licked his lips nervously at the expectation of what they might see. If the doors were open, then they were in deep trouble. If they were closed, then they should be safe enough.

They were closed.

THE LIGHTS WERE BLINDING. After the dimness of the tunnels, the array of comp-panels and whirring and spinning disks was dazzling.

Ahead of the six companions were the odd double doorways of the mat-trans chambers—one with the security coding of twelve, the other carrying the higher rating of nineteen.

"Which one, Doc?" Ryan asked.

"I'm sorry, my dear fellow. I fear that my thoughts were on too many mornings and a thousand miles behind. I was wondering how our lofty Apache shaman would cope in the world of Claggartville. What think you?"

J.B. answered the question. "Donfil had a real skill. Best you'll ever see. Skill like that costs, and costs plenty. He'll be loaded with jack and die a rich baron."

"Ah, I do hope so," the old man said. "I do so much hope so. Now, there was a question from you, my dear Ryan, was there not? Something about which doorway we should use? The one to the gold or the one to the dragon?"

"Yeah. The one we came in through? Or the other one?"

"Other one?" Doc sounded puzzled. "I fear I don't quite recall about the other one. Could you . . . could you possibly . . . ?"

"Space suits in it, Doc," Ryan said briefly, irritated by Doc's lapses of memory. "The one that someone had just been using."

"Ah, it returns to me. Space. The final... What was it? A mission that would boldly go where..." His voice drifted away. "Sorry, my friends. It's quite gone. Yes. Overproject Whisper. Part of the Totality Concept. A self-sufficient station in space, hidden behind the far side of the moon. All the latest in regenerating food and... Those were the rumors that I heard."

"Can we try that gateway?"

Doc Tanner shook his head. "I think not, Ryan. They would have a separate system of coded sec locks and all manner of deep comp-traps. I doubt it would be just a matter of shutting the door to send us speeding to the Lord knows where."

"Could try it one day," Ryan persisted, fascinated by the hidden possibilities of this mysterious second chamber with its entrancing silver glass walls and door.

"Yeah," Krysty agreed. "One day, lover. But this day... let's go."

Oddly nobody seemed to want to make the jump. Each of them knew how physically draining it would be—a sucking unconsciousness with driving nausea. They wandered around the control room, no one making a move toward the main gateway that had brought them to New England.

Doc found himself a neat, dark green seat with chromed castors and rolled himself around the panels, peering at the infinite array of knobs, levers and dials.

"Wonderful," he said. "State of the art equipment here, the likes of which I've never seen. Must be for that second gateway. If only I had more time, I'm certain I could unravel its arcane mysteries and transport us...spaceward."

"How much time would you need, Doc?" J.B. asked.

"Not long. Two...perhaps three..."

"Days?"

Doc laughed, showing his peculiarly strong, white teeth. "By the three Kennedys! No. Months, my dear fellow. Two to three months."

Ryan checked the silver-walled room very carefully, looking for signs that it had been used in the days since they were last there. But even his keen tracking eye found no trace of recent visitors. The self-contained suits with their bubble helmets still hung neatly in a row.

"Bastard hungry," Jak complained. "We going or staying? Could go get self-heats from outside rooms. Yeah?"

"No." Ryan checked his wrist chron. "Tide'll be coming up again. Open the door here and it's goodbye to the gateway. But you're right, Jak. Come on. Let's move out."

THE WALLS of the primary gateway were a rich turquoise color, reminding Ryan of the fine jewelry they'd seen in the baking deserts of the southwest, which brought back a fleeting thought of Donfil More. But the Apache was now a part of the past.

Ryan had always been a man more interested in tomorrow than yesterday.

The six companions ranged themselves around the six-sided room, Ryan waiting by the heavy, armored door, ready to trigger the starting mechanism that would send them, molecules scattered, to some other part of the Deathlands.

As always, there was the doubt and fear that the uncontrollable machine, its instructions long vanished, might select a redoubt for them that was now buried in the heart of an active volcano. Or crushed beneath a mountain of rubble.

Jak sat down directly across from the door, his head lowered onto his knees, his fine veil of white hair tumbling over his legs.

J.B. copied the pose, knowing from experience that this was the most comfortable position to adopt for a jump. The Armorer looked up at Ryan and winked. "Here we go again."

Doc and Lori huddled close against each other, her young blond head resting on the old man's skinny shoulder.

Krysty folded herself easily into a variation of the lotus position, laying her hands, palms up, on her thighs. She closed her eyes and let her head droop to her chest. Looking down at her, Ryan felt a sudden, overwhelming rush of love.

"Ready?" he asked. "Let's go."

The door swung easily on its hinges, shutting with a positive clicking sound. The locking mechanism triggered the mat-trans unit. Ryan stepped quickly across and sat down next to Krysty, touching her softly on the arm, receiving a half smile from under the fringe of her vermilion hair.

They experienced the usual flashing lights, and the first tattered shards of white mist appeared. The metal floor plates began to glow, and Ryan heard the rising hum that always accompanied a jump.

He closed his eye, seeing the patterns of pressure building inside the retina. His ears started to hurt, and he swallowed hard to clear them. The sound was like the waves rushing beneath the stem of the *Salvation* as she bucked through the rolling swell of the Lantic Ocean.

Ryan pushed the back of his hand against his eye, trying to ease the speckled color of the deepening pressure.

His last thought before the swirling darkness enveloped his brain was to realize that the dancing patterns looked amazingly like flowers. Blood-red roses.

FACE TO FACE WITH A SPECTRE FROM THE PAST

The war for survival continues in the sixth chapter in the Deathlands saga. In the swirling dust that was once New Mexico, Ryan Cawdor discovers a group of mercenaries who have looted an isolated cavalry museum and plan to use their newfound weapons against the local Indians. Cawdor cannot ignore the Apaches when they plead for his help, unaware that he'll soon be at the mercy of an age-old foe...

Widely available from Boots, Martins, John Menzies, W. H. Smith, Woolworths and other paperback stockists.

PUB: JULY 1989   **GOLD EAGLE**   **PRICE: £2.75**

RIVETING ACTION

VIETNAM: GROUND ZERO

RED DUST

ERIC HELM

In the 13th chapter of the explosive VIETNAM: GROUND ZERO epic, tense new events arise to test the U.S. forces. Baffled by the sudden halt in Vietcong acitivity, intelligence sources reveal that a small village in North Vietnam is being used as a staging area for enemy troops. In a covert mission of life and death, Special Forces Captain Mack Gerber undertakes to stop their next attack – and he can't afford to fail.

December 1989 £2.25

Available from Boots, Martins, John Menzies, W.H. Smith, Woolworths and other paperback stockists.

GOLD EAGLE